COME AND
TAKE IT

COME AND TAKE IT

SEARCH FOR THE TREASURE OF THE ALAMO

a novel

LANDON WALLACE

Trinity River Press

Cover Images:

Map – Lee Godden, photographer – no changes made – license granted by photographer

Alamo cannon – Gilberto Gonzales, photographer – no changes made – license @ https://creativecommons.org/licenses/by/2.0/legalcode

Slave on horseback – Texas State Archives from the Timothy O'Sullivan Collection

Copyright © 2015 by Landon Wallace
www.authorlandonwallace.com

Trinity River Press
Fort Worth, Texas 76102

Printed in the United States of America
Published 2015

19 18 17 16 15   1 2 3 4 5
ISBN: 978-0-9861731-0-3

Cover design by Sheila Cowley

PROLOGUE

Darnell Gunn parked his car a block away from the target. He switched off his headlights, refitted the stocking cap over his tight afro, and looked over the neighborhood. He couldn't see much; the flickering street lamps barely cast enough light for him to make out the single row of dilapidated clapboard houses down the road. He glanced at his quivering hand, and his tattooed nickname, *Shakes*, glared back at him, mocking his attempts to stay cool. *What the hell am I doing here*, he wondered. As expected, Shakes saw no other signs of activity. He knew most of the old folks in this west Brewton community had locked themselves in their homes earlier in the night. Fear was an emotion he knew well from his youth in the crime-ridden streets of the Philadelphia Badlands.

Shakes turned to the hulking Serbian with the unusual scar on his face sitting next to him. He tried to avoid staring but couldn't help himself. *Damn, was it really a crucifix ... on his cheek? How nuts was this guy?* Shakes hadn't wanted a partner on this gig, especially one he trusted so little, but the boss lady had insisted: something about a black man going soft on a black victim. It had pissed him off at the time, but now that old man Travis's house was in sight, he realized she might have been right. Shakes didn't like the assignment. Not one damn bit. The hero living at 32 Gulf Shores Drive deserved better. But Shakes needed the cash and having a stone-cold killer by his side kept his mind focused. *Steady your hands and finish the job*, he said to himself.

"Ready?" Shakes asked.

1

Kruger grunted.

Shakes opened his car door and motioned for the Serbian to follow. A lone dog wailed from behind a rickety chain-link fence as Shakes led his partner down the cracked roadway. They stole by a long row of one-story homes, hiding once behind trees to stay out of sight of a passing car, and closed in on their mark.

Shakes looked around the tired neighborhood one last time before turning toward Travis's front door. Unlike most of the surrounding houses, this one had a tended garden, a freshly cut lawn, and no weeds in sight. From the little Shakes knew about Travis, that wasn't a surprise. He slinked over to an undraped front window with a light shining from inside. He signaled Kruger to stand guard behind a stubby oak in the side yard as Shakes peered into Travis's home. The old man had his back to the window and was sitting alone in front of his television.

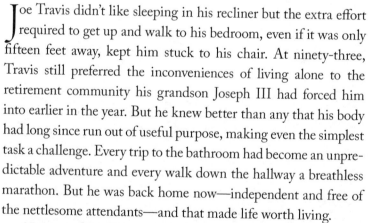

Joe Travis didn't like sleeping in his recliner but the extra effort required to get up and walk to his bedroom, even if it was only fifteen feet away, kept him stuck to his chair. At ninety-three, Travis still preferred the inconveniences of living alone to the retirement community his grandson Joseph III had forced him into earlier in the year. But he knew better than any that his body had long since run out of useful purpose, making even the simplest task a challenge. Every trip to the bathroom had become an unpredictable adventure and every walk down the hallway a breathless marathon. But he was back home now—independent and free of the nettlesome attendants—and that made life worth living.

Travis wrapped his gnarled fingers around the handle of his cane and tried to wiggle out of his chair, only to slump back in frustration. He pulled his tattered throw-blanket over his spindly, hairless legs. He'd be sleeping in his chair tonight.

Travis thought he heard a twig snap outside his window but had neither the interest nor the energy to investigate. He'd had plenty of experience dealing with the young hooligans of his neighborhood; they'd had their fun with him many times before. The ritual of gathering to drink beer and smoke weed in the alley behind his house had become so common that it no longer stirred his concern. Just so the kids knew enough to stay out of his gardens—that was all he cared about.

Travis picked up the new remote control from his scratched-up side table and considered which of his shows to watch—*Wheel of Fortune* or *Jeopardy*. The fancy recording device his other grandson Nat had installed was difficult to operate—it made his Apple laptop seem simple by comparison—but the convenience of watching the taped telecasts, even at midnight, made the hassle of all the confusing buttons worth the effort. He decided he'd start with *Jeopardy*, and while he waited for the system to activate, his gaze strayed to an aged photograph on the wall. There he stood in 1973 as a vibrant fifty-three-year-old man in uniform, alongside his only child, Sam, and his two young grandsons, Joseph III and Nat. Memories flooded his mind and Travis felt his body tremble momentarily. He couldn't believe it had been over thirty years since his Sam had died.

Even after the passage of several decades, Joe Travis had never ceased asking himself whether he could have done more to save his son. A thirty-seven-year-old divorced father, with two boys to look after, cut down in the prime of his life in a bout with alcoholism. To this day, Travis still had difficulty sleeping when thinking about that turbulent period. His Sam, a young man struggling to find his identity, having lost his wife, his purpose, and then, in the bottle, himself. And his precious grandsons left alone to fend for themselves without a mother and father, or any support network. He'd done everything he could for the boys, and they'd built remarkable lives despite their hardships, but he was still pained for that empty piece of their souls. The void only a father, his Sam, could fill.

The leaves in the yard crunched under trespassing feet and Travis knew the teenage prowlers were casing his house again. Still blessed with acute hearing despite his age, Travis thought he heard whispers from his porch and realized he'd been too lazy to close his front window shade. He hoped his late-night visitors, who were likely staring at him this very minute, would have their fun and go on their way.

The television started to come into focus and Travis studied the *Jeopardy* categories displayed on the screen. *Cooking, Words Ending in Z, Capitols, Paparazzi, Shifting Sands,* and the *Republic of Texas.* The last category was right in his wheelhouse. Travis had spent a large part of his adult life researching the pre-Civil War period of Texas independence and could answer virtually any question on the topic. His expertise had not grown out of any real fascination with the subject matter—he'd lived in Alabama most of his life, except for his years in the service—but he'd gained a PhD's worth of knowledge about the Texans' war with Mexico while investigating his genealogy and the life of his famous ancestor, Joe the slave.

A scratching on the front door interrupted Travis's thoughts and the old man realized the prowlers had more sinister purposes. Seconds later, a surgical incision separated the bolt lock from his front door and footsteps trampled into his small house. Travis tried to stand, leaning heavily on his cane, but a foot swung violently from behind him and kicked it forward, knocking him back into his chair.

"Don't move," said a gruff, heavily accented voice.

A giant hand swiveled Travis's recliner around and brought him face-to-face with two broad-shouldered men dressed entirely in black. One intruder was white with a distinctive scar across his left cheek, the other black, like him, with a stocking cap on his head.

"What do you want?" Travis asked without a trace of fear in his voice. He'd lived too long and survived far more harrowing events to allow a couple of thugs to scare him.

"Where's the m-a-a-p?" asked the hulking white man in broken, almost unintelligible English.

"Where's the what?" Travis replied.

"Just tell us where it is," the black man interrupted, "and we'll leave you alone."

Travis looked at his interrogators and smiled. He feebly reached toward his chest and squeezed the medical-alert button hanging from the chain around his neck.

"Fool," the white man exploded. He grabbed Travis by the shoulders, lifted him from his chair, and flung his ninety-eight-pound body to the floor. Travis's brittle bones snapped on impact. The white man then ripped the medical remote from Travis's neck and smashed it into pieces with his size-thirteen boot. In a haze, Travis saw the black man grab his partner's arm and yank him away.

"Are you crazy?" the black man spewed angrily. "We need him alive." He then knelt over Travis. "Help yourself old man," he implored. "Tell us where you're hiding the map."

Travis wheezed and gasped for air, unable to speak. Blood trickled from his nose. He already knew the fall had done too much damage. He soon felt his lungs constrict and sensed death was on its way, but in the moment he felt oddly triumphant. As life ebbed from his body, he felt closure, an odd satisfaction in all that he'd gone through to uncover the inscrutable secret of his ancestors. Yet, now, he regretted not having shared more about what he'd found with his grandsons. Why hadn't he explained the true reason for his obsessive search into his family history? Why hadn't he shown them the volumes of information he'd gathered about Joe the slave? Stubborn pride, an old man's fear his boys might think he'd gone soft, disbelieving him, had locked up his discoveries in the brain of a dying man. But at least he'd secured the USB drive. Even if the brutes found his laptop, they'd never find the hidden drive. Would they? Travis felt a gentle hand grasp his shoulder and willed his eyes to focus despite the searing pain.

"Come on, Travis," the black man said while leaning into his face. "Tell us where it is. You're a hero, man. I don't want to see you die like this."

The comments drifted past Travis as the final breath of life left his collapsed lungs. But death could wait a minute longer. Grimacing, Travis called on all the strength he could muster, pulled his arm away from his body, and extended a proud middle finger forward. "Come and take it," he gasped.

PART I

CHAPTER 1

Nat Travis stared at the ceiling, his sleep-deprived eyes moving through the darkness from one end of the room to the other, searching the uneven plaster for figures created in the shadows. Insomnia frequently tortured him during the football season, but tonight felt strangely different. It was only August and the recycling images of game film weren't the reason he'd tossed around for hours; instead, a sense of uneasiness consumed him, filling the cracks in his room with gremlins.

At times throughout the long night, his brain dwelled on the harsh realization that he had little to show for his life, a now-forty-nine-year-old high-school-football coach living alone in small-time Brewton, Alabama, with no wife and no children. But even while that was true, Nat was comfortable in his solitary existence, buoyed by the sense that high-school coaching, while hardly profitable, was the one thing he loved most. He thrived on the kids' pure enthusiasm, their work ethic, and their devotion to him and one another. For other coaches, the turn-on was all about the competition, the electric feeling of a close game, the soaring highs that followed a win, and the satisfaction of sending their boys, at least a handful of the talented ones, off to Ole Miss, Georgia, and of course, Alabama—maybe even the pros. But football meant more to Nat than even that. Coaching was his way of honoring those who'd helped him through his lost youth, a career through which he could offer the same firm, loving hand to young men—like the sixteen-year-old Nat Travis—who operated more on testosterone than good sense. No, he knew it wasn't some invading midlife crisis that was keeping him up this night.

Nat pulled the sheets away from his body and trudged toward the bathroom. He noticed the digital display on his alarm clock—2:00 a.m.—and, as if on cue, his iPhone beeped from his bedside table. He nervously reached over and picked it up. The readout said *unknown number.*

"Nat Travis," he answered groggily.

"Mr. Travis," said the voice on the other end of the line.

"Who's this?"

"Officer Parkhurst, Brewton police department. You're Joe Travis's grandson?"

Nat's heart rate accelerated with the question and he instantly knew why he'd been unable to sleep. "Yeah," he answered, "I am."

"Sorry to call you so early in the morning, but I have some bad news. Your grandfather's house was broken into last night."

"What?" Nat asked in a louder voice.

"His medical-alert button triggered a while ago and an ambulance was dispatched. That's all I can tell you over the phone," Parkhurst said apologetically.

"How's my grandfather?" Nat barked, without realizing he was yelling.

"We need you to come down to the station," the officer responded. "I'm sorry, but that's all I can say."

Nat intuitively understood the message. The police wanted to talk to him for a few minutes before taking him to identify the body. He'd seen this late-night scenario play out on television so many times that it felt surreal now that he was living it. "He's dead, isn't he?" Nat asked, his tone softening.

"I wish I could say more … I really do … but there are … regulations. Please come down to the station."

"Okay," Nat responded in a whisper. "On my way." Nat put

down the phone as tears pooled in his eyes. His knees buckled and he slid to the floor. The moment he'd avoided thinking about had finally arrived: His grandfather, his best friend, the man who'd saved his life after his father died, was gone. Even with Papa Joe's advancing years, the news still came as a shock. Of course, the old man was fragile, but he'd remained mentally sharp and he'd recently been cleared to return to his house after a short stint at the retirement center, which alone had seemed to peel away a few years. And he'd been so glad to be back. In fact, Nat had dropped by earlier this day and Papa Joe had looked relaxed and happy, telling old stories, and asking Nat questions about his team's prospects for the coming year. A robbery? Why would anyone break into the house of a ninety-three-year-old man with no material possessions other than a new television set, an outdated laptop, and a few wartime medals? It had to be the neighborhood. The horrible realization that he was likely the reason his grandfather was dead settled over Nat like a dark rain cloud. Why had he allowed him to go back to Gulf Shores Drive? To that house. Alone. Then, just as suddenly, Nat's bout of conscience gave way to overwhelming sadness. And pain.

Papa Joe was dead.

Nat said a brief prayer before standing and pulling on a pair of rumpled jeans and a T-shirt. He then walked into the bathroom, splashed cold water on his cheeks, and gargled with a mouthful of Listerine. He looked at his thinning hair in the mirror. The deeply etched lines on his face stared back at him, his forty-nine years passing before him in a blur.

———★———

On his way to the police station, Nat punched in his brother's phone number. He'd considered waiting until he had more information to make the call but his better judgment prevailed. No need to put off the conversation, even though he wanted to.

"Joseph Travis," his brother answered in a faint scratchy voice.

"Hey, it's me."

Nat heard his brother draw a deep breath, the kind he usually gave for dramatic effect, as if he was irritated by whatever Nat was about to say. "It's two-thirty in the morning."

"It's about Papa Joe."

Joseph remained silent for a moment, like a building volcano, before erupting, his default position wherever Nat was concerned. "I warned you," he shouted. "We never should have left him alone in that house! What happened?"

Nat considered hanging up but settled for biting his tongue. Sometimes all he could do with his brother was wait and hope that the few decent strands of his personality would win out. "I'm headed to the police station now," he responded, "but I'm pretty sure he's dead."

Nat felt Joseph regrouping. "Dead?" his brother stumbled. "I'll get the first plane down."

"Call me when you get here … I can pick you up."

"Don't worry about it; I'll rent a car. And don't make any arrangements till I get there. Papa Joe deserves a proper burial."

The dig was unmistakable and deep. Joseph's biting way of reminding Nat that a high-school-football coach wasn't capable of handling something this important. Their heroic grandfather's funeral had to be managed by the responsible brother, the one who could properly honor Papa Joe's life, the one who wouldn't leave him buried in a small town like Brewton, Alabama. Or, like an idiot, get him released from the nursing home where he had full-time care. Nat's anger spiked again but he let it pass. The scar tissue he'd built up over years of arguing with his older brother protected him from the sting of Joseph's words.

Resignation had now replaced anger and sadness was the only emotion he felt. The estrangement from his brother made the situation even more painful.

"Don't worry yourself," Nat finally answered. "Papa Joe handled all of his funeral details years ago." Nat paused, taking unwanted pleasure in Joseph's silence and the tacit admission that his grandfather had never mentioned any of the specifics to him.

"Fine," Joseph grumbled. "I'll call you when I land. Talk to you later."

Nat hit the red button on his phone, terminating the call, and breathed again. He then looked up and saw the single-story brick police department in the distance. Accelerating past the town square, he covered the final half mile and wheeled his Ford truck next to one of the parked squad cars.

CHAPTER 2

She knew her long black hair, parted and skimming across her shoulder blades, stood out among the perfectly coiffed updos surrounding the huge board table, but unlike the other women in the room, she cared little about her physical appearance. At her advanced age, what did it matter anyway? She'd chosen a simple navy dress, accented by a string of pearls bunched tightly against her wrinkled neck, and adorned it with a small cannon-shaped brooch with the letters A-l-a-m-o inscribed across the barrel. Angelina de Zavala Gentry lowered her head to avoid engaging in discussions with any of the San Antonio socialites scurrying about the room, but she missed nothing. For her, the coronation of the new president of the Daughters of the Republic of Texas, a woman she'd handpicked for the job, was not a cause for celebration, but rather the conclusion of a painstaking process. The worry lines etched across Angelina's face reflected the years of work that had carried her to this climactic moment.

The current president of the DRT, a chunky, neckless woman named Patricia Akers, pounded the gavel to bring the meeting to order. The room quieted. Akers then walked over to the private waiting-room door and knocked.

"Janet," Akers announced in a voice loud enough to be heard through the wood frame. "Or should I say Madame President? Please join us."

Janet Nelson, a photogenic, late-thirties city councilwoman from San Antonio, swung the door open and the assembled women erupted into a standing ovation. The board of directors of the DRT, the guardians of the cherished shrine of Texas liberty—the Alamo, had elected their new president general. The hundred-year-old organization, whose membership consisted entirely of women with allegedly direct bloodlines to the slain heroes of the epic battle with Mexico, had turned over power to Angelina's stealth protégé. Janet glided comfortably around the room, shaking hands with her fellow board members, hugging many of them, and breaking down many of the stern faces intent on pushing back on the celebratory mood. Angelina knew Janet's detractors would eventually fall in line once the new president was installed in office. They were so painfully transparent.

"Everyone be seated," said Akers. "Ladies," she continued, after the thirty-member board took their places around the marble-inlaid table, "I present to you the president general for the 2013–2015 term, the forty-second president of the Daughters of the Republic of Texas, Janet Bosworth Nelson." The women rose again and cheered their new leader in another prolonged tribute. Janet moved her runway-model figure to the head of the table, gently flipped her blonde hair, and raised her arms in triumph. She had the room under control.

"Thank you," Janet started, smiling through her Botox injections and making eye contact with each of the ladies as she spoke. "Proud Daughters of the Republic, I am humbled by your confidence and will serve you with the same pride and conviction that drove our ancestors to defend the Alamo against such insurmountable odds." She paused as if overwhelmed by the honor. "I will do everything in my power to fulfill your trust. Now, enjoy your lunch. We'll take up business in about twenty minutes."

Janet sat down next to President Akers and another of the seventy-plus-year-old leaders of the Daughters whose fingers were pried deeply into the organization as well—the outgoing treasurer, Valerie Butler. A woman whose sole rationale for her position had been that she'd married the owner of the San Antonio Spurs, a man who also happened to be the richest person in the city. Her wealth had earned her a seat at the table even though her lineage to the Alamo—which was loosely tied to a forgotten volunteer from Tennessee with no family records—stretched even the DRT's flexible standards to the edge. Angelina sat strategically across the table from the officers, far enough away to avoid conversation, but close enough to hear whatever they said. Akers and Butler, the two grand dames of San Antonio society, each sporting hair sprayed so tightly an earthquake couldn't shake it loose, clamped Janet on each side.

"Madame President," Butler started, "what's the latest with the AG's investigation?"

"You know that's our program today," Janet responded with a shrug of her shoulders, "so I'll only briefly preview my comments by saying that we've made significant progress. I think we've convinced the AG that the DRT's revised financial controls are sound and he's close to signing off on our plan. I'm confident we'll have a deal soon."

Butler and the women eavesdropping from nearby seats nodded, acknowledging that their glamorous new president had matters admirably under control. "Marvelous," Butler responded, and went back to playing with her field-greens salad specked with goat cheese and candied nuts. Angelina marveled at how easily the women fell for her protégé's lines. How foolish they'd become in their blind faith toward their new charismatic leader.

The rest of the luncheon conversation drifted to discussions about shopping, grandchildren, and other frivolous matters that Angelina held no interest in. She rarely had patience for these women and their narrow lives, which convinced her even more they deserved everything they were about to get. When the dessert trays of fresh fruit and hot chocolate dipping sauce finally made their way into the room, Janet stood up to address the crowd. Most of the women barely looked up from their plates.

"Ladies," Janet opened, "it's been a rough year for our

organization but I'm happy to report we're well on our way to putting our problems behind us. At your direction, I've spent the better part of the last six months working with Attorney General Craig's office to resolve the charges. To recount, there are three basic claims we had to address." Janet's white teeth glinted when she paused and smiled.

"One," she continued, "the AG was firmly convinced that several million dollars, much of it state money, disappeared from our treasury over the last decade. While the government auditors haven't said anything definitive, corruption charges are no longer my concern. By cooperating and providing full financial information, the DRT should be cleared. Remember, our auditors found nothing incriminating so I'm hopeful the AG's report simply admonishes us for insufficient financial controls.

"Second, the state's physical examination of the Alamo has produced a two-hundred-page report listing all of the needed repairs. Some of the items are minor, but many are those we've discussed in these meetings for years. A five-year plan for initiating the restoration work is being developed as I speak, and I'm satisfied you'll find the recommendations consistent with our goals. And, finally, the state wants a more active voice in the day-to-day operations of the property. That request is the trickiest of all. It's my responsibility to keep the Alamo within the DRT's management, but reality dictates we're going to have more oversight ... it's inevitable. How much I don't know yet, but I'm confident we can reach some resolution that won't endanger the independence of our organization."

Janet smiled and drew a deep breath. "And now the good news," she announced. "No criminal charges will be brought against the DRT. We'll be permitted to continue to operate without any threat of prosecution. The AG has assured me that compliance with the state's terms will give our organization the fresh start it needs. But as you might suspect, there is a price."

Janet paused before continuing. "So here are the details. The first is already done—you've installed new officers—thank you for that. The second is the agreement of this board that the Daughters will share all financial information with the AG's office for the next three years. And we'll have an embedded accountant from the state permanently in our office. That's underway. And third, and this comes with great sadness, President Akers and Treasurer Butler must immediately resign their positions in our organization."

A stunned silence fell over the room. Angelina suppressed a grin but felt a rush of satisfaction that Janet had followed her instructions perfectly, feeding her two old enemies to the attorney general. A nervous murmuring immediately started, and Angelina could see the indignant Akers and Butler squirming as if unsure what to do next. Angelina remained stone-faced but she sensed the old-timers at the table understood she'd orchestrated the scene. Finally, Akers and Butler stood, stared at Janet while mumbling vitriol under their breath, and reached forward as if to weaponize their butter knives. Akers then raised her right arm and pointed across the table at Angelina, muttering, "You ..." Janet motioned to a security guard but Butler stopped Akers first, grabbing her friend by the hand and leading her out of the room. The crowd stared with their collective mouths open.

Angelina maintained her stoic expression despite the finger-pointing episode and lowered her head. She then picked up her water goblet and discreetly saluted her accomplishment. For the first time in years, she felt her dreams were finally within reach.

CHAPTER 3

A small obituary in the *Brewton Standard* reported that Joseph Travis II, World War II veteran, hero, successful businessman, and community leader, had died from internal injuries resulting from a fall. There was no mention of a home break-in or violence. Nat had wondered why that detail had been left out until he heard that his brother Joseph had called the paper before he left Dallas.

Friends gathered at the Brewton Community Center the day before the funeral to pay their respects to Joe Travis and his two grandsons. Because the graveside service was to be limited to family only, Nat wanted to give the Brewton community a chance to say good-bye to his grandfather. He'd requested an open casket but the funeral director, Jerald King, had objected, claiming the old man's body was not presentable for viewing. Better to leave his medals and a few pictures on the table next to his flag-draped coffin, he urged. This was the one thing Nat's brother had agreed with Jerald about. Every other detail of the funeral plans had set Joseph off: the location of the grave site, the limited invite list for the interment, even the time of day picked for the service. But the funeral director had controlled matters for Nat, sparing him the conflict with his brother.

"Mr. Travis was very specific about his plans," Jerald had said, "and I'm not going to deviate from his wishes."

"Do you really want to challenge me on this?" Joseph had fired back threateningly.

"Your grandfather thought you might question his decisions,"

Jerald had responded coolly. "So he wrote his instructions down in case you wanted to see them."

Joseph grumbled but eventually relented in the face of the evidence, which brought Nat a mild sense of satisfaction. Nat had often found himself withdrawing from conflict with his brother as he grew older, unwilling to engage in Joseph's get-in-the-last-word debates, most of which ended only when Joseph got his way. Over the years, his brother had become a different man with a different perspective, and no one could move him off his ground, especially a small-town football coach from Brewton. There were times he missed the brother he once knew, the one he'd needed so much after his mother died of breast cancer and his father fell victim to the bottle. That Joseph was nowhere to be found.

They'd been close. Nat fondly remembered their days walking down to their father's workplace together, observing the sputtering grain elevators churn up and down, and hiding in his brother's secret place at the same time every day. "Watch this," Joseph had told his brother the first time and, like clockwork, Harriet Barnhill, the lady with the tightest dresses in Brewton, snuck into the room and started groping their father's boss. "Brother," Joseph had instructed, "this is our secret. You understand?" And after Nat hungrily agreed, he was treated to the first set of boobs in his life as Harriet reached behind her back and unclasped her bra. That image remained imprinted in Nat's mind even today. He'd never forgotten Harriet Barnhill.

The brothers had spent the rest of their time throwing rocks at the buzzards hovering around the rendering plant and waiting by the train tracks to see if the sparks flying off the rails might catch the grass on fire. They'd especially loved walking down the alley to Mr. Lumpkin's hardware store and waiting until the stooped-over friend of Papa Joe's brought them chocolate cookies. Joseph was the brother who'd always found time for Nat, who'd fished with him, protected him, and taught him to be a man. But a law degree and success—if that's what it was—had taken something essential away.

Nat stared across the community center at his brother. He'd once again seized control of his environment. Although many around him were dressed casually, a look that Papa Joe would have preferred, Joseph had his uniform on—perfectly tailored black suit and white shirt, well-placed American-flag lapel pin, freshly shined shoes, and a crimson pocket square that flowed across his suit in perfect symmetry with his Windsor-knotted tie. Although Joseph was shorter than Nat, his presence still commanded attention. He engaged both strangers and friends alike with a politician's zeal. Joseph moved fluidly from conversation to conversation, huddling with elderly women with his arm around their shoulders, commiserating with old friends, consoling others. Joseph hadn't known his grandfather, at least not the way Nat did, but no one in that room would have known. His brother's immense gifts were undeniable, even though they seemed particularly superficial at the moment.

Nat snuck to the back of the room, found an isolated corner, and threw back a couple of shots of Jack Daniels from a flask hidden inside his coat pocket. He drew a deep breath and tried not to brood. Then he saw his nephew, Emmitt Travis, and his mood brightened considerably.

"Uncle Nat. Great to see you. How've you been?"

Nat opened his arms and gave his thick-shouldered, twenty-two-year-old, Atlanta nephew a bear hug. "Emmitt," he said. "You're strong as an ox. Still pumping iron?"

"Nah, I'm getting soft. Too much studying, but I'm working out when I can. What are you packing these days, uncle? You look like you could still go deep."

Nat shrugged and then held out his large hands as though he was catching a long bomb.

From behind Emmitt, a thin-lipped, petite girl emerged. "Uncle Nat, I'm so sorry about Papa Joe."

Nat moved around Emmitt and squeezed his niece Amelia. "Hi, beautiful," he said. "How are you?"

"I'm great," she replied, looking down at her feet, "but I'm so sad about Papa Joe. I miss him already."

"He was so excited about your engagement," Nat continued. "He wanted to see you in that wedding dress more than you know."

Amelia's eyes welled up and she hugged Nat a second time.

Amelia's compassion again reminded Nat how foolish his brother had been to abandon his children and run off to Texas. Two young kids and a beautiful wife had been left behind in Brewton while Joseph romanced a white woman who had bigger ambitions than Alabama offered. The fact that his brother married the woman and had two more children proved he'd lost his way—and his soul. Joseph had chosen a political career and Karen Bartlett's money over his Brewton heritage, over his children, and over their mother, Renee, who'd been forced to uproot and move to Atlanta. Yet, from the ashes, Joseph's Alabama family had made a new life and succeeded without him. Nat always wondered if that had bothered his brother.

As Nat stepped back from Amelia, he saw Renee walk toward him with her arms outstretched. Her warm greeting comforted him.

"It's been too long," Renee offered.

Nat tried to suck the whiskey residue out of his mouth, embarrassed that his first encounter with his former sister-in-law in years would come with fire on his breath. "You look great, Renee," he stammered.

"Had to avoid the peacock over there. You'd think he's running for mayor of Brewton, the way he's carrying on. I haven't seen him since Amelia's graduation and he barely says hello. But what'd you expect? I need a drink. Can you help me out?" Renee gave him a knowing smile.

"Mom," Emmitt cut in, "Amelia and I are heading out now. We're going back to Grandma's house. Reggie's coming in later tonight. Good to see you, Uncle Nat."

"Make sure you say something to your father before you leave," Renee directed.

"Do we have to?" Amelia replied with a raised eyebrow.

Renee smiled. "Just do it," she admonished. "I'll see you back at the house. What time's that fiancé of yours getting in?"

"About ten o'clock," Amelia answered. "He's driving. And he'll be staying in the room with Emmitt, no worries. 'Bye, Mom."

Emmitt and Amelia kissed their mother on the cheek and angled toward the exit.

Nat watched his niece and nephew head out and then turned to their mother. He noticed a few lines below Renee's eyes but her smooth, bronze complexion had withstood time well. Genetics were definitely working in Renee Travis's favor.

"So how're you doing?" Nat asked. "And, I'm happy to put up the boys if you're cramped. My place ain't much, but I have plenty of room."

"That's sweet, but we're good. My mother would lock me out of the house if the kids didn't stay with her."

"So when's the wedding?"

"Still haven't picked a date yet and they're in no great hurry. Reggie won't finish grad school for another semester. Looks like I'll have something to keep me busy for the next year."

"Uh huh. And what about you? The last time I saw you was at Papa Joe's eighty-fifth birthday."

"Good memory. Some event, wasn't it?" She sighed. "I've raised a couple of good kids ... despite their father. But I'm not complaining. They're the lights of my life. Not much else has changed. I'm still teaching American history at Emory, but I finally earned a sabbatical so I'm taking the fall semester off. I guess it's one of the few benefits of getting older. I'm supposed to travel and refresh my batteries for the next four months, or something like that. Develop a book proposal while I'm at it. So what about you, Nat? Anyone new in your life?"

Nat shrugged off the question with a roll of his eyes. "Still alive," he said. "Got a good team this year. You need to come see us play."

"Typical." Renee laughed. "I'm glad I gave up trying to find you a woman long ago. But I can still hope." She grabbed him around the arm and whispered in his ear, "I'm so sorry about Papa Joe. I know how much you loved him ... and he loved you. You did a good thing watching over him all these years."

Nat felt the weight of his grandfather's death consume him for the first time since he'd received the news. The hectic pace of arranging funeral details coupled with greeting out of town well-wishers had left his emotions suspended. He rubbed his eyes. "Thanks, Renee," he whispered. "And you know how much he loved you and the kids."

"We're all going to miss him," she said. "I'll be around a few days if you want a shoulder. He was so good to me and my family."

Nat began to choke up when an elderly black man in a wheelchair rolled up through the crowd next to him.

"May I borrow this youngster for a minute?" the old man requested in a soft voice.

"Sergeant!" Nat exclaimed.

"How are you, son?"

Sergeant Anthony Ambrose was one of Joe Travis's oldest and dearest friends and a fellow combatant. Nat hadn't seen him more than a handful of times in his life, but he knew the wheelchair and the military dress, as well as Papa Joe's deep respect for the man. "Renee, meet Sergeant Anthony Ambrose. Served with my grandfather in the war. A genuine hero, just like Papa Joe. You've come a long way to be here, Sergeant. Good of you."

Sergeant Ambrose offered a mock salute. "I had to pay my respects to your grandfather. He was a dear friend. I also wanted to visit with you for a few minutes. Is there a place we could talk?"

"Of course," Nat answered. "Renee, we'll catch up later."

"Okay." She then pecked him on the cheek. "Call me; I mean that. Nice to meet you Sergeant."

"Cell number?" Nat asked before turning to Ambrose. "I'm going to take you and the kids to dinner before you get away."

Renee nodded, handed him a card, and plunged into the crowd. Nat watched her for a moment before pushing Sergeant Ambrose's wheelchair to a corner in the back of the community center.

"How're you holding up, son?" the sergeant asked.

"Barely," Nat responded. "More frustrated than sad in some ways ... we still don't know what happened. I'm hoping the police get off their asses eventually. I'm guessing it's one of those gangbangers from the neighborhood."

"That's why I'm here to see you," the sergeant interrupted. "There are certain things you need to understand about your grandfather. I suspect the neighborhood punks had nothing to do with his death. You might think I'm a crazy old man but you need to hear me out. Your grandfather had a secret. One that others wanted desperately, but that he shared with only one other person in his life. Me."

Nat wondered if he'd misheard the sergeant. He leaned down toward Ambrose.

"I don't have a lot of time left on this Earth," Ambrose continued, "and I don't want to carry your grandfather's secret with me to the grave. Joe Travis didn't trust many but he always said you were a good boy, that I should come see you if anything ever happened."

Nat's pulse quickened. Sergeant Ambrose hardly sounded delusional.

"Listen carefully," Ambrose said, his voice rising. "How much do you know about your Travis family?"

CHAPTER 4

Angelina de Zavala Gentry, a frown stretched across her face, watched the huge man with the scar on his cheek enter the hotel room with Shakes by his side. What started as a simple job had turned into a fiasco. Seeing the two men side-by-side for the first time made Angelina realize she'd made a mistake pairing them. Both were strong willed and unafraid but so different as to be incompatible. The huge white man was nothing but a mercenary, a trained killer; the black man anything but—he was jovial and loose, and the gold jewelry adorning his fingers and neck drew attention to his every movement. She'd known and trusted Shakes for a long time but when Frankie, the man who served as her eyes and ears, had seeded doubts about Shakes's loyalty, Kruger had become a necessary evil. And now it was too late to change; she needed them both, no matter how poorly matched.

"Sit down," Angelina ordered in her tinny voice, pointing the two men toward the open chairs in front of her.

"Ma'am," Shakes said with a nod.

"What do you have for me?" she asked.

"We found his laptop," Shakes answered. The black man removed the machine from his backpack and handed it to her. She noticed his long, manicured fingernails and wondered how he could do his job without breaking one of them. "We didn't have time to search the rest of his house, but we f'ed it up enough to look like a break-in. Whatever info the old man had is likely on his hard drive anyway."

"You think?" Angelina said with a roll of her eyes. "It

might've helped if you'd questioned him before tossing him around. I didn't want you to kill him!"

"No choice," the giant Kruger interjected in his heavy Slavic accent. "He punched his Life Alert bo-o-tton. We weren't trying to hurt him."

Angelina noticed Shakes cringe when he heard the word "we" and felt the tension build between the two men. "He was an old man," she said. "What did you think would happen if you threw him on the floor?"

"Time ran out," Shakes interrupted. "We had to make quick decisions."

Kruger shifted uncomfortably in his chair, as if he didn't want Shakes covering for him.

Angelina's concerns grew darker with each moment in the room. She doubted she could have the two men work together again in the future—they were just too combustible. "Old man Travis," she said, "has plenty of family in the area and a number of close friends in the military. For all we know, he's passed on the map to one of them ... or it's still in the house. Who knows? I'll review the laptop and see what I find. Shakes, did you get a copy of the attendees from the visitation at the funeral home? That should give us some ideas. For now, lie low. There'll be investigators crawling all around Brewton. Travis was a legend down there."

Kruger grunted but said nothing.

"Understood," Shakes responded. Sensing the meeting was over, he started to rise.

"Hold on," Angelina commanded. "I need to know everything Travis said to you. Is there anything you left out?"

Shakes and Kruger looked at each other and shook their heads. "He didn't say much," Shakes offered. The black man then drew a deep breath and stared at Angelina as if something had come to him. "Wait a minute." Shakes looked in the air and paused. "It may be nothing but just before the old man passed out he used a phrase that didn't make sense. Something bizarre … like … 'come and get it.'"

Angelina's interest was piqued for the first time since the men had arrived. She wobbled closer to them. "Tell me exactly what he said," she demanded.

"I'm not sure," Shakes responded. "Can't remember the exact words."

"I want the exact words!"

Kruger looked at his partner and held up his hand. "I know," he said.

"Speak clearly," Angelina shot back. She was having difficulty comprehending the giant's heavy accent.

He said, "'Come and take it!'"

Angelina's tight mouth relaxed into a grin when the huge man uttered the words. For the first time in all her years of searching, she had independent confirmation that the long-ago saga of Joe the slave and his map might be real. Old man Travis's dying words had to mean something—maybe even that he was hiding the secret. Angelina looked toward the two men and muttered her approval. "That's all I need for now," she said. "And I want you both to understand, this will be our last meeting. From now on you are to deal solely with Frankie. He'll be in touch soon."

CHAPTER 5

Nat tapped his foot while waiting for Renee and her children to arrive at the restaurant. They'd helped him through the long day, and with the funeral now behind him, he was interested to hear more about their lives. Nat gobbled up a few peanuts, knocked down a couple of Jack Daniels to take the edge off, and thought back to the service. It was a small gathering, only family and a handful of close friends, and he was satisfied he'd made his way through the difficult eulogy without making a fool of himself. Still, with his thoughts in turmoil, his voice broke more than once. It was the vision of Renee beside Emmitt, Amelia, and Reggie that drove him to discard his notes and finally speak from his heart. Their encouraging smiles had lifted an otherwise dreary day and brought him peace when Joseph's stern gaze beat him down over burying Papa Joe in an unworthy, run-down Civil War-era cemetery.

By the time Renee entered the restaurant, the alcohol had worked its magic, leaving Nat comfortable and relaxed. He was taken aback by Renee's clingy summer dress and straightened hair. She'd hidden her figure in her mourning clothes and kept her hair tightly wound in a bun. Until she walked in, Nat had forgotten how striking she'd been as a teenager at S.W. Niland High School. Renee had probably put on a few pounds since he'd last seen her in 2005, but who hadn't? And her confident stride suggested she was happy with her figure. Time had been kinder to her than most. For a woman in her early fifties, she looked easily a decade younger than she was.

"Glad you came," Nat said as Renee approached his table. "Where are the kids?"

"Take a guess," she responded, grabbing his shoulder and pecking him on the cheek. "Not the first time they've better-dealed me. I'm afraid you're stuck."

"Okay by me," Nat replied.

"Wow, this old joint still looks the same," Renee said, taking a seat. "Not much has changed about Brewton, Alabama."

That's an understatement, Nat thought. "I'd say Brewton still has a way to go to catch up with Atlanta. But we do have a Waffle House now. And a Walmart. And last I checked, pretty decent cellular coverage, too. What more do we need?" Nat chuckled.

"I always thought it was a charming place," Renee replied. "I've genuinely enjoyed seeing all of the familiar faces the last few days. You do remember at one time I expected to live here the rest of my life." She smiled wistfully.

Nat's mind shifted back to high school, when the quiet beauty had started dating his brother. Renee, a perfect combination of brains and looks, a mystery to most of the boys at Niland, and his brother, an extrovert with ambition oozing out of his pores, who succeeded with her where all others failed. A strange pair at the time but in hindsight a perfect match—the two shared a common bond of wanting to further themselves beyond the boundaries of Brewton. Renee's maturity at a tender age drove her to the boy with promise of a future and turned her away from the more popular crowd that Nat traveled in, all of them destined to remain in Brewton, many never even finishing high school.

"Tell me everything," Nat said. "By the way, do you want a drink?"

"I'd love a glass of white wine," Renee answered. "I don't suppose the wine list has changed much in the last twenty years." She smiled again, displaying a mouthful of perfectly white teeth that appeared enhanced by cosmetic dentistry. "The kids are doing great. Emmitt leaves for Texas law school in a couple of weeks and Amelia's just finishing undergrad. She claims she's taking a job at a social media start-up in Atlanta, but that remains to be seen. I suspect this wedding's about to take over her life. Reggie's got a good job with a financial-services firm. I like his family, too. They'll be a good team. What about you? What's new in your life?"

Nat hesitated. This was one subject that he really didn't want to discuss. "You know Joseph's still in Texas," he finally said, "so I rarely see him. With Papa Joe gone, I guess you'd say I'm on my own."

Renee eyed him sympathetically. "You know how sorry I am," she said. "But you can't tell me there's no lady in your life these days."

Nat grinned. "You know it's a cliché, but I'm married to my coaching. It's what I love to do. And you? Last time we met you were about to get married."

Renee held out her ringless finger and flipped her hand over. "That one didn't work. The closer we got, the more I saw Joseph. One bad marriage is enough for this girl. I finally realized that I have a bad habit of picking unreliable men. I'm better off on my own. Happier, anyway." She paused. "It's true," she said when she saw Nat cock his head as if to disagree.

After the waiter set down Renee's drink, Nat picked up his glass and said, "Well then, here's to truth and happiness … and to Papa Joe." They clinked glasses.

For the next hour, Nat and Renee rambled on about their families, traded stories about Papa Joe, and after a few more drinks, cracked a joke or two about Joseph's political career. The most surprising part was how connected Papa Joe had remained with Renee over the years. Nat had no idea his grandfather had taken such a genuine interest in Renee's life after the divorce.

The fact that he often emailed her to discuss her work at Emory, and to share with her his interest in black history, hit Nat from left field. Renee explained that she loved hearing from Papa Joe and that they'd grown closer over the years. Their conversation drew Nat to discuss a subject he hadn't planned to share.

"Do you remember meeting Sergeant Ambrose the other night?" Nat asked.

"Sure, the old man in the wheelchair?" she replied. "Why do you ask?"

"He told me a story the other night that I can't stop thinking about."

"That's intriguing. Tell me more."

"Sergeant Ambrose doesn't think neighborhood punks had anything to do with Papa Joe's death. It may sound hard to believe, especially now that I'm saying it, but … are you ready for this … he thinks the thieves were professionals."

"What? But why?"

"He said they were looking for something valuable, something Joseph and I apparently knew nothing about."

"That's hard to believe," Renee answered. Nat heard the skepticism in her voice.

"Ambrose told me he was the only one Papa Joe confided in but he couldn't keep the story to himself any longer. According to him, Papa Joe died with a secret. A very big secret."

CHAPTER 6

Sergeant Ambrose opened his closet door and pulled out a large storage box from the lower shelf—a collection of photos, letters, and mementos from his years in the service of his country. He always found himself reminiscing his way through this box whenever he lost one of his former comrades, but today's search had a different purpose. Joe Travis had committed him to a promise, one that Ambrose had privately questioned over the years, but one he was duty bound to honor. As a fellow survivor of the Omaha Beach landing, Joe Travis could have asked Ambrose to wheel himself to Washington and back and he would've done it. The lucky few living from the old Blue and Grey division had a commitment to one another that required no explanation, no matter the circumstances, not even in death.

Ambrose was struck by what he'd seen in Brewton, Alabama. A man who'd earned a Silver Star for bravery should have been buried at Arlington National, not in an obscure cemetery on the outskirts of nowhere. But, then again, that was Joe Travis. The choice was likely personal to him and no one would ever know the reason he'd selected that location. One of Joe Travis's grandsons, on the other hand, had been more than eager to soak up the adulation due his grandfather. In his remarks at the service, Joseph Travis had used every bit of his time to pontificate on his own accomplishments, rather than extolling the virtues of his heroic grandfather. A disgrace, Ambrose thought, even for a lowly politician. Thankfully the other boy, Nat, had shown the proper respect for his grandfather. Joe Travis had been wise to trust him.

Ambrose plucked out a couple of loose photos from the box and threw them on the bed. One was a photo of the 29th Infantry Division after securing Omaha Beach; the other a shot with Joe Travis in St. Lo after the Allies' hard-won victory and liberation of that small town in northern France. The same thought crossed Ambrose's mind every time he saw these pictures. Few Americans could appreciate what men like him and Joe Travis had gone through for their country.

Ambrose always felt as though he was peering into the life of some other man, into an alternative universe, when viewing these pictures. How much time had passed? How many books had been written? He sighed and shook his head. Even today, the memories of the German machine-gun fire raining down on his troops from Omaha Beach awakened him at night. At other times, the sounds of the Nazi panzers pounding through the French woods in pursuit of his men plagued him, the earsplitting blasts of their cannons still ringing in his ears. Each painful image had brought him closer to Joe Travis and the few survivors who shared his story. Only they could appreciate what the experience did to a man. Ambrose shrugged his shoulders, reached down into the storage container, and pulled out a small shoe box full of letters. He opened it and looked at the numerous handwritten and computer-generated notes he'd received over the years from Joe Travis. All had been sent to him after the war was over, save one—a worn two-page letter signed by a young private addressed to his four-year-old son days after the Normandy invasion. The words ripped through the old man like a bayonet as he scrolled down Travis's recounting of that terrifying day on Omaha Beach. His friend's words captured the horror of the moment—"body parts flew past our boat," "bullets whirred past my helmet," "one hit the soldier next to me in the face." The lines remained difficult to read, all these many years later.

Ambrose set the letter down and clasped his hands, soaking

up the quiet of the day and the ambivalent gratitude he still felt about surviving it all. Ambrose had preserved this letter ever since Joe's beloved son, Sam, had died and Joe had sent him a copy. He'd include it with his package for Nat Travis to remind the young man of his grandfather's heroism.

The numerous other letters from Joe Travis in the shoe box were personal and had collected in Ambrose's closet over the sixty years since the war had ended. Many were about Joe's life and his lost son but the more recent ones told a winding and incomplete story about the history of the Travis family. A story Ambrose believed had first gained Travis's interest after one of his closest friends, a young Hispanic soldier, died in his arms during the turbulent Battle of St. Lo.

The sergeant looked down at the huge stack of letters and felt a gnawing pain in his gut. Joe Travis's tale about a famous relative he'd discovered in his genealogical research must have been true. Why else would someone break into the old man's house and kill him? He felt little relief for finally having shared what he knew about Joe's research with his grandson, Nat, because it had come much too late. Then again, how could he blame himself if Travis never chose to share the story with his own family? At least he'd finally unloaded on Nat and given the next generation of Travises the opportunity to explore the mystery of Joe the slave. Maybe they'd take the time to figure it all out.

Ambrose picked up the letters along with the photos and placed them in a UPS box. He wheeled himself into the other room with the box in his lap and called the deliveryman.

CHAPTER 7

It had taken some work but Kruger had finally convinced Angelina to let him handle the next assignment alone. He'd reminded her several times how weak and unpredictable Shakes had become and the old lady had bought it.

Kruger knew that neither Angelina nor Shakes fully understood his motives or capabilities. He'd never told them that he'd grown up in the killing fields of Yugoslavia and been raised as a soldier. He wondered how they would feel if they realized he'd joined the Army of the *Republika Srpska* under the command of General Ratko Mladić as a boy and had been part of the bloodiest fighting force of Serbian president Slobodan Milošević. Or that he'd served in a specialized operations group within General Mladić's army that carried out the darkest missions of the war. Being branded on the face with the unmistakable Serbian cross had been part of his initiation into that brutal club.

He'd earned his place as a renowned killer, a man feared by even his own troops. These many years later, he was still unrepentant about the tactics he'd employed to protect his homeland and his comrades in the *Republika Srpska*. What the West had described as ethnic cleansing and genocide were the only ways true Serbians could control their lands and eliminate the despicable Muslims and Croats. Kruger and his men had done what was necessary. No apologies.

But despite his desire to stay in Serbia forever, Kruger had been forced to leave. When General Mladić and many of his brothers were persecuted for war crimes, he'd moved fast, paying his way onto a German merchant ship bound for New Orleans and the safety of the United States. After hiding in the shadows for several years, fate somehow brought Kruger to Texas and the Aryan Brotherhood in San Antonio. These were real men much like his Serbian comrades back home. Once adopted by the Brotherhood, he'd waited patiently to find just the right kind of work and eventually heard of a young Hispanic man, named Frankie, looking for muscle. When they met for the first time, Frankie had explained that the job was simple—provide security work for an old lady and "keep his mouth shut." Kruger sensed, however, there was much more to it than that. But after accepting the job, he got saddled with the pathetically undisciplined Shakes Gunn. Kruger knew immediately that the black man was a problem he'd eventually have to deal with.

Kruger stepped out of his car in front of the old sergeant's house in New Orleans. He patted his pocket to make sure the hypodermic needle was in place. The birds chirped from camouflaged locations in the trees as the huge man walked toward Ambrose's front door. Kruger licked his lips. The birds stopped chirping.

CHAPTER 8

Renee Travis fired up her engine and drove off to meet Nat. She'd felt a surprising connection when catching up with him at dinner the prior day, and when he'd told her the curious story recited to him by Sergeant Ambrose, she'd felt an improbable sense that fate had somehow drawn her back to Brewton. Part of the appeal was to the historian in her, but the story prompted memories of a suddenly meaningful series of probing calls she'd received over the last few years from Papa Joe. That the old man had kept in touch with her after the divorce to hear about Emmitt and Amelia had touched her deeply, particularly given his grandson's abject failure as a parent, but more recently he'd called with unusual questions about famous characters in the formative days of the Texas Republic. Many of the inquiries had been outside her area of expertise—she was a Civil War and Reconstruction scholar—but she'd known enough information to give him insight into books and new research that existed on the topics. Renee was happy to help Papa Joe and considered his interest in Texas history and his family's genealogy endearing, an engrossing use of a retiree's time, but little more. To discover there might be some greater historical importance to his questions, or better yet, a lingering mystery in the Travis family, now stirred her imagination. She was pleased when Nat had asked if she'd stay around and help him sort through Papa Joe's things to search for evidence supporting Sergeant Ambrose's story.

Nat had surprised Renee. The sullen teenager she'd known had given way to a thoughtful, pleasant man. The brooding intensity she'd always felt in his strained relationship with his brother had waned, and he seemed at peace with himself. He remained ruggedly handsome, only his drooping shoulders and full-retreat hairline giving evidence of his passage into middle age, but there was no vanity in his appearance. The transformation may have been natural with age, but she sensed the years with Papa Joe had brought Nat a great deal more balance in his life.

At dinner, they'd danced around their days at S.W. Niland and her eleven years with Joseph, but they'd laughed off the past without dwelling on her failed marriage and his troubled youth. She'd explained to him that the divorce had been a catalyst for her professionally, and that she'd spent the past fifteen years focused on scholarship, which now had her on the cusp of tenure at Emory. Much like Nat had found in coaching, she'd discovered research and teaching her true calling, neither of which she would have pursued if married to a controlling politician with a myopic focus on his own career.

"What about you?" Nat had prodded at one point, but she'd safely brushed the question aside with a sweep of her hand.

"Between raising two kids and my teaching," she'd explained, "there's been no time for relationships." They'd both smiled and moved on to other topics.

Her biggest concern as she pulled into Papa Joe's driveway was the fact that Nat understood so little about his grandfather's research. The two had been close, that much she knew, but Papa Joe's decision to exclude his most trusted family member from his work felt peculiar, maybe even intentional. She believed there had to be a valid explanation—perhaps Papa Joe worried the whole thing might be a hoax or dreaded that his grandson wouldn't take his findings seriously—but something was off. Maybe it was just an old man's stubborn pride. Whatever the justification, she was happy to help Nat, and she'd already decided to extend her stay in Brewton visiting her mother.

Renee parked her car on the street and sprang toward the front door of Papa Joe's house. The siding material on the exterior walls needed repair and the lawn a good mowing, but the place still retained its quaint charm. Memories of the perpetually positive Joe Travis filled Renee's head as she approached the covered porch, but her mood darkened once she saw the remnants of the crime-scene tape.

"Hi," Renee said when Nat stepped outside to greet her.

"Thanks for coming," he replied. "I'm not sure I could've done this by myself." He extended his hand.

"It still feels a little strange for me," Renee said, clasping his hand. "You sure you don't have someone you might prefer to help?"

"Funny thing, but I think Papa Joe thought more highly of you than anyone I know. He'd be pleased you're looking through his things. Some of them will bring back a few memories."

"And I did volunteer," Renee countered with a smile.

Nat nodded and Renee followed him into the sparsely decorated den in the front of the house. The lonely scene saddened her but she knew it was a setting Papa Joe loved. A motorized recliner chair tilted in a position even a contortionist would find challenging, a scratchy end table, and a worn television console were the only pieces of furniture in the room. "This is where he was the night they broke in." Nat pointed at Papa Joe's chair. "He slept here a lot because it was too hard for him to get to the bedroom."

Renee sighed. "I guess that explains the chair. Looks like you've straightened up most of the mess."

"I replaced a few drawers, stacked up the books, and reorganized the furniture, but there wasn't much else to do. Either the motherfu …," Nat caught himself, "sorry … the killers … found what they were looking for or they left in a big hurry. His bedroom was hardly touched."

"No need to apologize." Renee consoled him with her eyes.

"That's what confuses me about Ambrose's story," Nat continued. "If these were professionals searching for something important, why kill him? And once they'd searched, why leave behind a mess? If they hadn't, the police would've written off Papa Joe's death to a bad fall."

"You're right," she responded. "So where does that leave us?"

"Papa Joe never kept material things, other than his medals, and those are in a lockbox down at the bank ... with a few business documents. I want to go through his personal effects and see what's there. He kept pictures, letters, books, articles, so they may give us a clue what he might've been hiding. And maybe Ambrose was too dramatic. All he told me was that Papa Joe stumbled onto something valuable in his genealogical research about a slave named Joe ... but funny thing is my gut's now telling me this is real. So while I'm flipping through those things, do you mind searching his laptop? No telling what you'll find on the hard drive ... maybe even something about your ex-husband." Nat smiled, and they both laughed.

Listening to Nat's joke about his brother, Renee could feel the distance, the wall, that still separated them. It had been particularly painful when they'd discussed at dinner Joseph's political ambitions and how every advancement in his career caused him to further sever his connection to Brewton. Nat never appeared bitter about Joseph's success, despite having a few laughs at his expense, but instead seemed wrapped in melancholy regarding the deterioration of their relationship. And now with Joseph's ascension as a leading black figure in the heavily white, Republican state of Texas, Nat seemed resigned that nothing between them would ever change.

"Where did Papa Joe keep his stuff?" Renee asked.

"In his bedroom. Follow me."

Renee trailed Nat past a small kitchen into a bedroom with

a single wooden chair, a twin bed, and a knotty-pine bureau. A lone picture of Nat's father, Sam, sat on the nightstand. Nothing looked out of order. "I'll pull in another chair," Nat offered, retreating into the kitchen. He returned quickly with one of the dining-room chairs and placed it in front of Renee. "I'll go through his closet first," he continued. "There are lots of boxes on those shelves. The laptop should be in his bureau."

"Sounds like a plan," Renee agreed, "but something's been bothering me since our dinner. If it's true there's some deep, dark secret here, why didn't your grandfather tell you about it? Why only Ambrose?"

"I don't know," Nat replied with a shrug as he opened a shoe box from one of the closet shelves. "One thing I'm sure of—he must have felt there was a good reason to keep it private. I'd known he'd been doing research on our family tree for years, but I never thought much about it. I'm guessing now that it weighed on him pretty hard. Ambrose said the older Papa Joe got, the more worried he grew that people were looking for him, looking for his secret. He said the handwritten letters he's sending me in the mail describe Papa Joe's paranoia in great detail."

"And what about Ambrose?"

"Best friends with Papa Joe from the war. They were as close as two men who never saw each other could be. He's completely reliable."

Renee gently patted Nat on the shoulder. "So whoever broke in," she concluded, "could've stolen valuable information, maybe letters, and none of us would be the wiser?"

"Uh huh," Nat answered, "but I think Papa Joe would've been more careful than that. Or, at least I hope so. It's hard to believe a couple of thieves would need to kill him to get what they wanted."

Nat then turned to the closet and started to pull out his grandfather's private papers and photographs. Renee, in turn, began rummaging around the bureau looking for the laptop.

"What am I missing?" she asked after a short search.

"What?" Nat replied.

"I can't find the laptop," she said. "Did he keep it somewhere else?"

"That's not a good sign … may explain why there wasn't a mess in this room."

"They stole his laptop," Renee said as if the answer was obvious.

"Sounds like it, but let's look around the rest of the house to be sure."

After ten minutes of opening drawers and looking under furniture, Nat announced, "It's gone."

"Seems that way," Renee confirmed. "Any chance he knew how to back up his computer? Think he could have stored the contents somewhere else?"

"Doubt it; he wasn't that sophisticated … but wait a minute, I can't believe it, but several years ago he did ask me about backing up information on his computer. I didn't think much of it at the time but I did buy him a couple of USB drives with *Roll Tide* written across 'em. I have no idea if he ever did anything with 'em or would even know how to use the damn things. But I guess it's possible."

"Where are they?" Renee asked.

"No idea. I guess we should look around and see if he stashed 'em somewhere."

Fifteen minutes later, after poring through every drawer, cupboard, and cabinet in the house, Nat turned to Renee with a scowl on his face. "I knew it was a long shot. There's nowhere we haven't looked. Let's call the police."

"I want to take one last pass through the bedroom before we give up," Renee suggested.

"What's the point?"

"Instinct," she shrugged hopefully.

They both stood in the doorway of the bedroom and scoured the area. Short of a secret compartment or a loose board on the floor, Renee saw nothing that made sense as a hiding place for a USB drive.

"I give up," Nat conceded. "It's not here."

"Hold on," Renee shot back while pondering a new possibility. "What if a paranoid old man thought his computer might be stolen? Take another look."

Nat turned to Renee and followed her eyes to the picture of his father on Papa Joe's nightstand. "No way," he said as he walked over and picked up the frame. Nat shook it several times and his face burst into a broad, excited smile. He then carefully slid open the wooden back of the frame and a small USB drive with *Roll Tide* fell to the bed.

"Bingo!" she exclaimed.

CHAPTER 9

Angelina de Zavala Gentry had reveled watching her protégé kick her two old enemies out of their positions at the DRT. Having successfully wooed Janet Nelson to her side, Angelina now felt confident the young woman would do anything she needed. How Angelina loved working with politicians. So easy to predict, so simple to manipulate. Janet was proving no different from the many others Angelina had known over the years. The young woman's short career as a city councilwoman in San Antonio had perfectly fed her ego, and the fawning press, with gentle pushes from Angelina, had persuaded Janet she was destined for bigger things.

Angelina heard the knock on the outside door to her suite and dispatched Frankie to admit her guest.

A moment later, Frankie eased inside Angelina's office. "Señora Nelson is here," he announced. "Okay, you can go in now," she heard Frankie whisper to her guest. "*Buena suerte, Señora Nelson.*"

"Thank you, Frankie," Janet said as she entered through the heavy wooden door. Angelina saw Janet's eyes spring to attention when she began studying the décor of the oversized, dimly lit room. Arranged throughout were important historical artifacts and museum-quality novelties from the Alamo period of the Texas Republic that Angelina had collected over the years. A glass case holding a musket rifle supposedly used by Davy Crockett rested in one corner, a saddle ridden by James Butler Bonham was perched on a riding stand in the other, and a uniform from one of the Texans who died defending the fortress was filled out by a mannequin next to Angelina's credenza. Positioned in the middle of the room was a huge antique desk adorned with even more memorabilia—a lamp made from a nineteenth-century Mexican army pistol, a bronze bust of Sam Houston, and Angelina's huge letter opener that looked something like Jim Bowie's famous knife. Angelina leaned back in her chair behind Sam Houston's head and waited as Janet took it all in.

"Good morning," Janet said.

Angelina pointed the new DRT president toward one of the uncomfortable Early American chairs across from her desk. "You did a nice job at the meeting," she started. "Have you considered the new officer slate we discussed?"

"Yes, I have the list right here." Janet pulled a piece of paper from her purse and handed it across the desk. Angelina noticed the young woman staring at the dark, heavy bags under her eyes. She hadn't slept in several days and knew she didn't look well. Angelina pulled her glasses up from the dangling wire around her neck and started reading.

"Good." She nodded before continuing. "The list appears to be in order. There will be dissension from some of the old-timers but most of them are too scared to mess with you now. You should have no trouble running these through. Do you have the votes counted?"

"Yes ma'am. I believe we're in good shape. The shock over Akers and Butler will run its course and I think these new appointments will give us a solid working group. The Daughters will be structured just as you want."

"And the financials?"

"No changes from what we agreed on," Janet said. "I forwarded a complete set to Senator Cravens's office. He confirmed he has everything he needs for the hearings. Those will likely start next week. Akers and Butler have already received subpoenas."

"Then I can expect the board's vote on Kalender's proposal within the next few weeks?"

"Yes ma'am. That's the plan."

Angelina nodded but inwardly she was about to explode. How long she'd waited to get her excavation project approved. She soaked in the accomplishment, took a deep breath, but said nothing. Her pleased mood instantly shifted when she saw the uninvited guest. She punched down an intercom button and yelled, "Come here, Frankie."

The young assistant burst into the room and knew exactly what to do. He ran to the window and straightened the curtains, shutting out the sunlight glinting past the rust-colored fabric. "Do you need anything else, ma'am?" he asked.

"That's all," Angelina answered curtly, angered that Frankie had allowed sunlight to get near her prized possession hanging on the wall across from her desk—a tattered flag secured in a wooden frame with the famous words COME AND TAKE IT painted below a black five-pointed star and a cannon. It was one of the few genuine Republic of Texas Gonzalez flags. No item in Texas lore conjured up more symbolism than this marker of Lone Star defiance. Angelina had spoken to Janet of its important place in the story of Texas independence several times, but she wondered whether her young politico truly cared about it. She, however, knew the famous story down to the last detail. In late September, 1835, less than a year before the battle of the Alamo, the Mexican army had demanded that a cannon loaned to the town of Gonzalez, Texas, be returned to its owner. In defiance, the town assembled a fighting force and surprised the Mexican army before it attacked, driving them away and preserving the armament. In recognition of the achievement, two women in Gonzalez painted the COME AND TAKE IT flag on a cotton cloth and hung it in the town square.

"You know who gave that flag to me?" Angelina asked Janet once Frankie left the room.

"No, ma'am," Janet answered.

"My great-grandmother, Adina de Zavala, the Angel of the Alamo. Do you know who she was?"

Janet shook her head. "Of course, I do." It was the right answer for anyone aspiring to gain Angelina's confidence.

Most records suggested Adina died in 1955 with no living family or descendants, but that was before Angelina laid claim to her birthright. For two generations, the illegitimate line of Adina de Zavala had gone unknown, but Angelina changed that in 1997. At a press conference conducted in the long-barracks room of the Alamo, Angelina announced herself as the one true descendant of Adina de Zavala, that she would change her name to de Zavala Gentry, and that she was willing to commit her formidable personal resources to the restoration of the Alamo. Angelina's goodwill, however, lasted only as long as her husband, software innovator Gordon Gentry, survived. Upon his death in 2002, a battle as epic as the Alamo ensued over the use of his fortune.

Gordon Gentry's will set up a trust to support the DRT with a large portion of his estate but left his wife completely in charge of the administration of the funds. What started as a blessed relationship between Angelina and the DRT—Gentry's money being used to replace mortar, refresh paintings, and preserve artifacts—turned into a contest of wills over the construction of a monument on Alamo grounds. Angelina on the one side pressing for a statue of Adina de Zavala to be built in the center of the Alamo plaza, and the officers of the DRT on the other, refusing to desecrate the grounds with a tribute to a noncombatant. Angelina believed her personal largesse, along with her husband's bequest, would convince the DRT to approve her request to honor the Angel of the Alamo, but the leaders of the organization, most notably Patricia Akers and Valerie Butler, disagreed.

Angelina still bristled from her stinging treatment, particularly given that the leaders of the DRT had promised everything in the early years to get her money, only to turn on her when the time came for recompense. This was the same group who, despite their considerable means, never gave the kind of money to the Alamo that Angelina had regularly contributed. But they were the entrenched locals with deep ties in the city of San Antonio and they successfully outmaneuvered her. Eventually, Angelina grew tired of the struggle and resigned her position from the board in 2004, pledging at the time to freeze the DRT from her husband's trust fund and terminate her support forever.

But privately Angelina vowed her fate would be different from that of her great-grandmother. From this bitter experience, Angelina found a new purpose, redirecting her funds into exhaustive research about Adina de Zavala and the history of the Alamo. Angelina soon began traveling, collecting historical artifacts, and studying every document she could find about Adina and the old mission. It was in this turbulent period of discovery that Angelina's life cause was revealed. The unearthing of a secret in Adina de Zavala's story gave her new purpose—a famous treasure buried below the grounds of the Alamo, which Angelina would find and claim as her birthright. With that discovery, Angelina could then resurrect the de Zavala name to its rightful place of honor, and, more important, settle old scores with the DRT elitists who'd maligned her. History and glory would be hers, much like that of the great heroes of her beloved Alamo.

In time, Angelina formulated a plan, one that led her to

Janet Nelson, a treasure hunter named Frank Kalender, and an old man named Joe Travis, the descendant of Alamo commander William Barret Travis's famous slave, Joe. And buoyed by Kalender's assurance the treasure was real, she'd implemented her scheme. She had worked her way back into the DRT's good graces, by humbling herself and mending fences, and with her re-election to the board in 2010, phase one was complete. All of the rancor from the past appeared gone and forgotten. A happy family again. At least until the last meeting.

Her reverie was broken by a knock on the door.

"Ms. de Zavala Gentry," Frankie announced apologetically, "there's a gentleman here to see you. He said it's urgent."

"Urgent?" she growled, but she could see by Frankie's look that it was important. "Tell him to wait!" Angelina then turned back to Janet, but she was too distracted by the unexpected visitor to continue their conversation. "Thank you, Janet; you've done a good job. I'll review the rest of this information later. We'll discuss next steps very soon. Frankie will show you out."

CHAPTER 10

Nat marched toward the entrance to the diner while juggling the *Roll Tide* USB drive in his hand. Despite spending most of the previous night studying the stored files, he couldn't figure out if any clues were embedded in the documents. Dense articles, book excerpts, and genealogical studies jumbled together made for an overwhelming task for a football coach whose reading list started and stopped with *Sports Illustrated*. Nat needed help if he was going to make sense of it all, and he hoped to convince Renee to take on the challenge.

Nat had found comfort in the brief time he'd spent with Renee since the funeral. Despite their many years apart, there was a familiarity to their renewed friendship, and Nat felt a genuine connection through their love for his grandfather and for Brewton which, in spite of Renee's years living away, still owned a piece of her heart.

She was seated at a small corner table when Nat walked in just after 8:00 a.m. "How's your mother?" he asked while sitting down.

"If she had any more energy, I'd need a vacation from my vacation." Renee laughed. Her mother worked at the community hospital and was widely regarded as a fireball. "She's doing great."

Nat nodded with a grin. A waitress wiggled up to their table and set a cup of coffee down in front of Renee. "So the USB drive," he started while pointing at Renee's cup, indicating he wanted one, too, "appears to confirm Ambrose's story. There's a ton of crap, I mean information, on it—articles, genealogical documents, you name it—and the little I've seen leads me to believe Papa Joe really was onto something." Nat smiled at himself. "From what I can tell," he continued, "it appears he'd actually proven our family descended from this Joe the slave character. But I've only started reading through it all."

"Crap is a word I use with my research all the time," Renee laughed. "But what you're saying is both sad and exciting. Can't wait to hear what you find."

Nat looked at the picture of Paul "Bear" Bryant looming over Renee's shoulder and wondered what the patron saint of Alabama football would do in this situation. "I'm sure this isn't how you planned to spend your time in Brewton, but I was hoping you'd help me out a while longer. Whatever's out there is on this device," he said while holding up the USB drive, "and I could really use a trained set of eyes."

"That's some offer." Renee smiled. "A trained set of eyes."

Nat looked down, acknowledging his awkward proposal. "That didn't come out quite right," he said with a grin. "What I meant was I really need your help."

Renee laughed, which relieved his anxiety. "I understood," she said. "I was actually hoping you'd ask me. Hard for me not to be interested. I'd love to have a look."

Nat smiled and immediately felt a weight lifted by Renee's answer. Just as he was about to reach over to give her a high five, a ringing sound interrupted him. He looked down at his cell phone and saw his brother's number. Joseph and poor timing seemed to go hand in hand.

"Sorry, it's Joseph," he said. "I'm sure it's something about Papa Joe. I've been expecting his call. Give me a minute." Nat stood and walked to a private area of the diner.

"Joseph," Nat answered.

"Heard anything yet?" his brother asked.

"No, nothing. The police are still investigating but they don't seem too motivated."

"Could've guessed that. What about the coroner?"

"Got his report. Confirmed the fall caused Papa Joe's death. Collapsed lung, broken ribs, you name it."

"Have you figured out what the punks wanted from his house?"

Nat wasn't yet ready to share any more details with Joseph. At least not yet.

"The only things we've found missing were his laptop and credit cards, not that he had much more of value anyway. They probably didn't want the TV."

"None of that surprises me," Joseph responded, "but that's not the reason I called. I have some more bad news."

"Huh," Nat replied.

"Remember Sergeant Ambrose?"

"Sure, great guy."

"I just got a call from one of Papa Joe's friends. The old sergeant's dead."

"Jesus," Nat exclaimed. "What happened?"

"They found him slumped over in his wheelchair in his home. Apparently a heart attack."

"Incredible ... when's the funeral?" Nat asked.

"Couple of days from now in New Orleans. Any chance you can go?"

Nat hesitated but just for a second. "Yeah," he answered, "season hasn't started yet, and I owe the man that much respect."

"Good, I don't have time to get down there, but I was hoping you might."

Nat didn't respond to the subtle dig. "I'll pay your respects," he said. "Talk to you later, Joseph. I've got to go." Nat hung up the phone and hustled back to the table where Renee sat with an impatient look on her face.

"I can leave if you have business," she said.

"Sorry, but I have some bad news."

"What's happened?"

"Sergeant Ambrose is dead. Someone found him slumped over in his wheelchair this morning. Joseph said it was a heart attack, but the timing makes me wonder."

"I'd say so," Renee said with sympathy in her voice. "That's horrible. Something's definitely wrong. What in the world's going on?"

"That's what I want to find out. I told Joseph I'd fly to New Orleans for the funeral and pay our family's respects, but I have more on my mind than that." Nat hesitated. An idea had struck him. He looked at Renee and tilted his head. "This may sound crazy," he continued, "but I'm going to give it a shot anyway. Why don't you come with me? Think of it as a gift from Papa Joe—an all-expense-paid trip to New Orleans. If there's more to this story, I'd sure like your help figuring it out."

Renee sat quietly for several minutes as if calculating her options. Nat worried he'd made a mistake and felt embarrassed for putting her on the spot in such an abrupt manner. He opened his mouth, about to apologize, when Renee held out her hand to stop him. She then smiled and said, "You know I'm supposed to rediscover myself during my sabbatical, not chase down mysteries in the bayou. But what can I say? You have my attention. Let's see if we can figure this thing out. I'm in for New Orleans."

CHAPTER 11

Shakes massaged his head before securing his stocking cap in place. He then readjusted his coiled, leather bracelet and twisted his diamond-studded earring into place. Sitting outside Angelina's office, his mind drifted back to the two dead World War II veterans. Killing them wasn't something he'd signed up for. Two bona fide black American heroes snuffed out, and there was blood on his hands. Then again, he couldn't afford to wallow in guilt. Whatever was driving Angelina, she paid the bills and that's all he could afford to think about right now. Even then, he still couldn't believe it had come to this.

Shakes wasn't a killer and those heroes deserved better. Two men who'd fought at Omaha Beach, marched on the forward edge of the Allied forces in France, and been wounded in action deserved to die on their own terms. That's why he'd agreed to let Kruger handle Sergeant Ambrose. The beast with the strange scar on his face had no conscience. Young or old, black or white, hero or villain, it didn't matter. In reality, maybe Angelina was right to force Kruger on him; maybe she sensed he didn't have what it took to finish the job. Maybe ... he should have left when he had the chance. But for now Shakes knew he had to stay focused. He had the box of letters Kruger had brought back from New Orleans and hoped they'd please his client enough to keep her from turning on him.

The screw-up at Travis's house hadn't been his responsibility anyway. His only fault was not controlling Kruger's needless manhandling of Joe Travis. Why did the maniac have to spike the old man on the floor? Shakes had covered for his partner in their first meeting with Angelina, but he could no longer risk taking the fall for the Serbian.

The door flew open and the ninety-five-pound hurricane stormed into the room. "I told you never to come to my office," Angelina seethed. "Darnell, you were to wait for Frankie's directions. Didn't I make myself clear?"

Shakes had seen Angelina fly into rages more frequently in the past months and realized he had to hold his ground or it would get worse. She only called him Darnell when she was really mad. "I didn't think this could wait," he said in a slightly raised voice.

Angelina froze and riveted her eyes on him. "Sit down," she ordered. "Tell me why you're here?"

"Ambrose is dead," Shakes began. "I hope the big lug was more careful this time. He said he injected him with a needle and left him in his wheelchair."

"I know that," she shot back. "I ordered it."

Shakes didn't like the fact that Kruger had already communicated with Angelina and she'd so matter-of-factly approved the murder, but there was little he could do about it. His accomplice had clearly built a relationship behind his back. "Well, here is the box of letters he brought back. It looks like Ambrose was going to ship them to Joe Travis's grandson. I thought you'd want them right away." Shakes pointed to a box resting in a chair backed up against the wall.

"Darnell, you know better than to come to my office," Angelina pressed, her anger now ebbing. "Never, and I mean never, come back here again." She paused. "But thank you for bringing the letters. I'll take a look at them."

Shakes nodded.

"And, by the way, I understand your problems with Kruger. I'm counting on you to keep him under control."

"Yes ma'am. As long as you remember, I've had your back for

a long time. That dude could never have planted that evidence on those two old ladies like I did. And I've never let you down. He's more dangerous than he's worth, if you ask me."

"I understand your point," she replied, but Shakes could tell she didn't mean it. "I'm told both women," she continued, "have been subpoenaed to testify before a state senate committee. If that evidence shows up in their documents, I'll be very pleased."

"It will," Shakes said. "It will."

CHAPTER 12

When the wheels lifted off the tarmac for Louis Armstrong International Airport, Nat and Renee sat side-by-side cramped in a small regional jet. The plane quickly leveled off at altitude and the seat in front of Nat catapulted back into his legs. Renee snickered as Nat jumped up and faked that he'd been injured by the reclining menace. "Good thing this is a short trip," he whispered. Nat then sighed, reached into his briefcase, and pulled out his college-football-preview edition of *USA Today* along with a small laptop.

"We have different reading tastes," Nat said as he placed the laptop on Renee's extended seat-back tray along with the *Roll Tide* USB drive.

"Not really," she said. "I love reading about the upcoming football season. Where are my Dawgs in there?"

"A good Alabama girl rooting for Georgia?" Nat said incredulously.

"I've been a Georgian for some time now. You know I can't live in Atlanta and root for the Crimson Tide. And you also know my Emory hasn't got much of a team. Actually, we don't have a team at all."

Nat laughed and said, "Number eighteen for the Bulldogs ... problem is 'Bama's number one."

"Now you know why I'd rather study that USB drive of yours," she chuckled. "But I hope I'll find something that will shed some light on that sneaky grandfather of yours. Maybe one of these articles will remind me of some of the questions he asked over the years ... I bet they do."

"I'm sure glad you're here," Nat said. "My head's swimming from reading all of that historical information. I prefer Xs and Os ... and game films."

"Then gobble up that paper and we'll see where we are in fifty minutes."

They read during the flight without much conversation, both ordering Diet Coke when the flight attendant came by. Nat mindlessly scoured the scouting reports on six or seven SEC teams before his thoughts wandered off to the evening ahead. He and Renee would attend Sergeant Ambrose's public viewing and a short memorial service at the Charbonnet Funeral Home—Ambrose's burial would be in Arlington National Cemetery. Then, if time permitted, he would take Renee to dinner. He thought about booking a table at Commander's Palace or another of the city's great restaurants but decided to wait and to see how the night unfolded.

"What do you think?" he asked once they landed.

"You're right about one thing," Renee answered. "There's a ton of information on here. It's going to take a lot more time to figure out what it all means. I may need an increase in pay."

Nat laughed and stuffed the laptop and USB drive back into his briefcase as they headed off. "I'll check with my accountant," he said, "but times are tough. Maybe you can sneak a meal or two on the expense account."

After he and Renee checked into their rooms at the Pontchartrain Hotel, Nat cleaned up and changed clothes. They rendezvoused twenty minutes later in the lobby bar.

"So what do you know about Ambrose's family?" Renee asked as the waiter delivered her a glass of white wine and set a Johnny Walker Black in front of Nat.

"Not much," he answered. "Only what I remember from Papa Joe and a few sketchy Internet reports I found. Ambrose was a military man through and through. Most of his friends were those he met in the service, although I remember Papa Joe saying he spent much of his retired life working on a project at the National World War Two Museum in New Orleans. He supposedly volunteered so many hours that a special plaque was placed in his honor near the entrance. I think that he was a consultant on several of the exhibits—the D-Day Planning Gallery, the D-Day Beaches Gallery, and others—and a real stickler for detail. So much that he pissed off a few people along the way. I didn't see any record of a marriage, but I do remember Papa Joe mentioning he had a friendly relationship with one of the docents. I thought we'd look her up at the service."

"Name?"

"I think it's Miriam LeBlanc. I'm hoping she'll spend some time with us later tonight. I thought we could introduce ourselves at the visitation."

"Sounds like a plan," Renee responded enthusiastically. "By the way, what about the letters? Did you call your neighbors to see if they showed up yet?"

"I did and the answer's no. There aren't any notices from the postman on my door either. I don't want to call the police until we find out if Ambrose actually mailed them, but my gut tells me they were stolen. That's one thing I hope Ms. LeBlanc can help us with."

"It all sounds so incredible. If you're right, someone is cleaning up behind Papa Joe's murder. I can't imagine what he could've known, but it couldn't be worth killing over."

"I agree. Let's see where we get today."

As soon as Renee finished her glass of wine, Nat led her to the cabstand in the front of the hotel. A short ride later, they arrived at the Charbonnet Funeral Home where they were greeted by a few passing glances but for the most part went unnoticed. Many of the mourners milling around, both men and women, were dressed in military garb so Nat was able to immediately pare down his search for Miriam LeBlanc. It took no time to spot the smallish dark-haired woman who appeared to be the focal point of the reception. Dressed in a navy pantsuit with a white scarf on her head and a silver crucifix hanging from her neck, Miriam welcomed visitors much like a grieving widow. Nat and Renee got in line to meet her.

"Ms. LeBlanc," Nat said when they approached, "my name's Nat Travis and this is my friend Renee. Joe Travis was my grandfather. I'm very sorry for your loss."

"Joe Travis from Alabama? Oh my heavens, so nice of you to be here. Anthony loved Joe. Hard to believe we lost them both in the same week." Miriam grabbed her crucifix and held it in her palm.

"My condolences," Renee said, extending her hand.

"Thank you, dear," Miriam replied. Several people in the crowd pushed behind Miriam and temporarily knocked her forward. Frustrated, she leaned over to Nat's ear and said, "It's too busy right now to talk, but I plan on going back to Anthony's house after the service and receiving a few of his friends. Please come by?"

"That would be great," Nat said. "Very nice to meet you, Ms. LeBlanc."

"You as well," she said.

Anthony Ambrose's shotgun-style house wasn't too dissimilar from the small home Papa Joe had lived in most of his life. A front room, two small bedrooms, two baths, and a utilitarian kitchen. Modest accommodations for a modest man.

Miriam LeBlanc waited inside the screened front door as Nat and Renee walked up the sidewalk. "Glad you came by," she greeted them.

"Thank you," Renee replied.

Nat and Renee mingled with the small crowd of well-wishers for about an hour while Miriam hugged and cried her way through the evening. Nat spent most of his time listening to stories about Ambrose—many of them humorous anecdotes about a funny old man fretting over his bougainvillea and gladiolas while trying to maneuver around his front yard in a wheelchair. "A very determined man," remarked one of the guests laughing. Nat grinned along with the stories, many times remembering the same stubborn qualities shared by his grandfather. He tried to learn whatever he could about the circumstances of Ambrose's death but few in the room appeared to question his passing. An old man died—nothing more.

About 10:30 Miriam edged next to Nat and Renee and said, "My friends are leaving now so it's time to relax. I'm a good Catholic girl who likes her spirits but most of Anthony's *old* military friends don't drink. Alcohol-free makes things simpler. Go grab us something in the kitchen. Check the cabinet near the refrigerator." She grinned.

"You're sweet to do this," Renee said. "We know you must be exhausted."

"Don't be silly," Miriam responded. "You came a long way. I'll just need a minute."

"Why don't you help her out," Nat suggested. "I'll find that bottle and be right back."

The two ladies turned away and hurried back into the living room to escort the remaining guests out the door. Nat explored for a few minutes in the kitchen, found a Scotch bottle, and mixed three drinks. He walked back into the living room with his hands full.

"Not much of a Scotch drinker," Miriam said, "but tonight's different. So what do you kids want to know?"

"I guess we're not sure what to ask," Nat answered. "You

sound like you have a few stories about my grandfather so maybe that's where we should start."

"Your grandfather?" Miriam smiled. "Do you know how often he talked to Anthony? It wasn't every day but he might as well have lived here. Once they figured out how to email each other, and it took them a while, they really got dangerous. They were as close as two men living in separate states could be. Anthony loved Joe Travis."

"I never realized they were in such constant contact," Nat replied. "It just shows how tight-lipped my grandfather was. But I'm grateful Papa Joe had a friend like Anthony. Did you ever get a chance to meet my grandfather?"

"Not face-to-face but I talked to him numerous times on the telephone. He had such a sweet nature. But I do feel like I knew him given how much Anthony talked about him. So tell me, why are you here?"

For the next ten minutes, Nat carefully walked through the circumstances of Papa Joe's death, the letters that Ambrose was supposedly mailing to him, and the mysterious USB drive Renee had found in Papa Joe's bedroom.

"Oh my," Miriam said when Nat finished. She shook her head in disbelief. "So you think someone came to New Orleans, stole the letters, and killed Anthony during the robbery?"

"The thought's crossed my mind," Nat answered.

Miriam bit her lip and Nat could tell she was fighting back tears. "That's the worst thing I've ever heard," she whimpered. "Who could do that to an old man? He was such a kind, tender soul."

Nat involuntarily clenched his fist. "The police in Brewton still appear to think it was a bunch of neighborhood punks who broke into my grandfather's house and knocked him down during a robbery. They stole his credit cards and laptop ... and ran. The cops don't want to investigate—he was ninety-three—but their story just doesn't make sense."

Miriam nodded in apparent agreement with Nat's conclusion.

"I was waiting on Sergeant Ambrose's letters," Nat continued, "in hope they'd help me put more of this together. He told me they'd explain what my grandfather was doing when he died. Did Sergeant Ambrose ever discuss those letters with you?"

"Not specifically but I have some idea what was in them."

"Really?"

"Anthony talked a lot about your grandfather's research into his family tree. He said Joe liked to write him about what he'd found, where he'd searched, all those kinds of things. Those guys loved to write letters. But I'm not sure Anthony thought there was anything unusual. Lots of folks are into genealogy these days, especially as we get older."

"I'm sure that's true," Nat said, "but I believe there's more … something that goes beyond just family history. Something in those records that might even be worth killing over. That's what we're searching for."

"I can't imagine what it could be," Miriam said. "I wish I could help but nothing comes to mind."

"No worries, Ms. LeBlanc," Renee interrupted. "We appreciate the time you've given us. We're so sorry for your loss."

Nat didn't want to stop, but he understood Renee's direction.

"I'm sorry I couldn't help more," Miriam said, "but I guess Anthony didn't let me in on all of his secrets. Before you go, I do want to show you a picture Anthony kept in his bedroom that was very special to him." Miriam stood up and walked away while Nat and Renee waited.

"Look at these three young studs," Miriam proudly announced when she returned with a picture frame in her hand.

"When was this taken?" Nat asked.

"Anthony told me it was the day before your grandfather

saved his company from being wiped out in France. The day before he earned his Silver Star."

Nat choked up for a moment before turning to Renee. "What a great shot," he said. "I think I can make out Sergeant Ambrose but who's this other soldier?"

"Not sure I remember his name," Miriam answered. "Anthony once mentioned the young man was very close with your grandfather, but I don't know more than that. I think the poor soul was killed by the Germans soon after the photo was taken. I do recall that Anthony said they were inseparable while in the service, always talking, close as brothers. It was a deep connection."

Nat's eyes moistened. "Thanks for sharing," he said.

"Take the picture," Miriam offered while leaning forward. "I have no use for it." Her hands trembled as she handed the picture frame to Nat.

As the three huddled to say goodnight, Nat impulsively spread his arms around both women and held them in a bundle. They stood silently together several minutes and Miriam finally let go. Renee's tears soon followed.

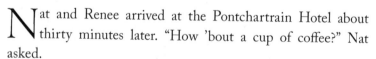

Nat and Renee arrived at the Pontchartrain Hotel about thirty minutes later. "How 'bout a cup of coffee?" Nat asked.

"Thanks, but I'm exhausted," Renee answered. "It's been some day. I'm beginning to feel like we're ... I mean you're ... onto something. There's more to this story—I can feel it—even if it doesn't make sense right now. I may go stare at the laptop awhile longer before I turn in. Want to meet for breakfast?"

"Deal."

"Goodnight, Nat." Renee patted him on the shoulder and

headed off to the elevator bank. Nat didn't move for several minutes. He watched Renee disappear into the distance and then tucked the picture frame he'd received from Miriam under his arm and headed up on his own.

CHAPTER 13

After a breakfast meeting at the Fairmont Hotel, Joseph Travis pulled into his high-rise parking garage in the West End of Dallas anxious about his full day of meetings ahead. Yet despite his busy schedule, he couldn't get his ex-wife off his mind. Seeing her at the funeral in Brewton had jolted him, and not in a way he liked. He rarely looked back—that was not his style—but he couldn't help pondering his stay in Alabama. What would his life have been like if he'd stayed married to Renee? What if he'd remained in Brewton? Neither option deeply appealed to him these days—his legal career and future in politics would never have materialized there—but the questions dogged him. The funeral had been a reflection point for a man rarely prone to reflection. And then as if to admonish himself, Joseph dismissed his thoughts. It was time to move on.

The more important issue on his mind was Renee's trip to New Orleans with Nat. He didn't want to care that they were spending time together, although the idea of his ex-wife and brother comparing stories did irk him. His son Emmitt had made it all sound so routine, yet the whole scene didn't feel right to him, as if they'd united to conspire against him. Sure Renee had the time, but why had she really gone with Nat to New Orleans?

Joseph pulled out his cell phone and dialed Renee's number just as he parked his Land Rover.

"Hello Joseph," Renee answered. "If you're looking for the kids, they're in Atlanta."

"What are you doing in New Orleans?" he asked.

68

The unexpected question made Renee bristle. "Is that any of your business?" she shot back. "But I'm glad to know you still care."

Renee's sarcasm irritated him. "Emmitt mentioned you'd gone down with Nat. I thought it sounded strange; that's all."

"Honestly Joseph, we're down here meeting a grieving widow and asking questions about your grandfather. What do you think we're doing?" she laughed. "On second thought, we're holed up at the Fairmont planning how we can sabotage your campaign for governor. Does that sound better?"

"Like I said, it sounded strange."

"You have to be kidding."

"What are you doing, then?"

"Seriously, I do appreciate this sudden burst of interest, but if it wasn't so out of character, I'd almost feel like you were concerned. But I don't think that's why you're calling."

Joseph had gone too far but he didn't care. "Well, what kind of questions are you asking? I thought Nat was going to pay our family's respects, nothing more."

The iciness in Renee's attitude oozed through the phone line. "God, Joseph," she sighed, "do you always have to be so suspicious?"

"Fine," he fired back. "I'll talk to you later, Renee." He punched the key to shut off his phone and then leaned back to ponder his thoughts. He hadn't considered it before, in his haste, but the timing of Papa Joe's and Ambrose's deaths did seem more than coincidental. He suddenly worried that Nat and Renee were hiding something from him. Maybe something very important.

CHAPTER 14

Angelina de Zavala Gentry had gone through Ambrose's box of letters and Joe Travis's laptop several times but had found little in the way of useful information. She seethed with anger over the incompetence of her associates. First Shakes, then Kalender, and now Kruger. And after hundreds of thousands of dollars and two deaths, she was no closer to the prize than she'd been months before. With these failures, she'd become even more resolute about her purpose, more steeled in her mission. There was no longer time for second-guessing or half measures. Success was the only thing that mattered now.

Angelina thought back to the events that had propelled her interest in her quest. Her life changed by a mystery etched on a small piece of paper tucked inside the jacket of her great-grandmother's Bible.

BZ – moved? Not in the LBR.
Find JB's trail. I had M.

The notation had taken some time for Angelina to decipher but it became entirely logical once she understood more about her great-grandmother's life. Adina de Zavala had scratched out a note revealing clues to a famous secret about the Alamo, one that had grown into such legend that most current scholars had written it off as myth or fantasy. But not Angelina. These many years later, after countless stops and starts, she still believed the note had meaning, that the mystery long speculated about in

Alamo lore was real. She caressed the copy of the note in her hand as she had on so many other occasions, seeking to channel her great-grandmother's communication, to find the answer that had eluded her for all of these years. Her mind drifted off to Adina's story.

———— ★ ————

Adina de Zavala was born in 1861, the eldest of six grand-children of Lorenzo de Zavala, the first vice-president of the Republic of Texas. She moved around early in life but settled perma-nently in San Antonio in 1886. Once there, Adina found a group of earnest women who shared a similar passion about their family's role in the story of Texas independence, and Adina enthusiastically joined them. It took little time for her small clique to find its way to another group of like-minded women from Houston who'd already taken steps to form a statewide preservationist organization called the Daughters of the Republic of Texas. The DRT, as it became popularly known, was a women's organization open only to those who could prove lineal descent from a man or woman who served the Republic of Texas. The nascent organization's mission perfectly suited Adina and her smaller group quickly folded in. To distinguish itself, Adina's San Antonio branch adopted the name De Zavala Chapter of the DRT in honor of Adina's famous grandfather.

Early on, the De Zavala Chapter directed its efforts toward pre-serving four Spanish missions south of San Antonio as well as the Mission San Antonio de Valero, otherwise known as the Alamo. By the late 1800s, all of these structures had been ravaged by relic hunters and were rapidly deteriorating due to a lack of financial support.

Adina soon became consumed with the Alamo, visiting the crum-bling building daily in a horse and buggy while calling on merchants all over town to contribute bricks, lumber, and other building materi-als to help renovate the structure. Adina's anger over the state's neglect of the decaying mission only escalated when she discovered that the government had no control over the grounds she was fighting to preserve. Most alarming to her, the convento, sometimes known as the long-barracks room, the famous indoor area where Alamo legend Jim Bowie was reportedly bludgeoned and bayoneted to death by Mexican troops, was owned by private commercial interests.

The convento's owner was a firm of wholesale merchants known as Hugo & Schmeltzer, a group with little reverence for the Alamo's important place in Texas history. Adina couldn't stand the sacrilege. She quickly determined to save the convento by convincing, or, if necessary, forcing Hugo & Schmeltzer to sell to the DRT. It was during these negotiations over the sale of the property that fate intervened to bring Adina into contact with the one woman she'd be forever linked with in history, Clara Driscoll.

Ms. Driscoll was an idealistic twenty-four-year-old heiress fresh from traveling abroad in Europe, who by 1903 was looking for a worthwhile cause to pursue in her new home of San Antonio. As a native of Galveston with roots to the Texas Republic, Driscoll was perfectly suited for the DRT. She also had the funds Adina's cash-strapped De Zavala Chapter desperately needed, and she soon joined the group to head up its fund-raising committee.

Driscoll's association with the De Zavala Chapter was more than timely. By 1903, Adina had struck out in her efforts to raise sufficient capital to purchase the convento from Hugo & Schmeltzer but had persuaded the merchant group to grant her a first option to acquire the building for $75,000. That's where Clara Driscoll stepped in. The heiress agreed to pay Hugo & Schmeltzer $500 out of her own personal funds and then financed an additional $4500 to secure the option.

Buoyed by these efforts, Adina and the other members of the De Zavala Chapter set up a collection booth outside the Alamo and held fund-raising activities to raise the money to pay off the Hugo & Schmeltzer debt. But their efforts were woefully unsuccessful and

Driscoll was once again left to make up the difference. She did that very thing, paying the final $70,000 to complete the acquisition. As news of Driscoll's generosity spread, many groups throughout the state, including the leadership of the DRT, petitioned the legislature to reimburse Driscoll and provide additional funding to support the Alamo. The cause went from insignificant to a political cauldron overnight. The DRT whipped the public into a frenzy over the state's inaction and by January 1905 the anxious legislature rushed through a bill to reimburse Driscoll.

As the battle raged on, Adina saw her authority within the DRT diminish. Clara Driscoll became the new darling, and as Driscoll's star ascended, Adina seethed. Unable to accept her demotion, Adina angrily pushed her De Zavala Chapter to secede from the DRT and restructured her organization to operate autonomously, free of DRT control and free of Clara Driscoll.

The DRT's embrace of Driscoll at the expense of Adina was the turning point in Adina's life. From that point forward, she embarked on a battle with the organization, challenging its every decision over the preservation, use, and control of the Alamo. When Driscoll sought to tear down the long-barracks room and create a large monument to the soldiers similar to those she'd seen in Europe, Adina dug in, claiming the building had to be left untouched and should be made into a museum. The dispute was both idealistic and personal and, because of the attention now focused on the Alamo, widely reported in the newspapers. The public was both passionate and divided. To quell the disagreement, the attorney general of Texas ultimately stepped in and issued an opinion that placed the care, custody, and control of the Alamo into the hands of the DRT and Clara Driscoll. By the ruling, Adina lost everything.

But even in defeat, she was not finished.

On February 12, 1908, the night before the long-awaited legal transfer of the convento from Hugo & Schmeltzer to the DRT, Adina took action. She illegally gained access to the convento, barricaded herself in one of the rooms, and refused to allow anyone inside. From February 12, 1908, until February 15, Adina subsisted in the convento, suffering "parched lips and a starving countenance." Her principled stand gained national attention but led many to believe that the woman had gone mad. Finally, on February 15, despite popular opinion in her favor, Adina was evicted from the convento building by court order.

A legend was born.

——★——

Most historians had never questioned Adina's reasons for protecting the long-barracks room from the DRT; in fact, reports regularly cited her self-proclaimed divine right to manage the Alamo as her sole and only motivation in barricading herself inside the building. Angelina had once believed that story as well. Until she found the note.

*BZ — moved? Not in the LBR.
Find JB's trail. I had M.*

The coded message cast a very different light on Adina's four-day odyssey in the long-barracks room. Angelina now believed her great-grandmother was neither a publicity hound nor a mad woman. The question had come to her as a revelation. What if Adina had purposely barricaded herself alone in the Alamo to search for something far more valuable than her legacy? Something only she had reason to believe was there.

A treasure.

A lost treasure so vast that it would make the inept acolytes of Clara Driscoll and the DRT fall over in their collective soup. The note told her several things about that treasure.

*BT - moved? - **Bowie's Treasure moved?***
*Not in the LBR. - **Not in the long-barracks room.***
*Find JB's trail. - **Find JB's trail.***
*S had M. - **Slave had map.***

Angelina's great-grandmother was not only a preservation-ist, as Angelina had discovered, but a practical woman as well. Bowie's Treasure was the prize Adina de Zavala had searched for during those four long days, a huge cache of silver hidden by a dying Jim Bowie that no historian, treasure hunter, or archivist had ever found. But Angelina had now grown convinced they'd all been looking in the wrong place.

Since the day she'd been forced to leave the DRT—much as Adina had been years earlier—Angelina had followed her great-grandmother's clues, embarking on a journey that had finally led to Joe Travis. Tragically, the supposed owner of the ultimate clue—*the lost map of Jim Bowie*—had proven to be another dead end. Precious time, actually years, had been wasted looking for an old black man and a map that may never have existed. Joe Travis knew the story of Joe the slave, that much was clear, but he neither possessed the map nor held any secrets about the precise location of Bowie's Treasure.

But one letter Kruger had recovered from Ambrose's house had provided a fresh lead. She still had time to confirm the information in that letter, narrow her search, and avoid any fur-ther mistakes once Janet Nelson obtained formal permission to go forward on the Alamo excavation project. Angelina desper-ately believed that her time was drawing near, that the discovery would soon be hers, and that Adina's epic struggle would be vin-dicated. Her great-grandmother may have died with nothing, frustrated by false leads and empty clues, but that would not be Angelina's fate.

CHAPTER 15

Once back in Brewton, Nat began reviewing the information that Renee had highlighted for him in Papa Joe's research. There were two large files on the drive, one titled "Genealogy" and a second styled "Personal." Among the documents in the "Genealogy" file were historical records, articles, and official documents, all tracing back to one man—a slave born in the early 1800s with the single name Joe. Unlike most nameless, faceless slaves from the pre-Civil War era, Joe had a documented history, one that had obviously been embellished over the years. An 1837 newspaper account from the *Telegraph and Texas Register* particularly caught Nat's attention:

Fifty Dollars

Will be given for delivering to me on Bailey's Prairie, seven miles from Columbia, a negro man named Joe, belonging to the succession of the late Wm. Barret Travis, who took off with him a Mexican and two horses, saddles and bridles. This negro was in the Alamo with his master when it was taken; and was the only man from the colonies who was not put to death: he is about twenty-five years of age, five feet ten or eleven inches high, very black and good countenance: had on when he left, on the night of the 21ˢᵗ April ult. a dark mixed sattinet round jacket and new white cotton pantaloons. One of the horses taken is a bay, about 14 ½ hands high very heavy built, with a blaze in his face, a bushy mane and tail, and a sore back; also the property of said succession, the other horse is a chestnut sorrel, above 16 hands high. The saddles are of the Spanish form, but of American manufacture, and one of them covered with blue cloth. Forty dollars will be given for Joe and the small bay horse, (Shannon) and ten dollars for the Mexican other horse and saddles and bridles.

If the runaways are taken more than one hundred miles from my residence, will pay all reasonable travelling expenses, in addition to the above award.

JOHN R. JONES, Executor of W. B. Travis
Bailey's Prairie, May 21st, 1837

Nat still had difficulty understanding why Papa Joe hadn't shared more information about his extensive research into Joe the slave. Although his grandfather mentioned his work on the Travis family history many times, Papa Joe had never referenced his study of this particular slave. The doorbell rang while Nat was pondering why.

"Thanks for coming over," Nat said while opening the screen door and bowing to Renee. He then ushered her into his small living room. "Not much to look at, but it serves the purpose."

"Very manly," Renee said with a smile as she studied the surroundings. She stopped momentarily when she trained her eyes on a small bookshelf in the corner of the room. She walked over and examined its contents. "Alabama High School Coach of the Year, 1999," she read. "Very impressive. You were in Mobile at the time. State champions in 2000 and 2002. But you came back to Brewton?" Renee tilted her head and let the question complete itself.

Nat froze when he heard the insinuation. "I needed a new challenge" reflexively rolled off his lips. "I certainly found it with this school. This is my fourth season with Niland and my first year with a real team." With that, he hoped Renee would be satisfied and leave it alone.

"A coach of the year at B. T. Washington High School in Mobile," Renee speculated, "one of the best football schools in Alabama, doesn't come back to Escambia County to take on a challenge like S.W. Niland. Coaching your alma mater couldn't be that big a draw."

"You're right; this drive looks like a treasure trove of information for a historian," Nat said in an attempt to change the subject. "I got interested once you explained it to me. Stayed up all last night looking at it. Want a cup of coffee?"

"You came back to Brewton for Papa Joe, didn't you?" Renee pressed.

Nat hesitated, knowing any answer he offered might give the wrong impression. There was so much about his life in Mobile he'd never shared, so much he'd buried, particularly his failed relationships, that he preferred to leave it alone. "I was ready to come home," Nat misdirected. "And Brewton is home." He turned, walked into his kitchen, and poured Renee a cup.

"So tell me what's on your mind."

Nat handed Renee the steaming mug. "I've printed some of the choice documents and want to go over 'em with you. I'd like your historian's viewpoint." He smiled while leading her to a nicked-up dining-room table that had several mug imprints burned into the wood. They sat down.

"Okay, let me have it," Renee said cheerfully.

"Here's the first one." Nat handed her the ad printed from the archives of the *Telegraph and Texas Register*.

"This is the one I mentioned," Renee responded. "Very interesting, isn't it? Looks pretty clear that Papa Joe thought the slave listed here was your ancestor."

"Agreed," Nat pronounced, handing her a second two-page document, this one entitled *Diary of Colonel William Fairfax Gray, Virginia to Texas, 1835–1837*.

Renee sipped her coffee and quietly read the document.

After a few minutes, she set the paper down and looked at Nat with a scholarly gaze. "So let me see if I can give you my take on this," she said. "I did some more reading last night and some of this is familiar to me. Colonel William Barret Travis, a lawyer in Alabama, came to Texas in the early 1830s with several slaves and little else. Once he settled near present-day Austin, he became consumed by the Texans' controversy with Mexico and was soon recruited to join the loosely formed Texas army. Later, he was requested to raise a company of soldiers to reinforce and defend the Alamo against a potential attack. According to Papa Joe's records, one of the twenty or so men he brought to San Antonio with him was a slave named Joe. The young man served by Travis's side during the battle but, unlike all of the others, survived to give an account of the attack to this Colonel Gray in 1837. Sometime after that, Joe became property of Colonel Travis's descendants, but later escaped with an unnamed Mexican and a couple of horses. Oh, and this is important, Joe was the *only* male survivor of the Alamo. Are we together so far?"

"Yes ma'am. But am I also right that Papa Joe's documents suggest Joe the slave was the last person to see Jim Bowie alive, witnessed Colonel Travis being shot in the head, and identified Davy Crockett's body for Santa Anna? I may not know that much about the Alamo but I sure remember those names."

Renee smiled. "It's quite a story—the single male survivor of that battle. How much is true ... who knows? But it still doesn't answer why Papa Joe kept his research a secret. And if the genealogy is accurate—and I bet it is; look how carefully he's connected the dots—he had to be so proud his family descended from Joe the slave. Makes you wonder if the old master from Bailey's Prairie is still looking for his fifty dollars. Is that what's behind this?"

Nat chuckled. "What about this one?" he asked, passing her a third article, a reprint from a document titled *Memorandum with Regard to William Barret Travis*, which bore the mark of the Alabama Archives and Department of History.

Renee read it quietly before turning to Nat with a puzzled look on her face. "Hmm." She reflected. "Didn't get to this one on the plane ... 'the Negro mentioned above, who himself was an Alamo hero, is buried in an unmarked grave near Brewton ...'"

"That's why I asked you to come over. I thought you might know if there were any historical cemeteries in Brewton that I don't know about ... or if this is just speculation by the writer. If Papa Joe believed our direct ancestor was the only male survivor of the Alamo and buried here in Brewton ... then that might explain some things."

"I hear you but I'm not aware of any slave-era cemeteries in town, although I'm not sure I've ever really thought much about it."

"Here's the other thing. As you know, most slaves typically took the surname of their owners so I presume that's what happened in Joe's case. By the time Papa Joe was born in 1920, I guess my great-grandfather decided to honor our family's past and named my grandfather Joe the second. I always wondered who my grandfather was named after. It had to be Joe the slave."

"Nice work, detective," Renee said. "I might need to hire you as my research assistant."

Nat smiled. "You motivated me while we were in New Orleans," he conceded. "The problem is, Joe the slave more or less disappeared after he escaped from Bailey's Prairie in 1837. One of the articles here suggests he resurfaced around 1877 near Austin but that sounds unlikely if he'd already moved to Brewton. But if he's buried here, what did he do all of that time?"

Renee cocked her head. "Good question," she replied. "That leaves a big hole in his life story."

"And one other thing. It seems Papa Joe also traced the genealogy of several men he served with during the war. I don't know why but there's three times as much material on a soldier named Ricardo Rodriguez than any of the others. Never heard of him, but since he's the only Hispanic Papa Joe followed in this material, I'm thinking he might be the one in that photo that Miriam LeBlanc gave us."

"Makes sense."

"It's the only explanation I have."

"Papa Joe was secretive, that's for sure," Renee said. "Sounds like you have a lot of investigating ahead."

"I'm gonna give it a try, but I'm open for any advice … or help … you're willing to offer."

"My advice is to keep looking for connections. So much of history appears random at first glance, but upon closer study, there's usually a logical explanation for people's actions. Some motivation that lurks beneath the surface. I'd like to help you figure this thing out but I'm leaving town for a few days. I promised to take my mother on a short vacation."

"Oh?" Nat said, while trying to act nonchalant about his disappointment. "Leaving tomorrow?"

"Yes. Mom doesn't get to travel much anymore and she's really looking forward to some girl time together. But I've already decided that while I'm gone, I'm going to read up on your ancestor Joe and see what I can find out. You should stay on the trail of these files, too. Just don't forget that football team of yours. My sabbatical lasts through the end of the year so I'm expecting to watch big things from your boys."

Renee finished off her coffee and stood up as if ready to leave. She stared at Nat. "It's been fun," she said. "It really has. Let's catch up next week when I get back."

"Thanks, Renee. You've already done more than I could have ever hoped for." Nat hesitated, unsure about what to do next. "Have a great trip," he said, already missing her.

CHAPTER 16

Janet Nelson waited in a private committee room for her moment on the stand. The closed-circuit feed on the wall-mounted television captured the members of Senator Cravens's committee assembling in the main room. She was confident she could handle them. Then again, she'd always been confident. From her time as a high-school cheerleader to her election as a city councilwoman from Alamo Heights, Janet had always been able to count on her looks and charm to get what she wanted from men. She'd culled her husband out of the crowd of up-and-comers in San Antonio the same way. Women, on the other hand, tended to distrust her at first sight, but she could typically win them by her support of causes dear to their neighborhoods and communities. And so the Alamo. Who wouldn't love a politician committed to saving the precious shrine of Texas liberty from profiteers and neglect? Today, however, the room was full of men with ebbing virility and inflated egos—men who could be enchanted by a mere flip of her hair. This would be easy.

The AG's complaints against the DRT were straightforward. The organization had been a poor steward of the Alamo property, had mismanaged millions of dollars in state funds, and had left the iconic structure in a state of disrepair. The fact that the DRT had a hundred-year history with the Alamo no longer mattered. State action was politically necessary.

Janet knew the choice between the two competing bills drafted by the legislature would be publicly settled through this committee. In one camp, Attorney General Craig and his cronies were ready to dump the DRT and have the state take over control of the Alamo through the state Land Office or Texas Historical Commission; on the other side, composed particularly of members representing the San Antonio political delegation, arguments would be made for more rigorous reporting requirements but retention of the DRT as independent manager of the Alamo. Janet's inside contact said the committee was being pushed hard by the AG to support his hard-line position.

Janet watched as Senator Cravens inspected the assembled horde, sighed, and took his position at the center of the ring. He gaveled the meeting to order, announced the schedule for the morning session, and then called the committee's first witness.

"State your name and position, sir," Cravens ordered.

"Roger Wilcox, first assistant attorney general for the State of Texas."

"Mr. Wilcox, have you performed an investigation into the stewardship of the Alamo over the past five years by the Daughters of the Republic of Texas?"

"Yes sir, I have."

"Tell this committee what you've found."

Wilcox looked like he was ready to devour the microphone. "The attorney general's office received a complaint about twelve months ago from an insider in the DRT," he started. "We received credible information from our source about significant problems with the organization's handling of state money. Upon receiving this complaint, our office began an investigation and sent out document requests seeking financial records for the last five years from the DRT. We had difficulty getting cooperation initially ... after several months some files trickled in ... but they were only a sample of what we requested. After reviewing these limited documents, interviewing a number of current and former members of the DRT, and sending a team of experts to inspect the condition of the Alamo, we reached a number of conclusions."

"And what are they?" Cravens asked.

"One: The state's resources have been poorly managed and there appears, at best, to have been inadequate financial controls in place within the organization. Two: Until very recently with the installation of the new president, Janet Nelson, there has been a complete lack of leadership and candor within the DRT. And, three: The Alamo building itself faces significant structural problems and unless immediate steps are taken to begin repairs, we may lose the historical character of the building forever."

A series of DRT witnesses followed Wilcox but few made a positive impact. Patricia Akers and Valerie Butler were particularly pathetic—two women Janet had helped Angelina set up but who in all truth didn't have the time on their social calendars to pull off a scheme to defraud the state. Yet, the documents that mysteriously ended up on their hard drives suggested they were sinister conspirators. Angelina's man Shakes had seen to that. In some ways, Janet felt sorry for Akers and Butler, but she'd learned to avoid letting her emotions get in the way of political necessity. As for the vendetta Angelina carried on against these two old women, that drama predated her arrival on the scene and was irrelevant to her mission. Even so, it seemed remarkably vindictive for Angelina to have harbored a grudge for such a long time.

Janet knew she'd be the final witness in the long line of DRT representatives. After being sworn in, she faced Senator Alife, universally regarded as the toughest interrogator on the committee, and smiled. In that moment, it was over. Alife moved quickly through his routine opening questions to get right to the point.

"In your time serving on the board of the DRT, have you had an opportunity to evaluate the finances of the organization?"

"Yes sir, I have," Janet answered.

"Have you reached any conclusions based on your review?"

"Yes, I have, Senator Alife. The DRT has not been a good steward of the Alamo or its finances. I can't lay the blame on any one person, or any two for that matter, but I certainly can't turn away from the obvious problems our failures have caused. As the new president general of the organization, I intend to do everything possible to change this, and from this point forward we are going to be completely transparent and accountable to the state. I don't want this committee or any of our benefactors to worry ... ever ... that their Alamo will lie exposed to roof leaks and termite infestation again." She paused and flashed her glorious smile at the camera. "I am here to serve you and the citizens of our state in a manner that will revive the Alamo to all of its former glory."

The media cameras clicked in rapid succession and Janet knew she'd turned the committee around, particularly since the normally sour Alife had returned her smile. Finally, he asked her, "Do you have a recommendation for the future management of the Alamo?"

"Yes sir," Janet answered, "I do. The DRT needs to earn back the state's trust. We recognize that. I believe that your recommendation, Senator Alife, to create an Alamo Preservation Advisory Board made up of the various constituent members represented here today—the DRT, the state Land Office, the Texas Historical Commission, the City of San Antonio, and the Bexar County Historical Commission—is by far the most thoughtful idea. If the new Advisory Board sees fit to allow the DRT to continue functioning in our traditional support role, but under greater scrutiny, then I think everyone here will be satisfied. I pledge to offer my complete commitment to ensure the success of that plan."

"And you would need someone beyond reproach to serve as president of this new Alamo Preservation Advisory Board, wouldn't you?" he asked.

"Absolutely; it wouldn't work otherwise."

"And do you have a recommendation for that role?"

"Yes sir," Janet answered, "I do." She paused and looked past Alife directly into the cameras. "There's only one person I could ever recommend for such an important job. It has to be Ms. Angelina de Zavala Gentry."

CHAPTER 17

Nat Travis gathered up his clothes, stuffed them into a duffle bag, and headed off to campus for practice. The start of a new football season always excited Nat, but this year he felt much of his traditional enthusiasm sapped by Papa Joe's passing. Nat wondered what football would be like without his number-one fan. What would he do without someone to pepper him with advice about the latest advances in the spread offense and 3-4 defense? Or pick him up after a tough loss? From his first moments watching the hound's-tooth-hat mobile floating over his crib, to his days as a wide receiver at Alabama A&M, to coaching high school in Mobile and now Brewton, football had always been the center of Nat's life. And Papa Joe his mentor, sounding board, and best advocate.

Seeing his brother at Papa Joe's funeral, however, reminded Nat that high-school-football coaching wasn't a particularly lucrative profession for a middle-aged man. While Nat struggled to get by on his modest salary, his brother, who'd developed his political talents as president of the S.W. Niland student council, had left him far behind. Joseph had seen his path at an early age, sharpened his skills in speech and debate, and worked tirelessly to build the right friendships. He was the energetic, well-spoken, young man with a future, inspired by the majesty of Martin Luther King's words and a thirst for advancement. A college scholarship, a full ride at the University of Texas law school, and then a brilliant legal career had sent Joseph into a different world. Now, all of these years later, things had changed. But while Nat resented Joseph's condescending ways, he still missed the relationship they once had. That feeling would never go away.

Back when they were boys, Joseph had been the leader, the revered older brother. But Nat wasn't one to take instruction very long, and by the time he was eleven, he'd reversed positions with his only sibling. Part of the change was due to Nat's growth spurt—he shot up three inches in two months—but just as much was a result of Joseph's evolving risk aversion. He grew increasingly calculating, unwilling to take chances, afraid to jeopardize his bright future, even as a teenager. Then, as Nat developed a love for the pool hall, a place he could bum a smoke, drink a beer, or experiment with virtually anything he wanted, Joseph drifted further away. Nat pushed all boundaries during that time, from stealing cigarettes from the convenience store to lifting tools out of his neighbors' garages. Eventually, though, Nat's bad-boy behavior caught up with him, with Papa Joe stepping in to take charge just ahead of the juvenile authorities, but by that time, Joseph had gone.

The coach's office at S.W. Niland wasn't much bigger than a closet. Nat had a small metal desk, a whiteboard, and an unstable visitor's chair that most of his assistants could barely fit in. But that didn't matter. The small office smelled of sweaty uniforms and muddy cleats, and Nat loved it. High-school coaches weren't allowed to hold formal drills until two weeks before classes started so Nat had a lot of work to do in a very short time. Playing one of Niland's biggest rivals over Labor Day weekend would've been enough for Nat to worry about, but now the mystery of the USB drive and Papa Joe's death weighed on his mind as well. In reality, he'd made little progress on the documents since Renee had left town with her mother. His apathy bothered him almost as much as the Brewton police force's inability to generate one significant lead into his grandfather's death.

The cell phone clipped to his belt buzzed. "Nat Travis," he answered without looking down at the digital readout.

"It's Joseph; have a minute?"

"Yeah, just got to my office. First practice this afternoon."

"Good luck with that," Joseph stated without much interest. "I won't keep you long." He hesitated. "I didn't mention this when we last talked but ..."

"What's that?" Nat interrupted.

"I hired a private investigator."

"You what?"

"I really didn't think much about it, but I was concerned the local police wouldn't be much help."

"You gotta be ..."

"Hold on, Nat— just listen for a minute. You may not believe it, but I cared for Papa Joe as much as you did. And based on your digging in New Orleans, I wondered if there was something more to the story."

Nat rolled his eyes and adjusted his position in his chair. "I don't know what you mean by that, but it's hard to believe you hired a PI in my hometown and didn't tell me about it. Give me a break."

"Dammit, Nat," Joseph interrupted. "I didn't call to argue with you. And I already got rid of the guy anyway."

Nat caught his breath. "I have practice. Is that all you have for me?"

"Not everything. Now shut up and listen for a minute. I had the investigator go through Papa Joe's phone records to see if he found anything unusual. Initially, he turned up nothing. Papa Joe talked on the phone quite a bit—but many of those calls were to you, Renee, and to his New Orleans friend who just passed. I have to be honest; I had no idea he was talking to Renee that much, but I guess that's not important. There was one number that caught my attention. Papa Joe placed a lot of calls to a 510 area code, which is Oakland, California. I figured it might be one of his old army friends, but I checked on it anyway."

Nat considered jumping in but held his tongue. "So what did you find out?"

"Actually, something very disturbing."

"What do you mean?"

"The number is a cell phone tied to the owner of a storefront business in Oakland. An antiquarian who sells novelty items at a place called *Treasuring the Past*. And get this … the guy has another, apparently lucrative, side business that keeps him far busier than his novelty shop."

Nat sensed a revelation. The anger he felt toward Joseph disappeared as he considered the importance of his message. "What is it?" he asked.

"The guy Papa Joe was talking to is a professional treasure hunter. His name's Frank Kalender."

Nat leaned back in his chair. The breakthrough tied together everything he'd learned from Sergeant Ambrose and the USB drive. His mind immediately raced back to the research materials and what they meant in light of Kalender's involvement. Had he missed anything? Nat sat quietly for a moment, thinking through it all, but quickly realized he didn't want to get into a deeper discussion with his brother over the phone. "This guy Kalender," he posed, "you think he knows something the Brewton police don't? Have you contacted him?"

"No, you're the first person I've called. I figured you might be better able to piece it together from what you've learned in New Orleans. What do you think?"

"Not sure," Nat responded.

"Well that's why I'm leaving it in your hands, little brother. I'm emailing you a copy of the phone records today. Despite what you think, I'm very interested in all of this. Papa Joe deserved better."

Nat had a dozen things he wanted to say but figured this wasn't the time. "I know that, Joseph," he said. "Thanks. I'll look into it."

CHAPTER 18

A one-day-turnaround visit to the Bay Area wasn't Nat's preferred way to prepare his team for its opening game of the season, but he couldn't get Frank Kalender to return his calls. He already suspected why this so-called "professional" treasure hunter had been communicating with his grandfather, and he wasn't about to let the man duck him without an answer. When his calls got nowhere, Nat confirmed Kalender would be in his office, jumped on the Internet, and bought a plane ticket to California.

Nat stepped out of his cab at 150 Grand Avenue in Oakland and stared at *Treasuring the Past* novelty store. Nat knew he'd found the right place because the storefront windows had bags of gold, treasure maps, and sunken ships painted across them. Seeing these elaborate designs left Nat even more certain that his grandfather had become mixed up with a hustler.

Nat had developed a serious distaste for Kalender while researching him online. Although the man was well educated, reportedly holding a master's degree in archeology from Cal Berkeley, and had gained some recognition for several books he'd written on antiquarianism, his scholarly endeavors were completely overshadowed by his more popular pursuit of treasure hunting. In Nat's view, Kalender was the classic celebrity born of the Internet, a tweet-posting, self-promoting carny-barker. Kalender's website was a patchwork of conspiracy theories, speculative thought, and links to sites devoted to the most famous legends in human history—the lost city of Atlantis, the Fountain of Youth, and the golden caverns of

El Dorado, to name a few. His website focused on stories of hidden treasure from around the world, from those of infamous pirates like Blackbeard to others buried in the ruins of forgotten civilizations. Kalender had figured out just the right mix of scholarship and speculation to lure any online visitor. The fact that Papa Joe had corresponded with him meant that he'd been sucked in as well.

Nat walked in the front door of the store and came into full view of a real-world version of Kalender's website. On one end of the building was a reproduction of a wooden pirate ship straight out of *Pirates of the Caribbean*; on the other an Aztec-looking pyramid with mannequins dressed as warriors bowing down to a golden idol. The theatric displays were intermixed with scenes of some of the great mysteries of the American experience. A small plane hung from the ceiling with a woman pilot, presumably Amelia Earhart, and a balcony display featured President Lincoln's box at Ford's Theatre. The place was wacky, bizarre, and entirely entertaining.

"Welcome to *Treasuring the Past*," a young female with orange hair greeted Nat.

"Hey," he responded. "I'm looking for Frank Kalender. Could you tell him Nat Travis is here to see him?"

"Cool, look around; I'll be back in a second."

Nat acknowledged the girl as she turned away and flashed him a zigzag tattoo on the back of her neck. He slowly made his way toward the huge pirate ship and studied the various novelty items and collectibles for sale in the store racks on the way. On closer inspection, Nat realized that Kalender's store was much more than entertainment; it was also crassly commercial. Wooden barrels full of fake gold doubloons, racks of Jolly Roger flags, and rows of cheap-looking peg legs for sale surrounded the display. Everything and more for the amateur pirate enthusiast.

"Nat Travis?" boomed a voice from across the room.

Nat wheeled around to find a bear of a man standing before him.

"Frank Kalender's the name," the man announced. "Glad you stopped by."

Nat caught his breath and perused the massive figure in front of him. Kalender filled up the room. His bright-yellow shirt with Oakland A's insignias looked like it could double for an outdoor tent and his wiry handlebar mustache expanded across his face like a serpent. Kalender was about six feet tall, broad shouldered, and had a stomach that extended out like an untapped keg barrel. He wore knee-length khaki shorts, flip-flops, and an oversized gold watch.

"Is there somewhere we could speak privately?" Nat asked.

"Sure, but don't you want a little tour first? Look over there—that's my latest addition. Quite proud of him."

For the first time, Nat was stumped by one of the figures—a Japanese general standing near a cave with a stick of dynamite in his hand.

"Don't know him, do you?" Kalender guessed. "Not unusual. General Tomoyuki Yamashita is the man behind one of the greatest unknown stories of World War Two. Secured billions of dollars' worth of gold bullion and other Asian treasure in a series of Filipino caves just before the end of the war. You can read all about him in my latest work." Kalender wheeled around and grabbed a hardback off a nearby shelf and shoved it in Nat's face. "It's my best yet."

Startled, Nat grabbed the book and looked at the cover. The title, *The Treasure All Around You*, appeared to capture Kalender's store. "What's your book about?" Nat asked while following Kalender to the Yamashita display.

"This one focuses on American treasure. I've only included Yamashita's story because the Americans claimed his stash as spoils of war. You'll be surprised to learn there's enough hidden treasure in the United States to keep me busy for the rest of my life. The untold story of the gold rush of the 1800s is that most of the treasure is still buried in mines all around California and the southwest. Give the book a read; you'll like it."

"Thank you," Nat said. "I'll do that. This is a fun place to look around, but I've come to talk to you."

"Fine, fine," Kalender said impatiently. "Follow me." The large man maneuvered around several other displays to a double door in the back of the building. He pushed his way through, turned to another door, inserted his key in the bolt lock, and stepped inside. "Have a seat," he said.

The flamboyant Kalender worked in a drab, sterile office with no decorations, no photographs, and no treasure paraphernalia. There were two huge, sturdy file cabinets that appeared bolted into the back wall, but little else. The only other furniture was a small desk with a large Apple monitor sitting in front of a lone window looking over the parking lot behind the building.

"I like to keep it spartan in here," Kalender said. "This is where I do most of my research and writing. So what's on your mind?"

"I think you know," Nat responded sharply. "I got the runaround from your secretary. I tried calling several times. You've been talking to my grandfather Joe Travis for several months and I want to know why."

"Sorry about not responding to your calls," Kalender apologized. "My assistant's very protective. But why didn't you save yourself a trip and just ask Joe yourself?"

Nat felt a rush of anger and waited for it to pass. "My grandfather's dead."

Kalender's mouth drooped when he heard Nat's response, and his mustache sagged over his upper lip. He seemed genuinely surprised by the news—but almost eerily expectant as well. "Very sorry to hear that," Kalender consoled. "I really liked your grandfather. An engaging man. And he told quite a story. I'm very sorry."

"I thought you might know something about …"

"Whoa big fella," Kalender interrupted. "Where you going with that one?"

"I'm not accusing," Nat countered, "but I believe my grandfather was murdered. His routine hadn't changed one bit in over thirty years, except that over the last few months he started talking regularly with a treasure hunter from California. You can imagine my concern."

Kalender stood up indignantly, paused to consider Nat's comment, and then sat back down. "Nat, you and I got off on the wrong foot," he said. "I'll take responsibility for that. I should've returned your call after I got your message—could've saved you a trip to Oakland—but I was worried about confidentiality. In my business, family members of my clients are often the last ones to know about what they're doing. And Joe Travis had quite a story. But if your grandfather's dead, then I'm willing to share his information with you. I want you to know I wasn't taking advantage of him, if that's what you're worried about. Your grandfather and I were working together and, by the way, he was sharp as a tack. Buried treasure is one thing—murder quite another. So where do you want to start?"

Nat sensed Kalender was telling the truth. On top of that, the large man's disarming personality made it difficult for Nat to stay angry with him. And for the first time, Nat thought there might really be an innocent explanation for Papa Joe's relationship with Kalender. "Take it from the beginning," Nat said.

CHAPTER 19

The time she'd spent in Charleston with her aging mother reminded Renee how rapidly the last twenty years of her life had swept by. Chasing a career and following Emmitt and Amelia from event to event had been fulfilling, but the hectic pace had left her untethered in so many ways. She'd missed the daily connection with her mother and had lost a true sense of home, the feeling of community that a small town like Brewton offered. The time away with her mom had opened her eyes.

"Seeing anyone new?" her mother had asked while they had sat reading on the waterfront one day.

"No," Renee had answered, but for the first time in years the image of a man came to her when contemplating her response. There was certainly no hint of a romantic attachment building with Nat Travis, but the quality time she'd spent with him in Brewton suddenly registered on her. Yet, she dismissed the notion quickly, not wanting to contemplate the immense complications that a relationship with her ex-brother-in-law would create.

Renee's cell phone rang just as she turned to walk out the back door of her mother's house to unload their bags from the car. It was Nat.

"How was your trip?" he asked, his voice energized.

"Nat, hi," Renee said while looking over at her mother, who raised her eyebrows and grinned. "We had a great time but we're glad to be home." She shrugged toward her mother, as if to ward off her suggestive look. "How's the research going?"

"That's why I'm calling. I had a breakthrough while you were gone."

"Really?" Renee countered.

"It all started with a prompt from Joseph."

"Joseph?"

"Yeah, I think you know the guy." Nat chuckled. "Listen to this. He hired a private investigator to look into Papa Joe's death and never told me about it."

"Are you surprised?" Renee asked, taking a seat.

"No, I guess not. At first, I was hot ... I figured he'd hired the guy just to look into me, but I got over it. But the PI did find something totally unexpected."

"You have my attention."

"Joseph's guy reviewed phone records. It appears Papa Joe's research into our family tree had a far different purpose than we thought. My grandfather was looking for something much more specific than our genealogy. Something you and I never imagined."

"Okay," Renee said. "You have my undivided attention. What was he up to?"

"He was searching for a treasure."

"A what?"

"A treasure. Papa Joe was communicating regularly with a professional treasure hunter named Frank Kalender. So I went to see Kalender in Oakland the other day ..."

"Whoa," Renee interrupted. "You flew to Oakland?"

"Yeah, and it was well worth the trip. After spending an afternoon with Kalender, I finally understand what Papa Joe was doing. And Kalender really thought they were onto something. He said they believed our ancestor Joe the slave held the secret to a Mexican treasure buried somewhere inside the Alamo. Kalender called it the lost treasure of the San Saba mines, or Bowie's Treasure. He and Papa Joe were dead serious about this thing."

"But why would ..." Renee stopped, trying to hide the

skepticism in her voice, "why would Papa Joe have kept something like a buried treasure a secret, especially if he believed in it so much?"

"I had the same question," Nat answered, "and I'm not easy to convince, as you know. But Kalender said more than once that Papa Joe was worried I'd think he was crazy if he said anything. He was using Kalender to validate some of his findings before coming to me. Kalender said Papa Joe wanted an independent expert's confirmation first. I've now spent the better part of the last twenty-four hours reading about Bowie's Treasure—it's been written about more times than you can imagine—and I now see the pattern in Papa Joe's documents. There's something to this story; I'm sure of it. Kalender's an eccentric … you can see that on his website … but he really knows his stuff. He's very convincing."

"I'm not doubting you," Renee countered, "but that's a lot to digest. Hard to believe Papa Joe learned something no other so-called treasure hunter ever figured out. Have you said anything to anyone else?"

"Other than talking to Kalender, you're the only other person who knows. I considered telling Joseph but thought better of it. And that leads me to this call. I know it's a lot to ask but I was hoping you'd come back and look at these records a second time with me. You're much more likely to see things that I've missed."

Renee hesitated, but not because she wasn't interested. She just didn't want Nat to think she was too anxious. "Any chance this Kalender may be behind what happened to Papa Joe?"

"That was the first thought that crossed my mind, but I'm convinced he didn't know Papa Joe was dead. He's a treasure hunter through and through—and likely milked my grandfather, but a killer … no. Just looking at him would tell you that much. He reminds me of one of those fat guys at a Green Bay football game who paints Packers across his gut and goes shirtless in twenty-degree weather. Bigger than life. And the fact he's writing a new book ... and hopes Bowie's Treasure will be the centerpiece ... says a lot. The bottom line—he's crazy to find this treasure and believes he was getting close with Papa Joe. My guess is whoever broke into Papa Joe's house might have been looking for the same thing."

The Kalender angle fascinated Renee. In researching history, she'd often found unusual turns in her work: More often than not they'd proven to be dead ends, but any chance at discovering unique information always excited her. "What do you have in mind?" she asked.

"Help me give this thing a shot. If we don't find something in the next few days, we'll bury Papa Joe once and for all. What do you say?"

Renee paused, but she'd known her answer from the beginning. After waiting a few more seconds, she said, "You have a deal."

PART II

CHAPTER 20

The Alamo—1836

Joe looked around the Alamo compound and could sense the soldiers were preparing for death. Tiny figures were beginning to form on the horizon, the Mexican army of doom, and the twenty-year-old knew it was only a matter of time before General Santa Anna launched his invasion. Colonel William Barret Travis, Joe's master and the commander of the Alamo fortress, stood in the center of the garrison dressed in full military garb, a portrait of bravery, but his steel was no match for the overwhelming force forming across the river. The harrowing letter Colonel Travis had drafted and recited to Joe in his headquarters several days before indicated as much:

Commandancy of the Alamo
Bejar, Fby 24ᵗʰ 1836

To the People of Texas and all Americans of the world,
fellow citizens and compatriots—

I am besieged, by a thousand or more of the Mexicans under Santa Anna—I have sustained continual Bombardment and cannonade for 24 hours and have not lost a man—The enemy has demanded a surrender at discretion, otherwise, the garrison is to be put to the sword, if the fort is taken—I have answered the demand with a cannon shot, and our flag still waves proudly from the walls—I shall never surrender or retreat. Then, I call on you in the name of Liberty, of patriotism and everything

dear to the American character, to come to our aid, with all dispatch—The enemy is receiving reinforcements daily and will no doubt increase to three or four thousand in four or five days. If this call is neglected, I am determined to sustain myself as long as possible and die like a soldier who never forgets what is due to his own honor and that of his country—Victory or Death.

P.S. The Lord is on our side.

Inspiring, Joe thought, but not enough to dissuade him from considering his escape options. But he was loyal to Colonel Travis and knew that his best hope for making it out alive rested on surviving the onslaught and then seeking mercy from the Mexican army. Until that time, Joe would stand alongside his master, rifle in hand, and if called to do so, die nobly in battle. Joe's fate and that of all of the soldiers in the Alamo was now in the clutches of His Excellency, General Antonio Lopez de Santa Anna.

——★——

The next morning, Joe watched the Mexican army parade into the streets of San Antonio less than a half-mile away, their standard-bearers proudly carrying the red and green colors of the Mexican government. However, the powerful eagle clutching a serpent in its talon in the middle of the Mexican flag was not the only image that captured Joe's attention. There was a new flag, previously unknown to the Alamo soldiers, unfurled at the top of the San Antonio church tower at the end of town. But Joe knew what it meant. "The blood-red banner," Travis had told him, "is the Mexicans' symbol of no compromise—General Santa Anna's message that he intends to kill every last one of us." Joe watched Travis spring into action upon sight of the dreaded flag. "Let's give them our response," the colonel *yelled. Travis then darted between his men. "Load the cannon," he directed, and the Texans returned their answer—a thunderous cannon shot that flew the eight hundred yards separating the Alamo from the Mexican army before falling harmlessly at the edge of town. Surrender, Joe realized, was no longer a possibility.*

For two weeks, Joe had watched General Santa Anna's troops lay siege to the Alamo from their protected positions across the river, using cannon fire and howitzers to relentlessly pound the crumbling fort. Day by day, the Mexican lines had inched closer to the fortress, a python slowly constricting its kill, waiting for the right moment to strike. Joe and all of the men beside him could feel what was coming, and it was only their faith in the cause, and the faint hope of reinforcements from Colonel Fannin's troops in Goliad, that kept them going.

Joe was glad that Travis had picked his boyhood friend, James Butler Bonham, to handle the job of securing additional troops for the Alamo. The two men were close, and the soldiers trusted Bonham to carry out Travis's orders. The native South Carolinian had ridden to the Alamo's defense months earlier along with his fellow riders, the Mobile Grays, and had become a favorite among the men. The trip to Goliad required not only courage in evading the Mexican forces but an equal amount of confidence to convince Colonel Fannin to come to the Alamo's defense. Joe could sense from Travis that Bonham's job was virtually impossible, but the men needed hope and Bonham was fearless.

Travis called Joe to prepare Bonham for the trip. Joe readied the lieutenant's cream-colored horse, placed key documents in his saddlebags, and loaded ammunition. It was February 26, 1836, when Joe stood alongside Colonel Travis and his co-commander of the garrison, the feebly ill Jim Bowie. As Joe rechecked Bonham's saddle, the South Carolinian finally arrived, huddled with Travis and Bowie, and recited a brief prayer. He then rode out—and Joe and every man in the Alamo held their breath. A short time later, the tower watchman rang the bell to report Bonham had cleared the Mexican line safely. The spirits of the men were lifted.

Santa Anna's relentless siege took its toll on the fortress during the week Bonham was away, and Joe watched Travis's mood darken. But hope returned on March 3. Joe watched from one of the parapets as Bonham galloped through a hail of bullets past the Mexican army and through an open gate near the Alamo corral. Joe cheered with all of the Texans as Bonham flew past the stunned Mexican soldiers without lifting his head from his horse's neck. Good news had surely arrived.

Bonham had none. The reluctant Fannin wouldn't bring his troops to the garrison's defense and the only other hope for support was still reportedly a several-days' march away in Gonzalez. Despite the grim report, Joe sensed Bonham's confident return through enemy lines had bucked up the morale of the troops and energized them for battle. If victory wasn't possible, why would a man who'd ridden to safety come back to a certain-death hole? Bonham's courageous act revived hope for victory.

Then, as if Santa Anna knew it was time, an eerie quiet fell over the Mexican army and the town of San Antonio. Troop movement. Formation. The attack loomed. Joe felt fear grip the beaten-down soldiers of the Alamo once again but Colonel Travis would have none of it. He rallied his men, summoned them to the center of the garrison, and drew a line in the sand with his sword. "Those prepared to give their lives in freedom's cause, come over to me," he implored. The assembled group knew exactly what this meant—if they stepped over the mark, they were likely to die. Every man, save one, crossed the line.

———— ★ ————

March 6, 1836
After a fitful night of preparations, Joe finally convinced Colonel Travis to rest. Joe set the colonel's sword and double-barreled shotgun by his side and helped Travis stretch out on his bunk. He then walked across the room and closed his eyes. He'd not even fallen asleep

when a voice hollered from outside the headquarters. The second time the voice cried out, the words were unmistakable.

"Colonel Travis, the Mexicans are coming!"

Travis jumped out of bed, grabbed his rifle, and strapped his sword on his hip faster than Joe could pull on his shoes. The colonel then sprinted from the headquarters across the plaza toward the buzz of activity at the northern end of the fort. Joe did his best to keep up. Travis quickly assumed a position by the north battery station and surveyed the area. There was no sign of the enemy in the morning fog but the eerie trumpet blasts, sparks of weapons fire, and distant Mexicans' cries of "Viva Santa Anna" signaled they were coming.

Joe looked back toward the plaza at the anxious Texans who were stumbling and running in every direction. Travis noticed the panic and attempted to bolster his men by exhorting, "Come on, boys. The Mexicans are upon us and we'll give them hell!" Travis continued shouting, urging his men to hurry to their positions. As Travis faced the plaza yelling instructions, Joe turned around and saw the first wave of Mexican troops emerge from the darkness, ladders extended, attempting to scale the northern wall.

Travis wheeled around, aimed his double-barreled shotgun at the gathering force, and fired. Several Mexican soldiers screamed when the buckshot rained down, piercing their hands and faces, inciting chaotic movement among those at the base of the wall. Within seconds, a volley of return fire whizzed by Joe's head. The slave dropped below a parapet to avoid the incoming round but his master didn't fare as well. Joe heard a thud and turned in shock as Colonel Travis recoiled, his head wobbling as if detached from his body, and fell backward to the ground. Joe jumped down after Travis but immediately knew it was too late. The blood streaming from the gunshot wound in Travis's head told Joe what he already knew.

Joe then turned around and saw several other defenders struck by incoming fire and he knew the Mexicans would soon be inside. He darted through the crowd of soldiers and sprinted toward the southern end of the plaza away from the battle zone. His hands shook as he flung open the door to the low-barracks room and raced inside, momentarily forgetting the building had been set up as a quarantine zone for the sickly Bowie. The once-mighty warrior was alone in the building, having relinquished his co-command to Travis as the undiagnosed ailment ravaged his body and rendered him immobile. The entrance area was dark but Joe saw candles flickering at the far end of the hall. He sprinted toward the light and froze when he came upon his bedridden former leader, whose head barely lifted from his pillow. Bowie was covered with blankets but had two rifles positioned across his chest and his trademark Bowie knife teetering on a side table next to him.

"What's happening?" Bowie asked in a faint, scratchy voice.

"The Mexicans, sir, they're coming over the wall. They already shot Mr. Travis."

"Well," Bowie responded before coughing, "we knew this day would come. They'll be looking for me soon enough. My scalp's worth something to Santa Anna's men. Go over there and hide in one of the closets. All of the ladies have gathered down the hall." He pointed at a room across the way. "Don't come out until I'm dead and the shooting's stopped. Do you hear me?"

"Yes sir," Joe answered nervously. "God bless you, Mister Jim." Joe made a move toward the closet just as gunfire exploded outside the doors. Colonel Bowie then yelled out with all of his remaining strength, "Come here, son."

"Yes sir."

"They'll kill all of us, you know?" Bowie continued. "Of the men still alive in this place, you're the only one likely to survive. Ol' Santa Anna claims he never kills black slaves or women. Come closer—I've got something for you." Bowie feebly reached under his pillow and pulled out an envelope. He handed it to Joe. "Whatever you do, don't let the Mexicans have this. Tear it up or burn it if you have to. But *if you make it out of here alive, remember Jim Bowie and remember the Alamo."*

Loud Mexican voices filled the low-barracks room and Joe realized time had run out. He dove into the closet across from Bowie's bed and held his breath, stuffing the envelope deep into his pants pocket. He said a quick prayer and waited, trembling, preparing to die. Within seconds, multiple gunshots rang out and Joe heard the trampling of feet, the thunder of a death squad, moving closer to Colonel Bowie.

The sounds that followed haunted Joe for the rest of his life.

CHAPTER 21

Angelina de Zavala Gentry moved around the interior of the Alamo grounds hoping she'd feel a sign that would remove all doubt from her mind. In her many years of false starts and wrong turns, chasing the treasure that had bedeviled her great-grandmother, she'd never found definitive evidence of the location. But now that she'd come this far, there was no more room for indecision.

Angelina was finally in a position to move. Janet Nelson had cleared the way for the excavation project that was certain to vindicate all of her efforts. If Angelina discovered the most famous secret of the Alamo, after one hundred and seventy years of speculation and disappointment, she would rehabilitate her family name overnight. The de Zavalas' place in Alamo lore would be secure, forever etched alongside the legendary names of Travis, Bowie, and Crockett.

Janet's wrestling of the Alamo away from the clutches of the Akers-Butler faction of the DRT, which had torpedoed all of Angelina's former "archeological" projects, had cleared the last obstacle in her path. Even the meddlesome politicians—who'd become so enamored with Janet that they'd turned over the new Alamo Preservation Advisory Board with virtually no restrictions—were out of the way. But even with all of this good news, Angelina grew more paranoid every day that the slow process had worked to others' benefit, that someone like Joe Travis was about to blow her cover, or worse, beat her to the finish line. Killing the old black man had solved one of those problems, but she sensed others lurked around the corner.

Frank Kalender was one of them. She'd taken a significant risk by hiring him to lead the Alamo project—the man was uncontrollable and a shameless self-promoter—but his credentials were good and his oversized personality permitted Angelina to maintain her low profile and avoid scrutiny. She'd always worried that finding her expedition leader on the Internet through a Google search was foolish but, in reality, Kalender had been the perfect tool for the job. He'd kept Angelina regularly updated on the latest news about potential competitors, misdirected the boundless community of speculators who followed his blog posts with religious fervor, and thoroughly researched each rumor about the treasure.

But he had a habit of misfiring. She remembered the day Kalender had excitedly announced that he'd found a descendant of Joe the slave living in Brewton, Alabama. Angelina herself had trembled at the report, sensing Kalender had finally uncovered the ultimate clue, but like all of his other discoveries, it had proven a dud. Kalender's inability to get Joe Travis to produce the treasure map finally led her to take matters into her own hands, only to discover that the old man knew far less than she did. And because Kruger and Shakes had bungled their job, she now found herself an accomplice to murder. The Travis fiasco convinced Angelina that the existence of a game-changing clue like a map was purely a Kalender fantasy. She berated herself for believing in his false leads and far-fetched ideas.

But even then, she still needed him.

Kalender had provided the expert testimony necessary to convince Janet's new handpicked board that an excavation event was just what the Alamo needed to reinvigorate the public's interest in the iconic structure. His project offered the group a gateway to notoriety for the decaying mission and a vehicle for free publicity and fund-raising. Yet, even with the approval granted, and the dig waiting only on a final plan, Angelina still worried the location remained too unsettled. Kalender had not convinced her that his latest suppositions were accurate. But finding Joe Travis had accomplished one important advance in her research—it had led her to Anthony Ambrose and fresh support for her long-held suspicion about the treasure's resting place. In particular, there was a specific paragraph from one of Travis's letters that dovetailed perfectly with her great-grandmother's note. Angelina perused it again:

BT – moved ? Not in the LBR. Find JB's trail. I had M.

Bowie's Treasure moved. Not in the Long Barracks Room. Find JB's trail. Slave had Map.

The trail had always been the key. Where was *JB's trail*? What did those few words mean? One of Joe Travis's letters to Ambrose provided what Kalender believed was confirming information:

My ancestor Joe was a slave who was owned by William Barret Travis, the commander of the Alamo. He had many responsibilities in serving Travis. He fixed meals, took care of his animals, and stocked supplies from the stores in San Antonio. His most important job however was pumping water from the one well in the fortress. The men never had enough water. Joe beat a path to that well so many times that Colonel Bowie nicknamed it Joe's trail.

"*JB's trail*," Kalender had concluded, "is the final resting spot for Jim Bowie's treasure! This has to be a reference to Joe's trail to the water well."

But even while intrigued, Angelina remained skeptical. She knew exactly where the Texans had drilled their lone water well in the Alamo, and she'd long understood it to be the perfect hiding place for Bowie's Treasure. But Joe Travis's letter was anything but definitive. Frustrated, Angelina had reluctantly signed off on the location, but her gut still told her she'd missed something.

Angelina thought back to the 2005 television show *History's Mysteries*, which speculated that an old abandoned well was the burial site of a previously unknown treasure hidden inside the Alamo. She remembered during those nascent days of her own personal quest, just after her long feud with the DRT had ended, how worried she'd become that some opportunistic Geraldo Rivera-like TV crew from the History Channel might usurp her prize. She'd known so little then but to this day remained shocked how close the ill-equipped explorers had come to making *her* discovery. Angelina had remained fraught with tension every day during those weeks that one of the TV researchers actually knew what they were doing; that was until word leaked out that the director was relying entirely on readings from some Kalender-like treasure hunter with a metal detector. Only then did she finally breathe.

The failed excavation project left the world and the DRT believing the treasure story was a hoax. But Angelina knew differently. She understood, unlike most others, that the television crew never considered the existence of a map, nor did they properly research the precise location of the well. Yet, the TV crew, despite their inept efforts, had only been off the mark by some fifty yards. Angelina realized then that the treasure could belong to no one else. And after the embarrassed DRT vowed never to allow a similar sacrilege on Alamo grounds, she felt confident the treasure would remain safe until her time arrived.

Finally, in 2013, with Janet's ascension to the presidency of the DRT, Angelina was ready.

CHAPTER 22

The Alamo—March 7, 1836

Joe stumbled through the entrance gate of the plaza with the butt of a rifle stuck in his back. He winced as the bayonet wounds in his chest resumed bleeding. Another shove and Joe fell in front of a large chestnut stallion mounted by a man with sparkling knee-high black boots. His Excellency. Joe straightened up before the Mexican leader, amidst taunts from the soldiers of "el esclavo, el esclavo." General Santa Anna stared back at him with a puzzled expression, shook his head, and spoke in broken English. "I spare your life, slave; kneel down before me."

Joe did as demanded, pointing his head toward the earth in hope of not offending the general.

"Now stand," Santa Anna ordered. "Look at my troops. Take the memory of what you see here today with you. Tell the Texas traitors this is the fate that awaits those who do not submit. Comprendo?"

Joe nodded. Out of the corner of his eye, he spied the Mexican troops assembling the lifeless Texans' bodies in the middle of the plaza.

"Travis, Bowie, and Crockett—all dead," Santa Anna announced with spirit in his voice. "I want you to point out their bodies to me. Go!"

Santa Anna followed on horseback as one of his officers rammed Joe through the crowd of soldiers to a long row of mutilated corpses. Many were carved up beyond recognition, but Joe knew most of the Texans by their clothing. He first walked over to his master, Colonel Travis, said a prayer to himself, and pointed.

"Colonel Travis," he declared.

A loud cheer went up from the Mexicans.

Joe then walked farther down the row, convulsing over the sight of his dead friends, before stopping in front of the grotesquely dis-figured body of Jim Bowie. He closed his eyes and trembled. Bowie's mouth was sliced open on both sides and his eyes gouged out from bayonet thrusts. Part of his scalp had been carved off. Dried blood had coagulated on the numerous gaping puncture wounds all over his body. A human piñata.

"Colonel Bowie," he announced.

Another huge cheer from the troops. "Viva Santa Anna," they cried.

The Mexican officer stuffed the butt of his rifle in Joe's back one more time, forcing him farther down the line. He walked past another fifty men before he came upon the buckskin clothing of Davy Crockett.

"Mister Crockett," he yelled.

The Mexicans saved their loudest cheer for Crockett, the man who supposedly killed more Mexican soldiers than any other Texan.

Santa Anna rode up to Joe and looked at him. "You've done well," he said approvingly. "I will allow you to live." At that moment, a rifle shot rang out and Joe caught a glimpse of Crockett's limp body bouncing up from the ground. "Take the slave to the room with the women," Santa Anna directed to one of his subordinates before turning back to Joe. "Remember this, slave," he pronounced. "The same fate awaits your General Houston and anyone else who defies me. Do you under-stand?" Cheers again rang out from Santa Anna's men.

Joe avoided looking directly at the general but again nodded his agreement. For the first time since the attack began, he thought he actually might survive. For once, his black skin had finally proven an asset.

Night fell on the Alamo compound and the nauseating odor of burning bodies wafted through to the small band of Texan sur-vivors. An unknown officer had locked Joe and four women down in a small room in the sacristy portion of the church with minimal surveillance. The minute night fell Joe unlatched the hidden trapdoor in the back of the room and crawled beneath the Alamo floorboards into the adjoining storage area. He then peeped out another trapdoor and slithered into the open. From there, Joe eased his way down the corridors of the church past several snoring Mexican soldiers to a window. Joe lowered himself through the opening and silently made his way along the perimeter of the Alamo fortress to the river. He slid into the water, flattened out on his stomach, and followed the current away.

Twenty minutes later, free from the Mexican troops, Joe reached deep into his pocket for the now-wet envelope Colonel Bowie had given to him in the long-barracks room. Joe was illiterate but Bowie's message didn't require him to read. The markings and directions were unmistakable.

Colonel Bowie had given him a map.

CHAPTER 23

The call had come in unexpectedly from Frankie. "Madame Angelina," he reported, "would like you and Mr. Kruger to help her at the Alamo excavation. I'll give you further instructions next week."

For the first time since he'd begun working for the old lady, Shakes felt uncertain about taking on a new assignment. But it wasn't the risk of the job that concerned him; it was the risk of his client. Angelina had changed. The quirky woman with the Alamo obsession had become more and more unreliable, maybe even dangerous.

It hadn't always been that way. When he'd first met her in 2010, Angelina had seemed harmless enough, an old lady he could take advantage of without much trouble. He was a grifter by trade and figured he'd see plenty of opportunities to score working for a wealthy blue-hair with limited staff.

When Shakes had arrived in San Antonio to chase a con on a group of military retirees, he'd never expected to stay around long. And when his original plan went south early on, he'd charted a quick getaway. The temporary work he took on as a cook was just to get enough cash to get home, but that's where fate and Angelina had stepped in. It was at the greasy, five-table diner where Shakes worked that he first met the sawed-off Francisco "Frankie" Cruz. The young Hispanic, who came in regularly for breakfast, liked to bullshit about sports and other topics while Shakes worked the griddle behind the counter. "What do you think about the Spurs chances next year?" he'd ask. "Did you see the soccer match?" "Damn, that Kardashian gal's a nut job." And on and on. After a couple of months of this routine, and just after Shakes announced he planned to leave town, Frankie gave him his number and told him to call if he wanted a new job.

The interview had been simple enough. Frankie's boss, he was told, was an older woman who needed someone to handle a variety of surveillance jobs, primarily to watch the movements of a couple of equally aged socialites. Shakes had jumped at the chance, convinced that he could use the job to start a new grift ... stealing from the naïve young assistant and his rich lady boss. But Angelina proved more cautious than he'd hoped. She'd kept her distance for the first six months, never communicating directly with him, and always inserted Frankie between them. But Shakes was patient and figured that he'd eventually get his shot.

And in the seventh month, he did. Frankie invited Shakes into Angelina's home and asked him to take on bigger assignments, primarily those Frankie didn't want to handle, like driving. He was surprised that his flashy appearance was a nonissue, but that was confirmed when the boss lady quietly stepped into the room, looked him over, and left almost without a word. "Hire him," she'd grunted on the way out. Soon Frankie was offering him more money and new responsibilities. Shakes was granted the role he wanted, replacing Frankie in performing Angelina's errands and in fetching her Starbucks each morning. His employer, whose manic eyes revealed far more than her words, loved her strong coffee, and Shakes smartly played along. Within weeks, he had a new routine—arriving at Angelina's back porch at 7:00 a.m., drinking a double-shot breakfast blend, and listening to her talk about her favorite subject: her ancestors and their prominent role in Texas history. During these talks, Shakes smiled a lot, complimented Angelina's stories, and worked hard to gain her confidence. The grift was moving his way.

But just as quickly, things turned south. Frankie unexpectedly reinserted himself into Shakes's relationship with Angelina and announced that his boss needed to add extra security to her staff. With that introduction, Kruger entered the scene. It was immediately clear that the huge beast was a threat. And when the Serbian killed old man Travis, Shakes became an unwitting accomplice to murder. He wondered how he'd let it happen. Why hadn't he done more to stop Kruger from manhandling the ninety-year-old war hero? Feeling guilty, Shakes had started to pack his bags to leave town after the break-in. Yet, despite it all, something held him back.

Shakes had never intended to become party to the level of crimes Angelina now seemed willing to commit without conscience, but he finally figured out there was a reason for her change in tactics. He'd secretly listened in on one of her conversations with the big oaf, Frank Kalender, and learned of their plan. What Shakes had originally thought were the petty acts of an embittered old woman, the kind of work he was suited for, didn't present the real picture. There was a bigger prize out there for the taking, one that could set Shakes up for the rest of his life if he played things right. Angelina was after a treasure buried deep inside the Alamo, one she'd kept secret from the rest of the world, but one Kalender supposedly knew how to find.

But even as his greed overwhelmed his good judgment, Shakes still wondered if he was making a mistake staying in San Antonio. Would Angelina now consider him a liability that would have to be handled? Was Kruger's real job merely to clean up behind her? To clean him up?

Unsure, Shakes decided to make his play, pocket a gob of money, and then get out of Texas as fast as he could. But with Kruger hovering around him like a shadow, he knew he'd have to be much more careful from now on.

CHAPTER 24

North of Calf Creek, Texas—1832

Jim Bowie crouched behind the rock escarpment and surrounding bushes and gnawed on a piece of beef jerky. His other men stretched out on their stomachs and peered over the horizon, safely camouflaged by the native vegetation and rugged sloping terrain. They waited. It might be several days before the Mexican silver train made its way through the narrow opening in the hills where they lay in ambush, but Bowie was wary of advance scouts discovering their location. They would stay concealed as long as necessary.

Bowie had left San Antonio three weeks earlier, in the early spring of 1832, on a northwest route toward the abandoned Presidio San Saba, declaring to all who listened that he was searching for clues about a lost Indian silver mine in the Red Hills of Texas. Bowie was careful to choose the abandoned mission fortress as his destination.

He often wondered how the Spanish could have been so foolish as to build a foreign settlement in the heart of tribal lands, particularly in the midst of Comanche country. In March 1758, shortly after the Presidio San Saba and its neighboring mission were completed, the unavoidable conflict occurred. A party of Comanches rode toward the newly constructed presidio in full war paint, intent on sending the Spanish government a signal about peaceful coexistence in the Indians' territory. Armed with native tomahawks and a variety of European weapons, including lances and swords, the Comanches collected the scalps of every man, woman, and child in the presidio, later torching the fort. The nearby mission fared no better. Everything that could burn went up in flames, and every human or animal capable *of moving was cut down and bludgeoned. The massacre left little of the presidio or mission standing and Spanish leaders never sought to rebuild it again.*

But the massacre only added to the legend concerning the Indians' silver deposits in the Red Hills. As time passed, many came to believe the Indian raid wasn't the hostile act of an indigenous people but instead a protective measure to keep the Spanish away from their precious treasure. These many years later, Jim Bowie believed none of it. By 1832, he'd tired of searching for the Indians' elusive secrets and had instead fixed on a more predictable target—the Mexican silver train from Sonora, Mexico. This caravan of mules loaded with fifty-pound silver bars and guarded by a small group of Mexican soldiers had to traverse the entirety of the Texas province from Sonora to New Orleans. There were plenty of spots to intercept the shipment along the way and Jim Bowie knew 'em all.

To throw further cover over his motives, Bowie had first gone to the abandoned presidio and left his mark for others to find, carving his name and the date into the rotting gateposts of the old fort.

BOWIE MINE
1832

Bowie then circled back into the hills and set up camp to wait for the Mexicans to arrive.

Bowie knew a typical Mexican silver train consisted of approximately two hundred mules loaded with as many silver bars as possible and would be protected by eight to ten musket-armed soldiers. The guards would be sequenced out over a single-file, rope-linked train, some eight hundred yards long, and clustered toward the front. Bowie also knew that at various times long expanses of the procession would be left unprotected. He'd decided to wait with his band of fourteen men in their concealed location, allow the majority of the caravan to pass, and then steal as many mules as possible. Depending on the positioning of the guards, Bowie believed he could steal dozens of mules without being detected.

After three days of waiting, Rezin Bowie came to his brother and announced the silver train was in sight. Jim Bowie picked up his field glasses, searched over the dusty landscape, and made out the first signs of the lead rider. He continued watching as the procession slowly came into view.

The mule train was heading in an east-northeast direction generally parallel to the San Saba River. Bowie's men hid in the hills above the river knowing the Mexicans would eventually move toward them to avoid the heavier brush and pecan trees growing in abundance along the waterway. Bowie had selected an interception point that appeared navigable for the mule team but with just enough bends and turns that the soldiers would naturally have blind spots once they passed. As the caravan grew closer, Bowie continued calculating, counting the number of mules, pinpointing the locations of guards, and assessing the amount of the load. Based on what he knew about prior expeditions, each mule carried about two to three hundred pounds of silver bars, approximately $40,000–$50,000 in value. Stealing ten mules would allow Bowie to pay off all of his men handsomely and still retain a good portion for himself, but twenty would provide him more than he could spend in several lifetimes.

Bowie decided to steal thirty.

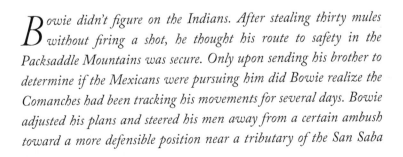

*B*owie didn't figure on the Indians. After stealing thirty mules without firing a shot, he thought his route to safety in the Packsaddle Mountains was secure. Only upon sending his brother to determine if the Mexicans were pursuing him did Bowie realize the Comanches had been tracking his movements for several days. Bowie adjusted his plans and steered his men away from a certain ambush toward a more defensible position near a tributary of the San Saba

River called Calf Creek. With the Comanches' attack imminent, Bowie's men swiftly constructed rock fortifications and prepared to defend their ground. The delay of the cautious Indians gave Bowie enough time to scout a location for hiding the stolen treasure. With the help of his brother and two other men, Bowie ferreted out a cave partially covered with brush, vines, and native vegetation and labored the better part of a day to hide the silver bars. None of the men quarreled with Bowie's decision to secrete the treasure; they had a far more pressing concern—survival.

A day later, the Indians surrounded Bowie's small band at Calf Creek. At dawn, over one hundred Comanches crossed through the thicket separating them from the area where Bowie's fourteen men lay in wait. The moment the leaders of the war party stepped into the open, twelve flintlock rifles fired and a dozen Indians fell to the ground. The Texans then grabbed their Spencer repeater pistols and fired off another volley of slugs while their two servants reloaded their rifles. More Indians dropped. The stunned Comanches quickly retreated into the brush. The same process repeated itself several more times before the Indians realized the danger of showing themselves in the open. Only once did the warriors get close enough to fire their own muskets and in that one exchange two of Bowie's men were hit. Over the course of a long day, the Indians lost almost half of their war party before they eventually withdrew to safety. But they only did so after stealing all of Bowie's horses and the canvas packs used to transport the silver bars. Bowie's men had survived the ordeal but would have to escape on foot to avoid further attack.

The heavy silver stash hidden in the obstructed cave had to be left behind. With no horses, limited gunpowder, and two wounded men, safety was Bowie's paramount concern. He'd retrieve the hidden silver bars another day.

CHAPTER 25

Nat strode up and down the sideline watching his players run through their final scrimmage before their opening game on Labor Day weekend. By the end of the practice, most of the kids were bent over at the waist, panting, and completely gassed. *Fatigue makes cowards of us all*, Nat thought, harkening back to his favorite Vince Lombardi line. But it was just the moment he wanted: his players physically spent, mentally worn, and captive to his coaching.

"Last play and then circle up," Nat yelled.

Both the offense and defense huddled and then hustled to the line of scrimmage. The ball fired back to the quarterback in shotgun formation and like a lightning strike, a wide receiver flashed past the defensive backs and caught a perfectly thrown spiral for a touchdown.

Nat concealed a smile. More than thirty years vanished in front of him as he saw himself crossing the goal line. S.W. Niland High School, circa 1979, and a senior named Nat Travis running into the end zone. He shook his head, amazed by how much his own football experiences still resonated in his mind. And then he smiled again. The irony of a player who once hated practice more than any on his squad now pushing his team to exhaustion never escaped him. He'd been such a different person then. Gifted but lost. Nat had been the kind of player he now hated to coach—too talented to bench, yet due to a reckless, insolent streak, and a lack of discipline, a cancer in the locker room. It had taken years for him to understand, and for Papa Joe to undo, the damage inflicted by his bad attitude.

But with Papa Joe pushing him after his father's untimely death, Nat drove himself to the best physical condition of his life and discovered talent he'd never even touched. He had the best receiving year in Niland history as a senior and gained recruiting offers from schools throughout the south. The fact that he chose Alabama A&M, Papa Joe's favorite college, paid homage to the man who'd saved his life. And coaching and working with kids, particularly those without hope or families, was his way of honoring that gift.

"Circle up boys," Nat said. "Great practice today. You're almost ready. Now get in here." The boys huddled.

When Nat pulled his head out of the pile of helmets after a closing prayer, he spotted Renee sitting in the bleachers. It appeared she'd been watching practice. He dismissed the boys and walked toward her. He was glad she'd agreed to join him for dinner so they could continue their work on Papa Joe's documents.

"Got 'em ready, coach?"

"Let's hope so," Nat chuckled. "I have no idea what I'm going to get but I do have a squad this year. Let me shower up and meet you in twenty. You can leave your car here."

"Great," Renee replied. "I'm just going to walk around the school campus and soak up some of the memories. I'll be around."

———◆★◆———

Nat greeted Renee in a blue golf shirt and freshly pressed gray slacks.

"You coaches clean up well," she said.

"Not every day a lowly football coach gets to break bread with the editor in chief of the yearbook," Nat joked. "Thanks for coming. I thought we could head back to my place for dinner and then start in on the documents. I have a lot to talk to you about, especially our new friend Kalender."

"Sounds like a plan," Renee responded.

Nat smiled, opened the door to his Ford truck, and helped Renee in. "I actually have a surprise for you when we get to the house. I think you'll like it."

After stopping to get gas on the way home, Nat pulled up to his driveway where several members of the S.W. Niland high-school football team stood milling around.

"What's this all about?" Renee asked.

"One of the boys loves to cook; the others love to eat. This is my surprise. I thought you'd enjoy meeting some of the team."

"Wonderful," she declared. "But I didn't think high schools allowed students to see coaches outside of practice. At least, they don't at Emory."

"You're right about that," Nat replied, "but I've had a tradition with my senior players my entire career. We always have a cookout at my place before the season starts. It's a bonding time. Technically, they're not in school yet so I'm not violating any rules … but I'd do it anyway. This is our way of building a team. We go bowling, watch college games in my film room at school … it's all about coming together so they can reinforce their pact not to drink or do drugs."

"I like that program." Renee flashed a perfect smile at Nat.

"This is a strong group," he said. "I have high hopes." Nat parked his car and flung open the door. "You boys ready to eat?" he yelled as he stepped outside.

A couple of the boys clapped their hands, and two raised their arms in triumph. The only white member of the group stepped forward and walked toward Renee. "Hello, Ms. Travis," he said, "my name's Wesley Phelps. Welcome to the annual senior-players' dinner."

A couple of the other teenagers mocked him.

"Don't listen to the rest of this crew," the boy cracked, "they have no class." He turned and grinned at his teammates before turning back to Renee. "You ready to eat, ma'am?"

"Thought you'd never ask," she answered.

"Cut the act, Phelps," Nat said with a wink and then waved his arm at the group, motioning them toward the house. By the time the boys reassembled in Nat's heavily treed, fence-lined backyard, one of the players already had the barbeque grill sizzling. Nearby, a rectangular picnic table with eight place settings waited. The checkered tablecloth was stacked with paper plates, knives, forks, and napkins.

"Where are your manners, Jenkins?" Nat asked abruptly. "Pour Ms. Travis a glass of wine." He chuckled when Jenkins scurried toward the ice chest.

"No you don't," Renee responded. "It's football season and I can drink iced tea just like these boys. Fill me up Jenkins." She giggled along with the rest of the players as the brawny five-foot-ten noseguard grabbed a Lipton's can from the cooler and poured it into a glass of ice.

"Almost ready," said Larry Roosevelt, the tight end turned cook. He studied the burgers, flipped several over one last time, and then piled them onto a server's tray.

Nat escorted Renee to her place in the center of one of the benches while the players placed several bowls of food in the middle of the table. There were baked beans, coleslaw, potato salad, and chips, surrounded by burger fixings of every kind. The boys then sat down and quieted.

"Hold hands," Nat directed. "You too, Jenkins."

Nat led the prayer and as soon as he finished a flurry of arm movements had tomatoes, lettuce, and onions flying around the table at lightning speed. By the time the group stood up from the table forty-five minutes and many stories later, only scraps were left. Roosevelt grabbed the last pickle and chomped it down. "Don't you boys have film to study?" Nat asked while grinning at the group. "Yes sir," they responded in unison. The players then jumped up, cleaned the table, and said their good-byes.

After the last of his players had taken off, Nat turned to Renee and said, "Thanks for sitting through that. I think Phelps kind of likes you."

Renee held her hand over her heart and patted.

"There are a lot of reasons I love coaching," Nat continued, "but that's the biggest one of all. There's a lot of power in a young group of men. If I can keep their energy directed in a positive way, I'll have done my job. Coaching football games is the easy part. To this day, I remember my senior season of high-school football like it was yesterday. These next few months will be filled with memories those boys will always remember. At least I hope so."

Renee looked at Nat and nodded. "That's a beautiful thing," she acknowledged. "I can tell you've done some good with those boys."

"We're both teachers," Nat replied with a knowing look, "doing the same thing. I just go at it a little differently."

Nat listened to the humming symphony of cicadas crying from their perches in the surrounding pecan trees and closed his eyes to breathe in the late-summer air. Though he missed his grandfather terribly, he felt in this moment, with Renee sitting beside him, that life couldn't get much better. He could almost forget the woman next to him was his brother's ex-wife. Almost.

"Let's go in the house and look at what I found in those documents," he said.

Nat and Renee huddled in his study as he poured them each a glass of red wine. They'd had a nice evening up to this point, but Nat now started to feel awkward alone in his home with Renee. No matter the bond he sensed forming, and despite the passage of time since her divorce, she was still the mother of Joseph's children. Nat had to keep reminding himself of that.

Nat's iPhone beeped and he opened a message that had come in while they'd been eating dinner. He immediately recognized the email address of the sender—thunter@Treasuringthepast. com:

I thought about our recent discussion and realized I'd not been completely straight with you. This has nothing to do with your grandfather's death but I did fail to mention a couple of things about his work. Please call me at your convenience.

Frank K.

"Look at this," Nat said.

Renee read the email on his screen and her face lit up. "It appears someone's got a guilty conscience. Let's give him a call."

Nat smiled at Renee and started punching in the number. "Way ahead of you," he said.

CHAPTER 26

Frank Kalender studied the plans he'd devised for the excavation project. Although he'd convinced Angelina that the long-abandoned water well was the location of the hidden treasure, he still had far too many questions to be certain. And questions were no longer acceptable to his financial backer. Angelina had been such a perfect partner when they started, a true believer like him, with firm roots in Alamo history and very deep pockets. Back then, she was engaged, inquisitive, and, most important, willing to spend whatever was necessary. They'd made a pact to find Bowie's Treasure even though she knew little, if anything, about Jim Bowie's story. But he'd been drawn to her because of her passion, her commitment, and a focus far different from the legion of Internet speculators he'd come to know in his business. She'd also proven to be a fast study, calling him to ask thoughtful questions about the historical movements of Bowie, the Texas legend who'd supposedly been an avid treasure hunter before joining the Alamo defenders. Energized by Angelina's enthusiasm, Kalender had soon grown to believe he really could find Jim Bowie's lost treasure.

But something had changed over the last six months. Maybe she'd run out of patience, or money, but Angelina's intensity had turned darkly into obsession. And once she'd found a way to gain control over the restructured DRT, thus giving her the opportunity to obtain the long-sought-after permits, she'd started to turn away from him. The change in their relationship had been gradual. She never stopped financing his research, but when she'd inserted the menacing Kruger into the mix he'd known it was trouble. This perpetually scowling man with the unusual scar on his face wasn't like Frankie and Shakes, the men he'd dealt with previously. Kruger was thoroughly intimidating, and now with the news of Joe Travis's death, Kalender's uneasiness about Kruger had turned into open fear. Angelina had known the old man never had the elusive map, but she'd killed him anyway. It was no accident.

Kalender's cell phone rang. He looked down at the 251 area code and figured it was Nat Travis calling about his email.

"Frank Kalender," he answered.

"It's Nat Travis, Mr. Kalender. I got your message. What's going on?"

"I apologize," Kalender responded. He sensed Nat had him on a speakerphone from the slight echo in the line. "It was never my intention to deceive you," he continued, "but you caught me off guard when you came to my office. I don't know what you think of me, or what you've heard, but you should understand that I take my work seriously. I don't write anything that I haven't researched thoroughly from both a historical and archeological standpoint. That's why I'm calling today."

"Go on," Nat replied.

"Everything I told you about my interaction with your grandfather was accurate. We'd made great progress reviewing his research and documentation and we both believed Bowie's Treasure was real and within reach. But, as I told you, most of our time was spent studying Joe the slave and trying to figure out what happened to him, not on treasure hunting. We traced Joe's movements across Texas and the south, even into Mexico, trying to find out if he truly ended up in Brewton, Alabama. I have to admit that most of my motivation was to find out what your grandfather knew about the treasure, but that never seemed to bother him. The treasure wasn't his primary concern."

"Yeah, yeah," Nat said impatiently, "you mentioned all of that to me the other day."

"Sorry to backtrack," Kalender said. "However, what I failed to mention was that my research really does suggest Joe the slave possessed a map showing the location of Bowie's Treasure. At one time my hope was your grandfather had it. I'd like to say my intentions were pure, but as it turns out he knew nothing about a map anyway. That's what I wanted you to know. I felt bad for leaving that part out."

"Why are you telling me this now?" Nat demanded.

Kalender sensed his new acquaintance from Alabama was growing angry. "I just wanted to put all of that on the table," he responded. "Your grandfather didn't have the map so it's a nonissue. Frankly, I've always had my doubts about the map story anyway. Even if it did exist at one time, it was likely lost in the fall of the Alamo. Although there is a popular story that a Mexican soldier stole it from Joe and then sold it the year after the Battle of San Jacinto, I'm doubtful. But I'm a treasure hunter—I had to follow my lead with your grandfather."

"But why call me now? What does it matter?"

"I can't give you a clearer motive, Mr. Travis. I just felt I needed to say something. Call it conscience, if you will."

Kalender could hear the wheels turning on the other end of the line, as if Nat was trying to figure out the real reason behind his call.

"Do you think someone killed my grandfather over this map?" Nat asked abruptly.

Kalender hesitated, taken aback by the question. "No, no, no, that's not what I meant, not at all. I just wanted to give you a fuller explanation of what my relationship was with your grandfather. Nothing else."

"So why do I sense there's something more to this map story?" Nat pressed.

"You've got good instincts, Mr. Travis. Just like your grandfather. And I do have one other thing I need to say. Even though your grandfather and I never located Bowie's Treasure, I've not given up on the hunt. After years of waiting for the opportunity, I'm going to be leading a dig at the Alamo to find it. The project has been planned for some time, waiting on permits, but I didn't want you to read about it in the newspapers and think it had anything to do with information learned from your grandfather. Like I said, I've been chasing this prize for a long time."

"And I'm supposed to take your word on that?" Nat asked.

"No, not at all. The dig will be on Alamo grounds in full view of public officials so it's nothing I'm sneaking around in the shadows doing. I've been hired by the new committee in charge of the Alamo—I think it's called the Alamo Preservation Advisory Board—but I wanted you to know about the dig. I felt I owed you that much."

An awkward silence fell on the line and Kalender heard whispering. "Did you say something?" he asked.

"No, I didn't," Nat replied. "Is that everything?"

"Yes, that's it. You know everything I do now."

Another silent period and Kalender wondered if the call was about to turn hostile. He worried that Nat had heard the hesitation in his voice when asked about Joe Travis's murder.

"One last question," Nat fired back. "When's this dig scheduled?"

Kalender knew he'd already crossed the line. If Angelina realized he'd given Nat any of this information, or even talked to him for that matter, there'd be hell to pay. But he'd already gone too far. "In two weeks," he said reluctantly.

"I don't trust that guy," Nat announced once he finished the call. "I think he duped me while I was in California with that goofy act of his. I should've known better."

"Take a deep breath," Renee responded, putting her hand on his shoulder. "I understand what you're saying, but think about what we just heard. I only have this one call to go on, but it didn't sound to me like Kalender is a killer on the loose. Sure I haven't met the man like you have, but I agree with your earlier judgment. He's an overzealous treasure hunter."

Nat nodded.

"I can't believe I'm saying it," Renee continued, "but I think you should call your brother. He's bound to know someone in Texas who can help you research this Alamo dig. Then you can figure out if Kalender's telling you the truth."

Nat's face tightened when he heard Renee mention his brother, but the notion had already crossed his mind. At the same time, Nat knew how his brother would react to Kalender's story. First, he'd mock Nat for taking it seriously, and then he'd dismiss the idea as a waste of time. Even then, Nat realized Joseph was his best option. He and his brother had a difficult time communicating, but they were blood. He looked at Renee, shrugged his shoulders, and acknowledged her suggestion: "You're probably right."

"Maybe not, but it's all I can think of right now," she said.

Nat stood up, walked into the bathroom, and splashed cold water on his face. "Not looking forward to this one," he said, breathing deeply. He then walked back to his desk, picked up his cell phone, and punched in his brother's private cell number.

"Hello," Joseph answered. And with little interruption, Nat then took his brother through the whole story about Kalender. Predictably, Joseph audibly sighed when he finished and then said, "You're not actually buying into this treasure bullshit, are you?"

"Brother," Nat replied, "I don't know what to believe, but I do know Papa Joe spent a whole lot of time studying this character Joe the slave. Maybe he was onto something. I'm at a loss."

"Finding this treasure is about as likely as a liberal Democrat getting elected in Texas. And, by the way, I looked into Kalender myself and I think he's a nut. I assume you saw his place in California ... it's a haven for every crazy conspiracy theorist on the left coast. Think about it: Papa Joe had a lot of idle time on his hands at the end of his life. He likely had some mild dementia, too. A conniving treasure hunter took advantage of him. That's all I can see."

Nat regretted calling his brother, and he hated listening to his condescending tone, especially with Renee in the room. "Why didn't you tell me you were checking out Kalender?" he asked. "You could've saved me a lot of time."

Joseph's silence answered Nat's question.

"Look, I didn't call to argue over Kalender," Nat continued. "I called to ask for your help. And I think I knew Papa Joe well enough to understand that he wasn't crazy. All I want you to do is find out about the archeological expedition Kalender claims he's planning at the Alamo. I'll take it from there."

"Do you know any more about what happened to Papa Joe?" Joseph asked. "Any leads on his murder?"

"Why do you think I'm going through all of this?" Nat replied firmly. "I don't know about this treasure story, but I do think it could be connected to his death. One thing's for sure—the police don't care. Their investigation is closed from all I can tell."

"Maybe there's nothing more to be found," Joseph countered.

Nat felt his hand grip tighter on the phone but he held his tongue. "Thanks for your help, Joseph," he said. "I'll wait to hear from you." Nat shut down the phone, exhaled, and looked up at an approving Renee.

CHAPTER 27

Miriam LeBlanc flipped through the items Anthony Ambrose had collected from the war and thought again about how much she missed him. As painful as the reminders were, Miriam realized cataloguing Anthony's personal effects brought her closer to him and provided some consolation. She stacked the pictures, medals, and news clippings into separate piles and then grabbed a pad and pen. The museum wouldn't want all of the collection, but she wanted to give life to as much of Anthony's story as possible.

One by one, Miriam picked up the photos, placed them into separate plastic sleeves, and marked the subject matter for easy identification. It was slow work but again reminded her about the reach of Anthony's heroism. Each photo carried with it a unique story, and she couldn't help but stop and reflect on certain moments. About halfway through the stack, she studied a picture of three smiling men in uniform that she hadn't seen before. Two of the soldiers were easy to identify, Anthony and Joe Travis, but the third she couldn't place. Fortunately, Anthony had written on the back of the photo, as he had on so many others:

England, May, 25, 1944. Joe Travis (Alabama) and Ricardo Rodriguez (Georgia).

Miriam scratched her head for a moment, trying to remember where she'd seen Ricardo Rodriguez before. She shuffled through several of the other photos but couldn't find another picture of him, but that's when it came to her—the old framed picture Anthony had kept in his room that she'd given to Nat Travis. Three smiling warriors—Anthony, Joe Travis, and the previously unidentified Ricardo Rodriguez. The connection led Miriam back to the night when Joe Travis's grandson had come to visit her. She'd meant to follow up with him and find out if anything had come of his grandfather's murder investigation but had been too distracted managing Anthony's affairs to do so. She'd liked Joe Travis's grandson—he was a good man—and hoped he'd found some closure in dealing with his loss. Miriam set the pictures down, clicked through the contact list on her phone, and touched Nat Travis's number.

"Hello, this is Nat Travis," answered the voice on the other end of the line.

Miriam exchanged pleasantries but went quickly to her point. "Nat, I thought of you today when I was going through Anthony's things. It made me wonder if anything ever came of the investigation into Joe's death. What did you find out?"

"Sorry to say, I've got nothing. Old men, even heroes like Papa Joe, aren't given much attention these days. I'm not sure his death's high on the police priority list."

"I'm sorry," Miriam said. "Sad but true. I actually thought long and hard about ordering an autopsy on Anthony like you suggested, but I was ultimately talked out of it by his doctors. They said it would likely be inconclusive given his age, and … well … I was so worried …" Her voice trailed off as she grew sad over not having done right by her friend.

"I know all I offered was speculation," Nat comforted, "so I understand why you decided against it. I shouldn't have pushed anyway. But I want you to know I haven't given up on my end yet."

"You're kind, Nat, but I'm telling you that I'd dig up Anthony tomorrow if you found out anything more. If there's a killer out there, I damn sure want you to find him."

"Thank you, Ms. LeBlanc. That means a lot. I'm glad you called … it's good to hear your voice."

"Oh, and Nat," she remembered, "there is one other thing. You still have that photo I gave you of your grandfather and Anthony from St. Lo?"

"Sure I do," he answered. "A great shot."

"I finally figured out the other guy in the picture. You know—the soldier who Anthony and Joe were so close to … who was later killed in action? His name was Ricardo Rodriguez. Apparently from Georgia. Just thought you might want to know."

"Appreciate it," Nat replied. "You've confirmed my suspicions. I've seen that name in Papa Joe's genealogical research quite a bit and thought that it might be him in the photo. Glad you were able to verify that. Thanks very much."

"You're welcome, son. Good luck to you. Remember, you call me if anything turns up."

CHAPTER 28

*B**ailey's Prairie, Texas—1837***
    Joe stared out of the small, box-shaped window of his bunk-house waiting for the moonlight to recede from the stable area where the horses rested. It was still too bright and far too early to make a move. So he waited. Several excruciating hours passed before Joe finally saw action near the stable.

In the months since his new master had moved him to Bailey's Prairie, Texas, Joe had bided his time patiently, waiting for his chance to run. He never thought his life would lead back to slavery. Colonel Travis had told him that he'd be free once his military service ended, but with his advocate dead, he'd quickly learned that for a black man, slavery was a perpetual state, even for one who had fought alongside Colonel William Barret Travis.

When word had spread to Gonzalez, where Joe moved after escaping Santa Anna, of the Texans' great victory at San Jacinto, Joe had expected his life to change. Less than two months after the massacre in the Alamo, Sam Houston's ragged soldiers had cornered the Mexican army and driven them to complete surrender, in the process creating a new, sovereign nation. Joe had felt assured that Texas independence would mean his personal independence as well. Yet, less than a week later, after he'd traveled into the town square in Gonzalez expecting to find work, he was hustled into a wagon and transported to a barn at the outskirts of the city. He'd spent the rest of the week boarded up with a small group of black men and women—most had been left abandoned after losing their owners in the war with Mexico. What Joe hadn't realized while serving alongside Colonel Travis was just how prevalent slavery had become in the new western territories. The stories told by the other black men and women herded into the small barn reminded him that while Texas had gained its freedom, blacks surely hadn't. So there he waited, lost and alone, until a few days passed and his name was called out by a gruff white man with a rifle slung across his back. Joe was directed to a wagon guarded by two more heavily armed attendants. "Get in," one of the men barked, and Joe complied, his head down, devastated about the dreaded trip back into servitude.

But tonight he would right that wrong. It had taken some time but he'd befriended one of the Mexican stableboys on the plantation, Enrique, and together they were about to put their plan into action. He watched and waited as Enrique guided their two mounts toward the open land just beyond the men's living quarters. Both horses had preloaded saddlebags thrown across their backs. At that point, Joe tiptoed across the bunkhouse floor, grabbed his work boots, and eased out the front door. None of his sleeping cohorts stirred. He then laced up his boots and scurried toward Enrique.

"Arriba!" Enrique whispered as Joe approached.

Joe nodded and soon they were off, riding briskly, safely out of earshot of the snoring ranch hands.

The two escapees steered their horses into a nearby creek bed, obscuring their tracks as best possible, and headed on a course for Tevis Bluff. Once there, Joe planned to reassess their route before setting off for New Orleans. There would be danger in making any stops—a black man and a Mexican with two horses would arouse suspicion—but Joe knew of several caves and hiding places along the way.

About twenty miles clear of Bailey's Prairie, Joe realized his escape had not gone unnoticed. As the first rays of sunlight splashed on the ground, he looked back and spotted several thundering riders in the distance.

"Ves los gringos?" Enrique cried.

Joe nodded in acknowledgement. "Time to change course," he

directed in a calm voice. "We can lose them in the hills." He pointed to a bluff in the distance but Enrique whipped his head back and forth.

"No, señor Joe, no. Adelante." Enrique pointed past him toward the pasture ahead. "Adelante," the young Mexican yelled a second time, before grabbing the reins of his horse and charging forward, his chestnut kicking up huge swirls of dust as he bolted.

Joe froze in place. He had several bad options: ride after Enrique and hope to outrace the incoming posse; wait and seek mercy from his pursuers; or maneuver his horse into the hills and hope the trackers would chase Enrique instead. Joe decided his best chance was to go it alone.

He pushed his horse to the cover of a grove of trees about fifty feet up the nearest hill, climbed down, and walked into a position where he could observe the approaching riders. In less than twenty minutes, the posse arrived. The trackers encircled the spot Enrique's horse had galloped away from, dismounted to inspect the ground, and began yelling at one another. Joe's heart pounded when a tall man with a bushy red mustache looked his way, pointing toward the hill.

But luck was on Joe's side. The riders jumped back up on their horses and stormed off, chasing Enrique in the direction of Tevis Bluff.

Drenched with sweat, Joe climbed back aboard his bay and made his way down the hill. And then reality set in. Joe vaulted off his horse, ripped open his saddlebag, and stared in horror. The only things before him were packed bags of beef jerky and cornmeal. The stolen money was gone. More distressing, Enrique had ridden off with something of even more value to Joe.

Jim Bowie's map.

CHAPTER 29

Nat paced the floor in his bright-red S.W. Niland coach's shirt and black pants. Like a nervous student waiting on a final exam, his manic energy filled the room, a giant adrenaline rush looking for an outlet. It was opening day, five hours before kickoff. His study of the game plan and films for the past three days had him ready for his opponent, but his intense focus had pulled him away from Papa Joe's story. He hoped calling Renee for an update might ease his anxiety. He also wanted to confirm she was coming to the game.

"Hi Nat," Renee answered cheerfully.

"How's the work coming?" he asked. "You found something worth writing about yet?" Nat knew that Renee was looking to zero in on a research topic during her sabbatical—that, of course, in addition to the time she was already spending on Papa Joe. He held out some hope the two might come together.

"You sound a little wound up, coach. Trying to release a little pressure?" She laughed.

"Okay, good analysis, Dr. Brown. So, can you help this nervous old coach get through his pregame jitters? Tell me about your research. How's it going?"

"I actually have quite a bit to tell you," Renee responded. "I'm making progress—but I doubt Emory will be happy. I've been totally absorbed by one Ricardo Rodriguez."

Nat chuckled. "I won't say anything," he joked. "Tell me about it."

"Okay ... well, the minute you confirmed Ricardo Rodriguez was the man in that picture, Papa Joe's research became much clearer to me. It suddenly made sense why so much of his material had no connection to Joe the slave ... why he kept all of this personal information on Rodriguez. Now that I've stopped trying to tie all of his research together, I've been able to focus more on just Joe the slave's story. I still haven't found anything we didn't know about Bowie's Treasure, but I'm uncovering a remarkable story about the only male survivor of the Alamo. And you know what? I think I can stop looking for a writing topic for my sabbatical. Joe the slave is one interesting character ... with or without a treasure."

"That's exciting," Nat mumbled, glancing at his watch. "Oh, sorry to be so abrupt, but I need to go."

Renee audibly sighed. "I can tell you're distracted," she said. "I'll see you at the game tonight. Just remember, I'm not coming to watch your boys lose. Go get 'em."

"We'll do our best," Nat said excitedly. "Our team has the talent but you never know. And I'll miss having Papa Joe there. May have to change my pregame ritual ... I always looked to him in his little corner of the stands before kickoff."

"Find some new inspiration," Renee suggested. "Dedicate your season to him. You know he'll be out there with you tonight."

"Thanks, appreciate that ... more than you know. And sorry to be so distracted ... I'll be better once I get this first game out of the way. I'm really glad you're coming."

"Good luck, Nat. In the meantime, while you're busy studying that playbook one last time, I'm going to keep digging. Maybe Papa Joe buried a secret to a treasure map somewhere in these files. Wouldn't that be something? Talk to you later."

Renee stepped through the growing crowd of spectators to a spot in the bleachers near a rotund woman wearing a number-19 jersey and a round button with a picture of a player. The woman held a painted sign, an S.W. Niland pennant, and about three noisemaking objects.

"Mind if I sit here?" Renee asked before realizing she'd likely regret her decision.

"Sure, as long you're cheering for the Pirates." The flabby woman's body jiggled in four separate places as she laughed.

"I think I qualify as a fan," Renee offered with a smile.

"Nice to have you then," the lady replied enthusiastically. "My name's Betty Stuckey; my boy's the wide receiver on the team. Number 19."

At that moment, a thundering roar erupted from the fans as the S.W. Niland Pirates took the field. Renee spotted Nat jogging to the sideline. She raised her arm in a friendly salute, meeting his eyes somewhere between the bobbing heads in front of her, but was unprepared for what followed. Her heart skipped a beat. It was nothing—just a spontaneous reaction to the moment, but one that surprised her. Maybe she'd convinced herself that nothing was changing with Nat, that she'd walled herself off from any romantic feelings toward him, but the tingling sensation told her something different.

Renee watched Nat move over to the bench and put on his coaching headphones, and her thoughts drifted back to the rebellious kid she'd known in high school. Or, rather, barely known. She remembered a misguided but gifted athlete who seemed to run away from comparisons with his older brother and stayed lost for several years in search of his own identity. What Renee regretted most about those early years was never taking the time to get to know Nat. Through her own failings, she'd allowed her soon-to-be husband's distorted, and negative, views of his brother to become her own. And for the early years of her marriage, that was the image she carried around about Nat. "He's going to end up pumping gas," Joseph had said derisively, "or if he's real lucky, coaching high-school football." Of all of Joseph's rude comments about his brother, that one stuck in her memory more than any other.

In time, however, after her children were born, Renee began to see more of Nat at family events and got to know him better without the filter of Joseph's negativity. From those experiences, a different picture emerged. Nat had developed a quiet sense of confidence after high school, an almost spiritual grace that made her reconsider everything she'd learned about him. Nat shined every time the family gathered, even while her husband's boorish conduct, his self-indulgence, and his soaring sense of identity slowly drove the brothers apart. At times, Renee wondered why Nat, the far stronger and more powerful of the siblings, didn't just lean over and pop his brother in the face, but she also understood the humility and patience it took for him to absorb Joseph's blows.

She also knew that Nat had the foresight to understand that challenging his brother would risk maintaining a relationship with his niece and nephew. Nat genuinely loved Emmitt and Amelia and they loved him. He was always on the telephone offering a comforting voice and encouragement when needed, especially in the latter years when their own father was too busy tending to his new family in Texas. Nat's relationship with Renee's children was real, enduring, and an inspiration to a divorced mother who worried every day that her children would be permanently scarred by their father's abandonment. But through it all, Renee had never considered Nat as anything other than a supportive member of her extended family. And she knew it made no sense to see him differently now. And yet, that reluctance, that logical disconnect, still couldn't prevent the small glance through the crowd from taking her breath away.

CHAPTER 30

New Orleans, Louisiana—1837

Lake Pontchartrain was a welcome sight for Joe. Thankfully, his escape route had allowed him to reach the northern border of New Orleans without further trouble. Joe felt certain Enrique had either been captured or killed by the time he saw the dim lights flickering on the outskirts of the Crescent City, although he still held out hope the Mexican stableboy had made it there alive.

By 1837, New Orleans had grown to over one hundred thousand people and had become the largest city west of the eastern seaboard in the United States. The mix of Creoles, free blacks, French, Irish, and Germans provided good cover for a former slave to hide. Joe and Enrique had chosen their destination with care, knowing they'd blend in amidst the odd collection of smugglers, illegal traders, and runaways. Even then, Joe knew a lone Mexican boy who didn't speak English or French would have a difficult time melting into New Orleans. He also knew that most former slaves and servants like Enrique eventually found their way to the part of the city known as Fauborg Treme, a renowned gathering place for free blacks and Haitian immigrants known as the "back of town." A man of color could live without interference from the white leaders in the Uptown or Downtown district in Fauborg Treme.

Joe carefully made his way through the sparsely populated northern edge of town where repeated flooding made it impossible to live, until he came upon the first row of shotgun cottages that signaled he'd reached the higher ground of Fauborg Treme. These rows of narrow, single-story houses with flat slate roofs and single, postage-stamp windows lined the streets winding through the area. There was little stirring in the neighborhood and Joe moved quickly to avoid causing any disturbance. He then turned past a cemetery full of aboveground tombs that separated the cottages from the business side of the district into a dimly lit street where he hoped to find free lodging for the night. Unsuccessful, he ended up wandering around with his horse until daybreak.

At first light, a weary Joe rode farther south to the port of New Orleans along the lower Mississippi River. Here, he came upon a wave of activity common to the largest shipping center in the south. Although it was very early in the morning, workers were already scrambling around the wharf loading cargos of fruits, tobacco, and assorted products onto the flatbeds and steamships lining the piers. Joe asked around and soon learned of a cotton exporter looking for day workers. Several hours later, he was on the job, loading a barge headed for the east coast. While securing work, Joe also found room and board for the night, making a deal to sleep in the port master's warehouse in exchange for his horse. For the next few days, Joe worked during the day and trolled the streets in the evening hoping somehow to find Enrique.

A week passed with no news of his fellow escapee and Joe made the difficult decision to give up his search. It was only then that he stumbled into his first promising lead. A toothless, Creole pirate, who'd recently moved from Uptown to the docks, told Joe of a young Mexican boy who'd attempted to sell him a treasure map outside a pub in the French Quarter. Joe felt energized by the first hint of good news since he'd arrived in New Orleans. But entering the white area of the French Quarter at night was dangerous for a black man, particularly based on the advice of an unreliable pirate. He decided to go anyway.

Joe left the warehouse area on foot about 9:00 p.m. and traveled in the shadows toward Laffite's Pub. But the minute he entered the bright lights of Canal Street, Joe realized he'd made a mistake; there was too much exposure for a single black man to move freely in this part of town. Joe tried to hide behind lampposts and building walls, but just before he reached Laffite's, several white men standing outside the tavern spotted him coming their way. One of the men turned and looked directly at Joe and started mouthing something through a bushy red mustache. He pointed at Joe with his finger and gestured to his friends.

Joe remembered that mustache.

He swiveled around in panic and sprinted down Canal Street, back toward the safety of Fauborg Treme. His ankle turned on a large rock as he ran but Joe never slowed. Faster and faster, he whirred down the cobbled streets until he pulled up panting, his lungs ready to explode. He'd run for ten minutes at full speed but this was the first time he'd allowed himself to stop and look back. Joe breathed deeply and sighed. For now, it appeared the man with the bushy red mustache had not followed him.

Joe then ran all the way to the port and from there snuck onto one of the docked cotton barges, where he hid in a small compartment. He stayed on alert the rest of the night, listening intently for any sign of a search party. At sunup, Joe heard the hissing of steam rising from a nearby ship and assumed his boat would soon be leaving. He poked his head out of the tiny room and saw the letters forming Bama Rambler on the wall across from him. He couldn't read but seeing deckhands scrambling down the hall scared him further into hiding. Joe sank back into his hole and covered up with an old canvas tarp he'd found on the floor. Now invisible, he prepared for the long ride out of New Orleans, and it was only then, as the boat prepared to shove off, that he considered what leaving meant.

While he might have saved himself from harm by securing passage out of New Orleans, Joe had lost Colonel Bowie's map forever.

CHAPTER 31

Renee knew that Nat's attention span had waned for the mystery surrounding his grandfather's death. Although he remained superficially engaged, his limited time for study was now devoted to game film, not historical research. And his team's electrifying start, including an unexpected 40-6 thumping of Brewton Heights on opening day, had pushed him even further away. But that didn't matter to Renee; she was now fully engaged in Papa Joe's story and required no encouragement to keep digging. A largely undiscovered, untold drama about a footnote character in black history tied to a modern-day hero had fallen into her lap. An irresistible mix for a scholar. With or without Nat, she wanted to know everything she could about Joe the slave, Joe Travis, and all of the characters who connected their lives. Her sabbatical had yielded a reward bigger than any she could have ever hoped to find.

But that wasn't the only thing changing in Renee's life. Every day, she felt herself growing closer to Nat, even though with football started her forms of communication were largely text messages and quick hellos on the telephone. And then there was Brewton itself. She'd forgotten all about the qualities of small-town living that she'd enjoyed as a young girl. There was a charm and sense of belonging among her mother's friends that felt unique to southern Alabama. They rallied at Papa Joe's funeral, cheered for the S.W. Niland Pirates together, and checked in with one another regularly during the day, just because. Renee was starting to understand how her mother, and Nat, had found such contentment in this place.

Renee's days in Brewton had now fallen into a routine of morning coffee with her mother and then long hours on her laptop, investigating the various leads from Papa Joe's USB drive, and then some writing. By now, she'd followed the trail of Joe the slave's life, just as Papa Joe had, and learned a great deal more about the legendary treasure of Jim Bowie. Her thesis had developed into an inspirational story about Joe the slave and Joe Travis and how their unique acts of heroism had connected their family through two centuries. That they were related had now become an unimpeachable fact. But even as her story came together, the one thing that continued to puzzle Renee was Papa Joe's seemingly unbounded interest in the family of his wartime friend Ricardo Rodriguez. The close relationship between the two, bonded by their experience on Omaha Beach, explained much, but Renee sensed there had to be something else, something deeper, a tie that connected Papa Joe throughout his entire life. Ricardo Rodriguez's death at St. Lo might have scarred Joe Travis as a young man, but Renee didn't believe that single experience could propel his deep interest in the Georgia native's family. What was it about this one soldier that made him so compelling?

Renee had found historical family records in Papa Joe's file that took Rodriguez's roots back to Mexico and the Texas war of independence. She'd seen that his father, Jose, was the first U.S. citizen in the Rodriguez clan and that he'd lived in Louisiana for a time before moving to Georgia. There, he'd met his wife and they'd started a family. Jose Rodriguez had two children, a daughter who died at an early age and a son, Ricardo, the soldier who was Papa Joe's wartime comrade. The family history appeared to stop at Ricardo's death, although another Rodriguez, a successful Atlanta businessman named Enrique, who was born in 1936, appeared prominently in Papa Joe's files as well, even though he had no apparent family connection to Ricardo or Jose

Rodriguez. Renee had her suspicions about Enrique's roots, but they couldn't be confirmed from the records on the USB drive or those she'd subsequently found on the Internet. Now armed with more information than she could possibly want on Enrique Rodriguez, she decided to take her research to the next level.

That search took her to Lawrenceville, Georgia. She confirmed Enrique Rodriguez's address through an online directory and, after a call with a difficult woman, found out he'd be home the following Sunday. "He rarely leaves the house," the woman had said unenthusiastically, "so come on if you want." And with that, despite the lukewarm reception, Renee decided to make the seven-hour drive to Lawrenceville. Her navigation system eventually guided her to a gated residential community in an affluent area on the western edge of town. As she approached, Renee saw a large rock entry sign—*Friendswood*—surrounded by a manicured lawn, freshly planted pansies, and flowing native grasses. The gate arm to the development stood open, presumably because of the large number of drivers speeding in and out, so Renee hurried through. She maneuvered her way to a two-story, stucco, Mediterranean house with a large circular driveway and several Bradford pear trees lining the front sidewalk. By the look of things, Enrique Rodriguez had done very well, just as Papa Joe's records suggested.

Apprehensive, Renee parked her car on the street bordering the house, walked to the front steps, and rang the doorbell.

A few seconds later, the huge mahogany door cracked open. A young boy with jet-black hair peered out from behind.

"My mother doesn't allow me to speak with solicitors," he announced.

"Oh, I'm sorry, I'm not a solicitor," Renee replied, realizing the assertive youngster had probably never seen a black face in his neighborhood. "I'm here to see your parents. Are they home?"

"Who are you?" the boy asked abruptly.

"I'm an old friend of your family from Atlanta. Tell them I'm the one who phoned the other day. My name is Renee Travis."

"Wait a minute," he said. The door slammed in Renee's face and she heard the bolt lock turn inside. Several minutes passed before Renee realized the boy was likely not going to return. She turned away disappointed just as a tan Suburban wheeled into the driveway. The car stopped and one of the tinted windows rolled down. "Can I help you?" asked a voice.

The back door of the Suburban then opened and a thirty-something, dark-haired, brown-skinned man stepped out along with a blonde wearing a cotton sundress. They both walked toward Renee.

"I think I may have frightened your son," Renee said with a smile. "Are you Mr. and Mrs. Rodriguez?"

"Depends on who's asking," the man fired back. He didn't have a trace of accent in his voice. Any Hispanic roots in the Rodriguez family had apparently been washed away long ago.

"I'm very sorry," Renee apologized. "I've handled this all wrong. My name's Renee Travis … I'm from Atlanta. I called the other day about talking to Enrique Rodriguez. I thought this was his house?"

"Oh, you're the one interested in my father," the young man replied more calmly. "My wife mentioned you to me."

"Good," Renee said with some relief, throwing back her head. "I hope you don't mind if I talk to him. I'm doing some research on my grandfather's life and thought your father could help explain a few things. He apparently knew my grandfather well … at least, according to the records I've seen."

"That so?" the young man questioned. "My name's Ricky Rodriguez. This is my wife, Maxine. I'm sorry if my son was rude to you at the door. Kids." He held up his cell phone to suggest the young boy had already texted him.

"I understand," Renee smiled.

"Well, you're in the right spot, Mrs. Travis." Ricky's tone turned decidedly more upbeat. "My father's probably peering out that window right now." He pointed to the second story. "And I'm sure he'd love to talk to you. He's in poor health, but he'll yap your ear off if you're willing to give him the time. I'll go check. You can wait in his study." Ricky led Renee inside the front door, but she could tell that his wife, who remained a safe distance behind, had reservations.

The interior of the house was even more impressive than Renee had imagined. Marble floors, detailed stonework, and magnificent art pieces; Enrique Rodriguez had indeed done well.

"Please have a seat," Ricky directed, pointing to the room at his left. "I'll ask my father to come down."

"Thank you," Renee replied, stepping into a wood-paneled home office. The study was filled with books, two mounted diplomas from Vanderbilt University, and several framed photographs, one of them a generic, war-era photo of a platoon landing on Omaha Beach. She stood in the middle of the room, afraid to touch anything, and rotated from her fixed position to study the four walls.

A few minutes later, a bent-over, bald man with a breathing mask in his hand shuffled into the room, a portable oxygen tank in tow. He looked up at Renee with approving eyes. "Those youngsters don't know how to treat a lady," he announced. "Could I offer you something to drink?"

"No thank you," Renee replied. "I won't be here that long. Thank you for seeing me, Mr. Rodriguez. My name's Renee Travis."

"Enrique," the man said, holding out his hand. "And, by the way, I've got all the time you want. Old men like me don't get surprise visits from beautiful women very often."

"You're kind," she said, smiling.

"How can I help you?" Enrique asked. "Ricky said you heard

about me from a family member?" Rodriguez inhaled deeply from his oxygen mask. He sat down on the sofa while Renee eased into one of the chairs next to him.

"Actually, it was my former father-in-law, Joe Travis, from Brewton, Alabama. He died recently. Did you know him?"

Enrique's head snapped to attention when he heard the name. His eyes twinkled.

"I live in Atlanta," Renee continued. "I was once married to a man named Joseph Travis the third, who is the grandson of Mr. Travis."

Rodriguez straightened in his chair and his back stiffened. He breathed, nose in his mask, and nodded as if to suggest Renee should go on.

"At Joe Travis's death," Renee said, "I started helping his family sort through a few things. It's a long story but I have a picture I want to show you." She pulled out a copy of the photograph she'd first seen in Papa Joe's bedroom and handed it to Rodriguez. "These two men," she advised, pointing, "are Anthony Ambrose and Joe Travis. They've both died recently. I'm guessing the third gentleman is your father."

Rodriguez accepted the photograph, studied it carefully front and back, and set it down. He pondered several seconds and bit his lip. The color appeared to drain from his cheeks. He then collapsed forward, dropping his face into his hands. "*Jesucristo*," he muttered. "*Jesucristo.*"

"Mr. Rodriguez?"

"Just give me a moment," he responded. He sucked deeply again from the oxygen mask and stared at Renee, the twinkle in his eyes now a raging fire.

Renee waited patiently, unsure of what to do next.

Minutes passed as the old man turned up the dial on his tank and slowly started breathing normally again. "How did you know it was my father?" Enrique finally asked.

Renee's body shook with excitement. "Intuition and a lot of research," she answered.

"Then you're probably interested in what I'm about to tell you," he said. "My own family has never shown this level of interest in my story." He wheezed and chuckled at the same time.

"I'm more than interested."

The old man breathed one last time from his mask and sighed. "After my father, that man in the picture, died in Europe, I was placed in an orphanage ... I was a very, very young boy. A war baby—conceived before my father shipped off to England—and I lived in that orphanage until I was sent to boarding school in the third grade. I don't remember my mother." Enrique lifted his eyes to the ceiling and steadied himself before continuing. "I gave up searching for her long ago. Just as I suppose she gave up on me." He stopped and put up his hand in response to Renee's look of sadness, indicating he'd moved past the trauma long ago. "It wasn't unusual for women in those circumstances," he continued, "to give up their children, but this abandoned child had advantages most other orphans only dreamed about. I went from an Atlanta orphanage to Overland boarding school in Virginia where I spent the next ten years of my life. Overland was not just any place; it was one of the most prestigious schools in the country."

"You were fortunate," Renee agreed.

"Yes, I was. I didn't fully appreciate how much until I got a little older and realized I wasn't a ward of the state—that some-one, somewhere, had shown an interest in me. I had no other explanation, because there were few ... no ... no other minority students at Overland. And for a time the fact I knew nothing, nothing at all, about my background or my benefactor, who refused to come forward, stung me badly. But there were numer-ous children of servicemen in the school so I sensed there was a reason I'd been sent to Overland. After a short rebellious period,

I accepted my good fortune and decided to make the most of the gift. And so I dug in—and dug in hard. I made very good grades and found my way to the top of my class and then to Vanderbilt … where I was awarded a scholarship, I might add."

"What a great story," Renee beamed.

"It wasn't all that easy for me at Vandy. It's tough academically and I had to work thirty-five hours a week to help pay my way, but it was the best thing that ever happened to me. I learned the value of hard work."

"I can only imagine," Renee conceded.

"While in college, I started probing more deeply into my past, but the most I could find out was that my anonymous benefactor had set up an educational trust for me, administered by an Atlanta attorney. But beyond that, my questions only led to more dead ends. I ultimately concluded that my mother had changed her name and moved away after my father died and that my benefactor was some unknown member of her family … who felt some guilt." He paused for a moment, regrouping before moving on. "In college, I started working construction jobs and learned the business inside and out. By the time I graduated, I knew how to frame a house … and read a balance sheet. I understood what I wanted to do with my life."

"And you've done quite well, obviously."

"I've been lucky in so many ways. I couldn't imagine not working hard given the advantages God, and some incredible soul, provided me."

"Did any family ever emerge during all of this?" Renee asked.

"No, never. The first real sense of my parents actually came when I was ready to leave Overland. The headmaster called me into his office and gave me a packet of letters that my father had written to me from England while preparing for the invasion at Normandy. My mother had left them with me at the orphanage. Why did he wait so long to give them to me? I'll never know. They did things differently in those days, and perhaps they thought it was best to wait until I was old enough to process the information. But the gift of those letters is one I'll always treasure."

Renee's eyes grew moist as she imagined the young Enrique becoming acquainted with his father through a series of writings.

"Yes," he went on, "those letters have stayed with me and guided me ever since. I had a history through my father's correspondence, and I learned a lot about him ... and some about me. Mainly, that he had no family once he went off to the war, his only sibling having died as a child. His parents, my grandparents, had also died, which he explained to me was the reason he'd enlisted the first chance he got. I also learned that he was part of the landing team on Omaha Beach, a warrior, a patriot, but also sensitive and playful—but through all of his writings there's no mention of my mother's name. And they apparently never married, because I've checked everywhere for a marriage license. I guess knowing some things is better than knowing everything ... at least I like to think so." The old man shrugged. Life had, in the end, been good to him, and he'd clearly decided to just leave it there.

Renee nodded and tried to communicate her understanding with a compassionate look. She felt tears begin to well up in her eyes.

"Back to your question," Enrique said, shaking his head as if to pull out of his reflective mood. "Your picture of my father is one I've never seen. To this day, all I've ever really known is that someone gave me a chance at life that I didn't deserve. And yet despite my efforts, I've never known why." He started trembling and held his hand out to Renee. "Until today. It all makes sense to me now. Let me show you something."

Renee remained mute as the man shuffled over to his desk, opened the top drawer, and pulled out an envelope. She felt a nervous excitement that she could barely contain.

"This came to me recently from an Atlanta lawyer." He handed the envelope to her.

The letter inside was brief but the shaky scribbling was virtually identical to that she'd seen in Papa Joe's handwritten notes. On the outside, the envelope said, "To be delivered to Enrique Rodriguez upon my death."

Enrique,

Your father was my hero and friend. I made a promise to him when he died and now that God has come for me I want you to know how proud he would have been of you. God, family, and country have guided you just as they did your father. Some day, I expect to meet you in His Kingdom.

Love,
J. T.

Renee looked up from the note. "It all makes sense now, doesn't it?" she whispered. She then reached over to Enrique and cupped his hand. For several minutes, no further words were spoken.

Enrique Rodriguez called his daughter-in-law on the cell phone and asked her to bring tea to the study. He then spent the next hour telling Renee more stories about his life, his family, and his business success, and as he did, the articles archived in Papa Joe's USB drive attained new life. Throughout the discussion, Renee's mind wandered to the commitment Papa Joe made to the dying Ricardo Rodriguez on the battlefield in

France—and the sacrifices he surely had to make to honor that pact. She wondered how a man of limited means managed to carry such a big expense without anyone in his family knowing. A hero of great stature grew even larger in her mind.

"I can't tell you how much this has meant to me," Renee said as she sipped her tea. "And I can't tell you how fortunate I feel to have now answered one of the huge questions I'd been unable to resolve, until today. Papa Joe's fascination with Ricardo Rodriguez now makes complete sense."

"You said that was one of the questions. Do you have others?"

"You listen carefully, don't you?" Renee replied with a smile.

"I was an intelligence officer in the navy." Enrique winked and struggled to reposition himself on the sofa.

"I won't bore you with the details but Papa Joe did have more secrets than just those about the Rodriguez family." Renee then walked Enrique through the story of Joe the slave, Bowie's Treasure, and Frank Kalender. Although she never raised doubts about Papa Joe's fascination with the mystery, Renee inflected her voice to try to convey some of her reservations. Enrique listened intently without interruption. Then, as Renee finished, he said calmly, "Look over there on that shelf. See that carved wooden box. Could you grab it and bring it to me?"

"Of course." Renee quickly picked it up and handed it to him.

Enrique pulled out a key from his jacket pocket, inserted it into the small lock, and opened the box. "These are the letters I mentioned to you. I've read them many times throughout my life. Most are written from the perspective of a father to a small child so I assumed most of them were fantasies to gather my interest, but there's one in particular I think you'll find interesting." Enrique gingerly leafed through about ten letters before settling on one. "Here it is," he said. "I'll make you a copy and let you take it with you. Might change your mind a bit about whether Joe Travis knew what he was talking about."

Renee took the letter and read through it. Her heart raced when the words written over sixty years before came to life. "Oh, my God," she cried.

Rodriguez shook his head and smiled. "It appears Joe Travis's interest in escaped slaves, Alamo heroes, and hidden treasure really are connected. Sounds like his research was pointing you somewhere. If I were you, I'd go back and look at that USB drive again."

CHAPTER 32

Wednesday was game-plan day for Nat. His whiteboard had three trick plays drawn up and several special defenses designed to stop the defending champion Riverview Knights' lead option. He'd spent the last seventy-two hours in his office working on these new designs, player assignments, and generally fiddling with schemes he already knew by heart. Fully absorbed in game preparations, Nat hadn't yet discussed with Renee her exciting news about her trip to Georgia. His brain needed total immersion in football, despite her breathless call. They'd agreed to take it back up after the game.

Nat's phone rang and he reached over and grabbed the receiver from its cradle.

"Nat Travis," he answered.

"I heard Niland looks like the team to beat down there," said the familiar voice.

Joseph's friendly, conversational opening surprised Nat. His brother's calls were normally strident, all business. "Didn't think you had much time to follow small-town Alabama football," Nat replied as he pushed back in his desk chair. "So what's on your mind?"

"I've been busy since we last talked. Remember that Alamo dig you asked me to check into … well Frank Kalender's not quite the flake I thought he was. It appears he's about to get that archeological project underway. The crews are on the ground and the preliminary work has already begun. A small number of VIPs have been invited to observe the dig when it reaches the depth where the artifacts are expected to be found. At least, that's what the governor's office told me. No one's mentioning the possibility of buried treasure. The big event is this Saturday night ... and I've managed to get us invited."

An alarm in Nat's mind immediately went off. No matter how straightforward a situation might appear with Joseph, there was always an angle, and he sensed one with his brother's mini-confession. He couldn't figure out why Joseph wanted him down in Texas for the event. "Huh," Nat mumbled, "I appreciate the offer but I've got a lot to do right now. Playing the defending champs this week."

"And the game's Friday night. Right?"

"Yeah."

"So why not fly in Saturday morning and go home on Sunday? You won't miss a thing. C'mon, I pulled a lot of strings to get you invited."

Joseph's pushy comment pissed Nat off. His brother rarely wondered about Nat's reasons for doing anything, especially if they conflicted with his own, and this was another example. Joseph was demanding he come to Texas and Nat was supposed to fall in line. Yet, despite not wanting to spend any more time with his brother than necessary, Nat felt drawn to Kalender's show. But only if he could take Renee. And there was the rub. Faced with making this admission or choosing to stick with the plan, he opted for the latter. "Let me think about it and get back to you later today," Nat said.

"You're kidding ... right?" Joseph barked. "I banked every favor I had to get you on this site and you want to consider the offer? I even went to that sorry mayor in San Antonio and promised to support him in his race for Congress. This Alamo dig is locked up tighter than the Treasury Building. Damn, Nat."

Nat felt like slamming the phone down but held his tongue in check. "Thanks for the call," he growled. "Let me see what I can manage here with my schedule."

"Whatever, little brother. Let me know in the next hour or I'll have to cancel the whole damn thing." Joseph's phone clicked silent.

As Nat hung up, he wondered what he should do. He could deal with his angry brother, but what about Renee? Could he fly to San Antonio and not mention it to her at all? And how would she feel if he went alone? But did he really have a choice?

Reluctantly, he picked up the phone and called Joseph back.

CHAPTER 33

The game with Riverview was the biggest of the year for S.W. Niland. A perennial power, Riverview featured the state's leading rusher from the prior season, a speedy five-foot-ten block of granite who'd already committed to play at Alabama, and a bone-crunching defense that kept Nat awake at night. Any impartial observer of high-school football gave the Pirates little hope of knocking off the Knights; yet, despite the long odds, Nat liked his team's chances. His boys had practiced sharply all week, were playing at home, and were free of injuries. If his quarterback could control his mistakes, Nat felt an upset brewing. How much he wished Papa Joe could be there to share the excitement.

As he raced to the sideline with the team before kickoff, Nat looked up to the stands where Papa Joe had always stood, hands outstretched, in his pregame show of support. At first, all Nat saw was a congregation of fans, a group oblivious to the special significance of the area they'd randomly plunked down in. Then something else caught his eye. A fan's sign. He looked a second time and a smile creased his mouth.

This is Travis Country
Go Pirates!

At first, Nat couldn't see who was holding up the sign but then the figure emerged, and her face beamed through the throng of excited fans. Renee. She'd moved into Papa Joe's seat for this critical game. It was Renee who'd said "find some new inspiration"—and Nat knew he had. He smiled, gave Renee a wave, and dove into his team's frothing huddle.

By the end of the first half, Nat's Pirates had finally come down off their pregame high and their opponent's talent had taken control of the game. A quick 10-0 lead for the Pirates had turned into a 14-13 deficit and all of the momentum was now on the side of Riverview. The block of granite had scored two touchdowns and gained over one hundred yards in the first half. Nat had the important decision at half time of choosing whether to reenergize his team's emotional state or work more clinically to ensure better execution in the third quarter. As he walked to the locker room, the thought of the whiteboard in his office shot through his mind. None of the three trick plays specially designed for the game had been used in the first half. In truth, they'd not even crossed Nat's mind. He planned to spend some time with them during the break.

The Pirates lined up to kick off to Riverview to start the second half and trick play number one was put in motion. A perfectly disguised chip kick sailed over the Knights' first line of coverage and Niland's fastest player caught the ball in full stride just before Riverview's startled deep backs came up to make the play. The crowd went wild and the Pirates had the ball and the momentum back. A frenzied second half followed with the teams battling back and forth until Niland fair caught a punt with 1:48 left on the clock and one time-out remaining. The score: Riverview 28 – S.W. Niland 26.

A succesful series of plays had moved the Pirates down to the Knight's fifteen-yard line with three seconds left when Nat called the team's final time-out. Nat huddled with his players and instinctively glanced toward his special spot in the stands. He then turned back to the huddle and stared at his anxious kicker, the chance for a championship likely riding on his foot. The coach didn't hesitate. His third trick play was primed and ready. "Field goal formation, fake right, throwback."

Nat walked out of the stilled locker room to the parking lot. The game had been over for more than an hour and Nat felt a chill in the air that he'd missed during the heat of battle. Most of the cars were gone by this time; the only ones remaining were school vehicles and those belonging to maintenance personnel. Nat looked at the beaming scoreboard in the distance and shook his head, wondering what had compelled him to call a fake field goal.

"That was some call, coach," said a familiar voice from a car parked near his truck.

Nat turned and saw Renee emerge from a small Chevy, her face radiant in the moonlight.

"I didn't expect a reception," he grinned.

"Any football coach who calls a fake when a short field goal will win the game deserves to hear it from the fans." Renee walked toward him. "Good thing it worked." Renee stopped and smiled, as Nat edged closer to her.

"Thanks for being here," he said. "Sometimes Papa Joe and I met after the game and had a cheeseburger down at the Burger Depot. Another lost tradition." Nat now stood several feet away from Renee, alone in the parking lot. She looked even more beautiful in this moment, and his heart rate accelerated. But despite the setting, the confident football coach was struck with fear, bordering on panic. He wanted to take Renee in his arms, bend her backward, and kiss her, but he felt alarmingly frozen in place. The timing was right, the scene perfect, but he couldn't take the next step, the risk taker on the sideline now a bundle of nerves off it. Was it the looming specter of his brother, or was he really just afraid of what embracing her meant? "Well," he fumbled, "how about we begin our own tradition down at Burger Depot? They keep me a special booth down there after games and it's private enough we can discuss your trip to Lawrenceville. We need to do that before I leave for San Antonio."

"San Antonio?" Renee asked, jerking back several steps as if shocked by a live wire.

Nat instantly realized his mistake. What foolish instinct had compelled him to make this admission at the most inopportune time? Was he that dumb? And having already put Renee off after her enthusiastic phone call about her trip to Lawrenceville, he'd just doubled down on stupidity. "Joseph called and invited me to come down to Frank Kalender's dig tomorrow," he acknowledged. "Sorry, I didn't have time to call you because of the game. I'm flying down early in the morning."

"Why would you need to call me?" Renee snapped, backing even farther away. "I'm sure you'll have a great time with your brother." She turned and reached for her car door. The moment was ruined.

"Renee, wait," he said as she climbed into her car.

"Good luck in Texas," Renee snarled, yanking on her seat belt. She paused, as if contemplating saying something further, but then pulled her door shut and motored away.

A lone cloud edged its way across the night sky, masking the glow of the moon previously illuminating the parking lot. Nat stood motionless in the cool night air, frustrated, and feeling as empty as he did the day he'd watched Papa Joe lowered into the ground. His eyes followed Renee's car through the parking lot, past the stadium, and watched as it disappeared over a hill just as the gleaming lights announcing his big victory on the scoreboard shut off.

CHAPTER 34

B *rewton, Alabama—1876*
       Forty years. A lifetime had passed since Joe's capture as a
young stowaway on the Bama Rambler. *Now an old man, he'd*
spent much of his adult life enslaved on a cotton plantation in south-
ern Alabama, owned by the wealthiest man in Escambia County.
He'd felt fortunate to have escaped from New Orleans those many
years ago, but he'd fled right into the open arms of a vile, despicable
man. Winfield Montgomery hated blacks, and he regularly punished
his slaves with a blood-soaked cat-o'-nine tails. Yet despite the harsh
conditions, Joe had managed to find a wife in his new home, and that
relationship had sustained him despite Winfield Montgomery and the
wreckage of the Civil War. Like all slaves, Joe had been declared a free
man in 1865 by the Great Emancipator, but freed blacks in Alabama
were in many ways no better off than before. Sadly, sharecropping
held them as penned, inside their farms, as the master's plantation
gates once had.

Joe had wanted to return to Texas since the moment he'd been
captured as a stowaway on the Bama Rambler, *but the opportunity*
hadn't come. However, now, in 1876, with his wife passed from fever
and Montgomery finally dead, he was ready. Travel was no longer a
risk except that Joe wasn't as nimble as he'd once been when escaping
Bailey's Prairie. But his time in the Alabama fields had hardened his
muscles and kept him strong. He was fit enough for the long journey.

A month later, saddle weary and worn, Joe rode into Clarksville,
Texas, a community just west of Austin. He'd purposely sought out
this small town full of freed blacks because he figured it would serve
as a perfect launching spot for his search, the quest he'd never, not for

one day, stopped thinking about. Colonel Bowie's still-undiscovered treasure.

Joe fit in easily in Clarksville and made a good life for himself with the other former slaves and felt comfortable calling Texas his new home. Soon he set about piecing together whatever information he could find about Bowie's lost map and formulating his plan. But then fate interrupted. In March of 1877, the city of Austin announced a celebration of the fortieth anniversary of San Jacinto Day, the date Sam Houston defeated Santa Anna and the Mexican army, and a call went out to all Texans whose families had served in the war of independence. Joe's celebrity had leaked out among the residents of Clarksville and as the lone surviving male from the Alamo, he was summoned to Austin for the event.

───◆───

C. R. Bailey was an Austin land speculator and opportunist whose business had taken a bad turn during Reconstruction. By late 1876, with his creditors circling, Bailey had a revelation. He could reform his real estate company, announce a discovery from the silver mines surrounding Austin, and fend off his creditors with promises of rich rewards for their forbearance. As a result, the C. R. Bailey Company became the San Saba Mining Company. Although Bailey's sole mission was to buy time, raise money, and avoid his looming insolvency, the arrival of Joe in Austin with all of the other Texas veterans gave his plan a fresh makeover. Bailey's minions quickly spread the word that their boss had secured secret information from Colonel Travis's former slave that pinpointed the exact location of Jim Bowie's legendary treasure. Through this lie, Bailey was able to secure funding from a few wealthy locals, which bought him time—and thrust Joe into the middle of his scheme.

───◆───

*S*everal nights into his stay in Austin, Joe had grown comfortable in his new role as a hero of the Alamo. In that short time, he'd somehow forgotten that even as a celebrity, he was still a black man at the margins of a white man's world. C. R. Bailey soon reminded him of his place.

Walking back to his quarters one evening, Joe was confronted by two heavyset cowboys in an alley.

"Come on over here, boy," called a voice from the shadows.

Joe inspected his surroundings but knew that at his age running was not an option. "Who's speaking?" he responded nervously.

Two big men dressed in dirty range wear appeared in full view to his right. "Step over here, boy," directed one of them. He motioned with his arm, which exposed a pistol hidden inside his belt.

Joe hesitated. "What do you want?" he asked.

"We ain't here to hurt you, if that's what you're worried about," said the other man, who was missing most of his front teeth. "We've got a business proposition fer ya. Now, come over here." The man rested his hand on his pistol.

Joe inched toward the alley but remained guarded. "Tell me what you want," he said defiantly.

"Our employer thinks you have information that might be useful to him," answered the toothless cowboy. "We're authorized to pay you a pile of money for a map to Colonel Bowie's treasure." The man flashed his gums and a wad of paper money bigger than any Joe had seen in his lifetime.

"What if my memory's not so good?" Joe asked.

"Just draw it up as best you can, sign it, and leave town. Mr. Bailey can handle the rest."

"What do you mean leave town?"

"We mean tonight. And never come back to Texas. That's what we mean."

"Can I see that roll of bills again?" Joe pressed.

At sixty years old, Joe could live as he never had with the kind of money the cowboys flashed at him. And after all his years in servitude, Joe could finally get paid off for the famous map he'd lost when Enrique had bolted off in panic, even if his new map was pure fiction. So an hour later, the two brutes handed Joe the money, reminded him that he was a dead man if he repeated what happened, and rode away with Joe's imperfect hand-drawn map to nowhere tucked safely inside one of their saddlebags.

As soon as the men disappeared, Joe rushed to the nearby livery and bought the best horse he could find. For the first time in his life, Joe had real money in his pocket, enough to care for all of his friends back in Brewton. Mounted on a brown-and-white stallion, he galloped off on what he knew would be the last ride of his life.

CHAPTER 35

Shakes felt something was off about his meeting with Frankie and Kruger. There was no good reason Angelina needed him at the Alamo excavation when there was already a full crew of permanent security personnel. Frankie explained that Angelina didn't trust the "regulars," but that statement didn't hold water. That and the fact she was paying him a shitload more money than normal for a gig like this had him on edge. Kruger's disinterested stare and occasional grunts during the meeting only made him jumpier.

Despite his worries, Shakes had decided to stay in town and see the project through. One, he needed the $1500 Angelina was offering him; and, two, he sniffed an opportunity for more money, a great deal more money, if he could figure out a way to scam Angelina and Frankie. He wasn't sure how things might come down, but he had options.

Shakes had staked out Angelina's house every morning for the past week to see how her routine had changed since he'd been forced out as her driver. He'd determined what time Frankie arrived each day (about 8:00), when he picked up Angelina's paper from the front yard (about 8:15), and when he left to take her to the office (about 8:45). In every case, Shakes had seen Angelina in the back seat of her town car scanning the newspaper as Frankie pulled out of the driveway. The most important detail Shakes had established was the one-hour gap between the time Frankie and Angelina left the house and the maid arrived. That was enough time for him to get in, find what he was looking for, and bail out before the housekeeper caught him.

Shakes had figured out the other details necessary for his burglary in his normal way. Although Angelina had been careful never to punch in her alarm code in front of him, Shakes had heard the beeping of her four-digit sequence many times. From the first day, he'd kept an eye out for the code and had finally stumbled upon it when spying on Angelina at an ATM machine. He'd only caught the first two entries of her password, but once he confirmed those numbers corresponded to the month of her dead husband's birthday, it didn't take long to crack the others. And the fact she'd repeated the sequence on virtually every one of her other passwords was no surprise, as Shakes knew that was a dumb habit shared by many of his marks. A man could trade on that kind of stupidity, and Shakes had always remained ready. Information was his currency and amassing alarm codes and other sensitive information was never far from his mind. In fact, that's how he'd uncovered Angelina's secret hiding place for her house key as well.

The Friday morning before the Alamo dig, Shakes hid in his dark-tinted Chevy Lumina a block away from Angelina's house. The minute Frankie's town car drove past him he jumped. He raced to Angelina's property through a gravel alley that bisected the neighborhood, and then he scaled the brick perimeter fence behind her backyard at the precise location where her house was obscured by a large pecan tree. From there, he darted to Angelina's patio door and dug out the hidden door key from a giant fern planter on her porch. Both the key and alarm code worked as expected and Shakes instantly had free rein.

Shakes suspected the most likely hiding place for evidence concerning the excavation project would be the study where Angelina regularly worked. He'd seen glimpses of it when cruising the hallway but most of what he remembered was a large Apple computer screen and lots of books. Shakes hurried to the room and was suddenly reminded Angelina had left it filled with the heavy masculine décor of her dead husband. The study looked like time had passed it by: The dark-brown wall paneling was badly faded, the hardwood floors gouged and worn, and the inset bookshelves sagged from the weight of their numerous volumes. To finish off the dreary look, Angelina maintained an 1800s-vintage desk that dated to the de Zavala part of her family in the center of the room, flanked by two heavily cushioned chairs with cracks in their rough leather upholstery. They were the furnishings that Gordon Gentry had apparently spent most of his time among before his death, and Angelina had carefully preserved them to keep his memory alive. The only thing that looked like the rest of the house was a winged desk chair with colorful fabric, where Angelina liked to sit, and a patterned rug that covered most of the floor.

Shakes squatted behind the long, narrow, de Zavala desk but was disappointed to find that the wooden drawers were locked. He opted for efficiency over stealth. Using a steel letter opener from the desk, he pried open the top drawer and started riffling through papers. Nothing. He followed up unsuccessfully with the other drawers and quickly grew frustrated with his lack of success. He banged his fist on the chair before turning and staring at the bookcase behind him, searching for a new idea. In front of him were over one hundred volumes on the Alamo, from antique manuscripts with tattered spines to historical classics like Walter Lord's *A Time to Stand*, but nothing stood out or caught his attention. As he sat there racking his brain, Shakes noticed that one of the old books on the second shelf notched out a bit farther than the others, which were otherwise lined up perfectly evenly. An untrained eye might have missed it, but not Shakes. He pulled out the irregularly placed book and immediately realized it was not what it appeared to be. The spine seemed authentic but the inside was a hollowed-out core containing a secret compartment. Shakes jerked it open and found two keys.

He plucked the first one out and tried it in Angelina's desk. He smiled as it glided in. He then held the second key dangling from his finger on a chain while he looked for its home. There were no other locks anywhere to be seen.

Shakes began opening and closing the desk drawers in frustration and then noticed the edge of the rug had been pulled back so it wasn't trapped by the leg of the desk. Shakes's heart skipped a beat when he reached down, pushed the wool fabric away, and exposed a key-holed compartment carved out of the hardwood. He placed the second key in the lock and it opened. With sweat running down his forehead, Shakes bent down farther and picked up a handful of papers stuffed on top of a passport and two $5000 straps of cash. Just as he began studying the documents, Shakes heard the screeching of tires, as if a car was pulling into the driveway. He jumped up and looked outside the window, but it wasn't the housekeeper's Kia or Frankie's town car entering the property. It was a blue Taurus with a huge figure in the driver's seat. Kruger. With no time to straighten up, Shakes grabbed the $10,000 from the safe, stuffed it with all of the papers into his pants, and ran.

He cleared the back fence just as Kruger entered the house.

CHAPTER 36

Shakes pulled down the sleeves on his leather jacket and steadied himself before entering the breakfast diner where he'd once cooked eggs. Although convinced he'd cleanly escaped Angelina's house the day before, he understood the risk in approaching Frankie without an escape route. But jumping town before finishing the Alamo job, admitting his guilt by his actions, was the worst of all options. Frankie waited at a corner table sipping coffee when Shakes walked in. He was alone, a good sign.

"What's up?" Shakes asked while sliding into the metal chair across from his handler.

"You'll be on your own tonight," Frankie responded. His face tightened and Shakes could see the anger behind his brown eyes. "Kruger's out. Miss Angelina fired him."

Shakes tried not to react, although he nearly exploded out of his chair when he heard the news. He shifted slightly to his left and accepted a cup of coffee from the waitress. "Never trusted that dude anyway," he said casually.

"Kruger's my problem," Frankie snapped with a frown. "Be at the east exit of the Alamo church at six p.m. tonight. You'll get a uniform there and be shown to your post. Your job is to keep our guests from wandering, confine them to the observation deck, and herd them out the exits at the end of the program. When they're gone, come by Miss Angelina's office and you'll be paid. *Comprende?*"

"Yeah," Shakes confirmed. He wanted to question Frankie about Kruger but he could tell the young Hispanic was not interested in discussing the matter. He didn't want to press his luck anyway. It appeared Kruger had been blamed for the robbery, and that was good enough for him.

Frankie pushed back from the table and stood up. Before turning to walk away, he stared down at Shakes, cocked his head, and asked, "And if you happen to hear from Kruger, you'll let me know? Right?"

Shakes saluted in acknowledgement, ending the conversation. He then watched Frankie drive away in Angelina's town car. What had just happened? Was he incredibly lucky or had Kruger actually been up to something? In either case, Shakes couldn't have planned things any better. He would no longer have to worry about watching his back and could now finish his work with Angelina, set up his plan, and leave town without arousing suspicion. *Damned straight*, he thought.

Shakes leaned back in his chair and considered the night ahead. He had to expect Frankie would have more than one set of eyes on Angelina's guests, particularly the Travis brothers, who he'd learned from one of Angelina's stolen papers were on the guest list. That had triggered an idea, and he knew that all he needed was a moment to communicate with one of them. He'd then draw them in by leaving copies of some of the notes he'd found in Angelina's file in their hotel room. Extracting money from a rich Texas politician and his brother from a distant, and safe, location would be a better bet than taking on further risk with Angelina Gentry. He figured the Travises would pay plenty to know what he'd found out about the old lady's plans and her connection to Joe Travis's death. And if they messed with Angelina later, what did he care. The crazy old bitch deserved it.

Shakes hadn't figured out everything from the documents he'd lifted from Angelina's safe, but he knew enough to understand the brothers were getting closer to her than she wanted. The old lady's documents confirmed an alternative location was planned for Kalender's excavation in the Alamo, one she'd not revealed to the public, and her angry scribbles by the Travis's names on the guest manifest screamed they'd become problems. Angelina was apparently trying to make the discovery on her own terms, for her own benefit, without anyone else knowing, especially Joe Travis's grandsons. How she pulled off her scheme was of no concern to Shakes. He had the intel on her plans and that's all that mattered.

Shakes surveyed the Alamo grounds from his perch above the excavation site and spotted the two men in the distance, Nat and Joseph Travis, the grandsons of the war hero Kruger had murdered. Although it was 9:00 p.m. and there was limited visibility in the outdoor courtyard, it was easy to spot the brothers. They were the only black faces in the crowd. The lawyer Travis in his blue three-piece suit and bright-red tie drew attention away from his brother by his constant movement.

A spotlight flashed to a small stage and a blonde woman in a tight red dress appeared just to the right of the excavation site. "Good evening," she greeted the crowd. "My name's Janet Nelson, city councilwoman for the Alamo District, and on behalf of the Alamo Preservation Advisory Board, I want to welcome you to a historic occasion. Tonight we hope to uncover a rare part of our state's history. A missing piece of our Texas heritage. To help us, we are fortunate to have one of the world's foremost treasure hunters to guide us through the next hour. So without further ado, I present Mr. Frank Kalender."

A polite cheer went up from the small audience.

Shakes pulled the security-guard hat down over his head and watched the spotlight move to the oversized Kalender. The large man walked to the podium wearing tan work clothes and a hard hat. His trousers were spattered with fresh dirt stains, which gave the impression he'd been working in the pit all day. Shakes doubted that. "My name's Frank Kalender," he bellowed into the microphone, "and I'm excited you're all here to take part in the opening of the lost well of the Alamo. Our monitors suggest we're within five feet of our objective and we'll be dropping the cable down to our miners in hope they'll lift out our first priceless artifact. In a few short moments, you will all be witnesses to history."

A second subdued cheer went up from the guests, who craned their necks to observe the semi-lit crater in front of them.

Kalender then activated a large motorized hoist that hissed and whined like a locomotive before it dropped into the hole. Kalender shouted instructions to his men below and started wildly swinging his arms, milking the moment for full effect. While this process went forward, Shakes looked across the way to where Angelina stood just outside the sight lines of her guests, the darkness shielding whatever facial expression she wore as the spectacle unfolded.

A few minutes later, Kalender announced, "Folks, we have contact. I believe the hoist has something attached, something very big."

The crowd stopped talking and stared at the now brightly illuminated hole, waiting for the newfound treasure to rise from the earth. Moments later, a long cylindrical object caked in dirt came into view. A murmur whirred around the courtyard.

Kalender directed the laborers operating the machinery to a barren spot to his right and only then did Shakes start to see the more defining characteristics of the object. An iron surface, roughed up with age, with wooden remnants of a base for support. "Ladies and gentlemen," Kalender declared, "we've uncovered a piece of ordnance, or in modern terminology, an

Alamo cannon. There are other objects below and it appears the well is full of artifacts."

Shakes smiled at the half-assed applause from the crowd.

He then turned his attention back to Angelina, who'd stepped farther into view and had a pleased look on her face. Little did tonight's observers know what Shakes understood—that the artifacts, while real, were only being hauled up to deceive them. The real prize Angelina was after would never be displayed to this group. The whole show was bullshit.

"Oh my Lord," Kalender roared, "a musket. Could it be Davy Crockett's very own Betsy?"

Another muffled cheer from the crowd.

Thirty minutes later, after more bluster and several new discoveries, including two cannon balls and a nineteenth-century lamppost, the charade was over. Kalender pronounced, "Thank you all for taking part in this historical event. These objects will provide our Alamo historians with years of study and a wealth of knowledge about the heroes who died here defending your honor. Not exactly the treasure we sought, but treasure nonetheless. You will all be provided a signed copy of my latest book, *The Treasure Beneath Your Feet*, when you leave. Please move toward the security guard on your left, who will escort you out."

At this point, Shakes stepped toward the guests and ushered them toward the exit. He waited patiently for the two black visitors to separate from the rest of the group but they stayed huddled up, in the midst of the other dignitaries, frustrating his plan. With little time left, he made his move.

"Sir," he said to the taller black man, who made eye contact with him. "You dropped your program."

Nat Travis acknowledged Shakes but waved him off.

Shakes contorted his expression while continuing to push the small crowd down the narrow hallway toward the exit. "Sir," Shakes said in a raised voice.

Nat muttered something to his brother and then turned toward Shakes. He drifted to the back of the crowd as Joseph pressed forward.

Shakes carved him away from the pack and whispered, "I have information about your grandfather and the treasure. I'll contact you later." As soon as he finished speaking, Shakes was joined by several other security guards who herded Nat and the remaining members of the party out the doorway.

Satisfied, Shakes pivoted the other direction and hurried away to Angelina's office.

CHAPTER 37

Nat had been pushed outside the building by a wave of uniformed personnel and was unable to force his way back in. After several frustrating minutes arguing with the guards, Nat realized his impatient brother, who'd hustled ahead to retrieve the car, was probably growing angrier by the minute.

Nat bit his lip when he approached the parking valet, where Joseph waited. "Sorry, call of nature," he explained as he slid into Joseph's sedan. Questions raced through Nat's mind as he reclined onto the car's leather upholstery. What had the guard intended by his comment about Papa Joe and the treasure? Why throw out such a cryptic statement and then disappear? Was he right to withhold the shocking comment from his brother? But instinct, and past history, told him to keep his mouth shut. Having spent the afternoon and evening with Joseph, Nat felt even more certain that his brother's decision to help out was not based on some newfound interest in their grandfather's life story, but rather on simple political opportunism. Joseph appeared far more interested in rubbing shoulders with the other VIP guests at the event than establishing the accuracy of Nat's research about the treasure. And while he continued to discount the validity of Nat's story, Joseph seemed more than ready to capitalize on Kalender's work if any of it proved true. Nat visualized his brother's picture on every front page in the state proclaiming his great discovery at the Alamo, which would gain him the type of notoriety he longed for.

It was in this strange suspended moment, just after the unknown man had suggested a tantalizing connection between

Papa Joe's death and Nat's research, that his feelings for Renee crystallized. He wanted so badly to talk to her, to ask her opinion about what he'd just heard, to hold her. But he also felt deeply troubled about the way their last meeting, at the stadium, had ended. In this whirl of regret and disappointment and the thought that he'd hurt her, a deeper sense told him that he loved her. The reservations he'd allowed to creep into their relationship because of Joseph seemed utterly foolish now that he was sitting in a car next to him.

Nat remained quiet the rest of the way to the hotel. And it wasn't hard to do since his brother was busy listening to his phone messages over his Bluetooth system, ever the important politician. When they finally arrived at the Munger Court, Joseph clicked off the phone and looked at Nat and said, "Well, sorry this was such a nonevent. But I guess I got drawn in by the treasure story, too. Let's meet for breakfast before you get off in the morning."

Nat nodded, careful to avoid any outward sign of emotion. "Breakfast's good," he said. "And thanks for setting this up. I'm glad I came down and witnessed that BS, even if it was more of a show than anything else. I don't see any reason to waste your time meeting Kalender now. I'm sure you can tell he's a world-class self-promoter."

"Yes, well ... maybe we can let Papa Joe rest in peace now ... forget this treasure fantasy."

Joseph's comment didn't faze Nat. He'd become so familiar with his brother's subtle digs that this one bounced right off him. "Let's say six thirty tomorrow morning," Nat suggested as they entered the lobby.

They rode up the elevator for eight floors before Nat stepped off and headed to his room. When he threw back his door, exhausted and ready to call it a night, the first thing he saw was an 8x10 manila envelope lying on the floor. Nat reached down, snagged the package, and tore it open. Seconds later, he dropped it back to the floor.

The mysterious security guard had made good on his word.

Shakes turned off the lights to his Chevy and walked inside the all-night coffee shop with the red-neon sign that he'd spotted from the highway. He'd driven for two hours after being paid by Frankie and was tired and hungry. Inside the one-room diner, Shakes noticed three Hispanic men sitting at the counter and a lone waitress punching in numbers at the register. In the back, he could see a short Asian cook working the griddle. Shakes plopped into a small booth as far away from the front door as possible.

As the waitress filled his coffee mug, Shakes reached down and felt the fanny pack attached to his waist. He'd never had so many Benjamins on him before, and the weight of carrying such a large sum made him uncomfortable and jumpy. He thought about his brief conversation with Frankie again. Angelina's man had paid him his fee without any questions, said he'd be in touch, and dismissed him in less than two minutes. Something about how that went down didn't sit right. The relief Shakes felt after hearing Kruger had been dismissed was replaced by a fresh set of fears. Frankie had never been so distant, so aloof, and his attitude suggested something had changed. For that reason, Shakes hadn't even bothered returning to his hotel room to collect his gear after the meeting and instead drove immediately to the highway, pointing his Chevy northwest toward Midland. He was not taking any further chances staying in San Antonio.

Shakes ordered the largest burger on the menu, downed his coffee, and rethought his plan. He'd wanted to convince the Travis brothers they should pay for more information with the nugget he'd left with the bellman, but he now realized he needed to wait—maybe even abandon the whole idea. With the threat level raised in his mind, Shakes needed to get a safe distance away from Texas, cool off for a few days, and then reassess from a position of safety. He ordered another cup of coffee and then walked to the men's room. By the time he returned, a large man in a hooded sweatshirt had plopped down in a booth at the other side of the diner. Shakes couldn't see the man's face but his immense shoulders raised the hair on Shakes's back. He thought about running, unsure if it really was him, but returned to his seat where he quickly snuck one of the dinner knives off the table and pushed it into his sleeve. A moment later, Shakes watched Kruger unwind his massive body from his booth and stalk over. There was no way out.

"I need the papers back," Kruger demanded in his trademark broken English. "And the money you stole." He poured himself into the seat across from Shakes.

Even with a knife, Shakes was no match for the Serbian and immediately ruled out taking him on. "You and Frankie played me, didn't you?" he asked.

Kruger shrugged. "I've always known what you're about. Now, are you going to make this hard?"

"I've sent the documents off to protect myself. You can't touch me."

"That was a mistake. You had some value to me until I heard that."

Shakes saw the evil he'd come to know in Kruger's eyes, a look that suggested nothing he said would matter. "You'll never get that treasure without me," Shakes offered.

"Let's walk outside together," Kruger directed. "Just give me what I want, and I'll let you drive off wherever you want to go. You're no longer my concern."

Shakes knew Kruger's true mission, and his staying alive

was not part of it. But he recognized that hanging in the booth was not an option. Kruger could drag him out by the scruff of his neck if he needed to. "Let's go then," Shakes said.

The other patrons paid no mind to the growing drama near them, barely looking up from their plates when Shakes stood up. He'd already decided that his one shot at escape was the kitchen and he had about two seconds to make his move. Without hesitation, he swung wildly with the knife, catching a piece of Kruger's hip, and then lunged over the counter in front of the three Hispanic men. He then scrambled to his feet, sprinted past the large griddle, knocking the cook over, and slammed into the back door. Kruger flicked the knife aside and dove toward Shakes but came up empty. The counter rumbled and plates flew into laps as he caromed across the linoleum. The giant then grunted, jumped up, and charged in the opposite direction toward the front exit.

Shakes tore through the back door to a barren parking lot. The night air was eerily still, and Shakes realized the other customers weren't coming to his aid. He also understood that his next move would determine whether he survived. He spotted an alleyway across the parking lot behind a row of storefronts that would provide an escape route if he could safely cover the open hundred yards before him. Shakes crossed himself and raced over the pavement, stretching every muscle in his legs to capacity, covering the first fifty yards in a blur. In the scramble, he thought of his days as a kid, running from the Philadelphia police, and remembered his knack for always keeping one step ahead of the law. But Kruger was nothing like those locals in Philly. Shakes knew he had to duck and weave as he ran, limiting the target area for the shot he sensed was coming.

A rifle blast cracked from the direction of the coffee shop and Shakes felt a piercing metal slug rip through his left lat muscle, entering his lung. He collapsed to the ground and his legs went numb. Like a winged dove he lay stranded, waiting for the executioner.

Within seconds, Kruger was standing over him with a pistol extended from his hand. "Give me the money belt," he growled.

"Come and take it," Shakes replied as blood formed in his mouth. He'd barely spoken the words when Kruger fired the next shot.

CHAPTER 38

Angelina de Zavala Gentry paced around her office waiting for Kalender to arrive. She stared at the COME AND TAKE IT flag resting peacefully in its glass case on her wall and wondered if the famous banner would forever remain the crown jewel of her collection. Jim Bowie's treasure seemed so frustratingly far away now.

"Good morning, ma'am," Kalender said as Frankie led him into the room. The treasure hunter had saddlebags under his eyes, the kind caused by piled-up hours without sleep, and his body slumped forward as if the weight of his fatigue was forcing him to teeter over. His hair lay matted down in patches across his scalp and a dirt-ring indentation creased his forehead. He had sweat stains all over his clothing.

"I've waited my whole life for this moment," Angelina grumbled, "and you still have nothing?" She slapped her knotty fist onto her oak desk to emphasize her displeasure. "Nothing?"

"Ms. Gentry, the well is just where we thought it would be," Kalender explained while lifting up out of his crouched position, "and we've uncovered additional artifacts, but there's just no treasure. We've run out of places to dig." A defeated frown spread across Kalender's face.

"No treasure," her voice rose with agitation. "After all of the money I've spent? You've got to have something. You better!"

"What else can I say?" Kalender pleaded. "I thought we were going to find the treasure last night. Even as late as four o'clock this morning, I thought we had the site targeted. But there's nothing else in that well. Nothing."

"Then where's the treasure?"

"If I knew," Kalender answered, his arms raised in surrender, "I'd have it in your hands right now. I thought it was in the well just like you did. All signs pointed there, as did Adina's note. I've miscalculated somewhere. I just need more time to work back through my research. I need to recalibrate."

Angelina swung her head back and forth, her black hair bouncing across her face like branches from a willow tree. Hadn't she already killed two, now three men with Shakes, in pursuit of the treasure? Acts she could never have even imagined a few years earlier. And now she was fully aligned with a dangerous killer. A man who appeared to be watching her every step as if ready to make a move on her. All of this couldn't be for nothing. "What's that supposed to mean?" Angelina screeched. "Recalibrate?"

Kruger quietly entered the room and stood by the door. Angelina noticed Kalender peer over his shoulder.

"Where's my damned treasure?" Angelina yelled. She glanced at Kruger, nodded, and the giant moved toward Kalender.

"There is something," Kalender blurted out. "Old man Travis did leave one other clue."

Angelina motioned for Kruger to stand down. She walked over and stared Kalender in the eye.

"I'm waiting," she demanded.

Once Kalender finished offering his latest spin on the mystery, Angelina returned to her desk and fell into her chair again. She could feel the clock ticking in her head, forcing bad decisions on top of the bad ones she'd already made. This clown had played her for a small fortune and now, at this late hour, was volunteering a new story, one she'd never even heard before. It had to be self-preservation. A lie. How could she even consider allowing Kalender to haul her off on another crazy jaunt? But even though reason told her different, Angelina couldn't let go, her whole being so wrapped into the prize that she couldn't give up. She knew that the treasure hunt had become a narcotic, as powerful an obsession as a junkie's addiction, but it didn't matter. She sighed and decided to give Kalender one last chance. What other option did she have? "This better be it," she warned the sweating Kalender, whose acrid body odor now enveloped the room like a leaky septic tank's. "Remember that!" Angelina signaled Kruger to show the defeated treasure hunter out of the room.

Alone in her shrine to Alamo history, Angelina thought back to what she'd been through. It had taken years to rebuild her position in the community, years to research the story of Bowie's Treasure, and hour upon hour of working with Janet Nelson to prepare her for the take-over of the DRT. All of these efforts had to pay off. She alone deserved to uncover the greatest mystery in Texas history. Jim Bowie's treasure had become her baby as much as any mother's child.

CHAPTER 39

Nat arrived back in Brewton early Sunday afternoon. He'd never had a chance to talk to Joseph about his unexpected encounter with the security guard at the Alamo, even if he'd wanted to, because his brother hadn't shown up for their breakfast meeting. Instead, Joseph had checked out early with a note of apology left behind at the front desk. Nat wondered why he continued to hold out hope for improvement in his relationship with his brother, but the trip to Texas had just about cured him.

Nat's focus, however, was not on Joseph. All the way home from San Antonio, he thought about ways he could resurrect Renee's trust. Flowers came to mind, but Nat knew he needed more than a gesture to repair her damaged emotions. By the time his plane touched down, he'd decided the only way to deal with Renee would be to go see her. And he was surprised, but gratified, that despite her frigid temperature on the phone she'd agreed to come by his house that night.

"So how was San Antonio?" Renee asked when she walked in his front door about 7:00 p.m.

Nat could feel the tension in her voice and her formal handshake conveyed more than words. "I appreciate you coming over. I have a lot to tell ... and show you," Nat said.

"You mentioned that on the phone," Renee snapped. She stood a safe distance away from Nat and didn't remove her jacket. Her body language said it all: *I'm short on time and you need to get to the point.*

"I'd like to say something first," Nat started. In truth, he hadn't planned a script for this moment but hoped some form of inspiration would guide him to the right words. He knew one thing—he couldn't play it safe now, or protect his feelings—he had to expose himself and show a vulnerable side he'd avoided with Renee, in some ways avoided his whole life. "The other night ..." he started.

"Let's not go there," Renee interrupted. Her face was taut and she clenched her fist.

The tender reunion Nat had hoped for was terminated before it started. Renee wanted no part of him, and Nat knew instantly that more patience would be needed ... quite a bit more. "Please sit down," he said while reorienting his thoughts. He pointed to the small dining table just outside his kitchen. "This may take a while." Nat pulled out the notes delivered by Shakes and laid them on the table.

"What are these?" Renee asked.

"Please sit down," Nat implored the still-standing Renee. "Like I said, this may take a while."

"Okay, but I can't stay long," Renee answered before finally taking a seat and removing her jacket, revealing a crisp white blouse and navy skirt. "I have dinner plans at eight," she said.

"I'll go fast." Nat then hurried through his story, discussing the time he spent with Joseph in San Antonio, the Kalender show at the Alamo, and his encounter with the black security guard. "I expected to hear from that guard by now," he said, "but there's been no word. He obviously knows something or why else would he have left these notes behind in my hotel room? What do you make of it?"

Renee said nothing while Nat talked, but she pored over the handwritten papers with great interest. Nat looked down at the primary note Renee had been deciphering, which read:

This clue from Adina de Zavala provides information about the location of the treasure your grandfather was looking for with Kalender. I know more, much more, about it. I introduced myself tonight so you'd know who I am when I call. You'll hear from me soon. My name is Shakes.

BT - moved? Not in the LBR. Find JB's trail. S had M.

"So, if I'm buying any of this," Renee said, "I have to believe this note is real and it has some logical connection to the treasure and your grandfather's research."

"Yeah, that's the way I see it," Nat replied. "I have no idea what else the guy wanted. He's got to either be trying to help me or setting up some kind of scam."

Renee cocked her head. "Maybe he's doing both," she posited.

Nat's phone beeped. He looked down and saw a text message from Joseph. His first thought, in light of all the trouble his brother had caused, was to read the text later. But he couldn't help himself and swiped his finger across the phone's face. He read the message, straightened up, and looked at Renee with a blank stare.

"What is it?" she asked.

Nat handed her the phone. "It's from Joseph. Take a look at this."

The text said: **Nat, sorry I had to run this morning, but work never waits. I just got a message from a friend at the Capitol which said that a black security guard from the Alamo was murdered last night. Strange, huh? Thought you'd want to know. J**

"Your guy?" Renee asked.

"Not sure I saw another black security guard down there. Most were Hispanic." Nat paused, looked at Renee, and said, "I can't do this without you, Renee. Can you stay around a while longer?"

Renee looked down at her watch and nodded. "Let me make a call," she said.

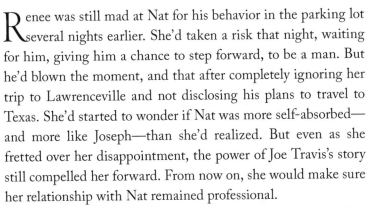

Renee was still mad at Nat for his behavior in the parking lot several nights earlier. She'd taken a risk that night, waiting for him, giving him a chance to step forward, to be a man. But he'd blown the moment, and that after completely ignoring her trip to Lawrenceville and not disclosing his plans to travel to Texas. She'd started to wonder if Nat was more self-absorbed—and more like Joseph—than she'd realized. But even as she fretted over her disappointment, the power of Joe Travis's story still compelled her forward. From now on, she would make sure her relationship with Nat remained professional.

"If he was the only black security guard," Renee started as Nat shut off his phone, "I would guess it's the same man. And, by the way, I think you were smart not to say anything more to Joseph. I can already see his brain working the angles in that text."

Nat smiled so she could see they were aligned on that issue. "What are you thinking?" he asked.

"How all of this fits together. If this murder is connected, I'm wondering if it somehow ties into what I learned in Lawrenceville."

Nat looked down as if to apologize when Renee mentioned her trip to Georgia. "Tell me more about that," Nat requested. "I was completely selfish in not taking the time to listen earlier."

Renee had understood Nat's anxiety about his big game with Riverview, but she still felt bruised. Even so, she'd uncovered so much during her visit with Enrique Rodriguez that she was dying to break the shackles off her story. "This is quite a tale," she said. "Listen carefully." Renee then detailed her meeting with Enrique Rodriguez and his emotional reaction to her story and methodically built her way up to the point when Enrique unveiled Papa Joe's handwritten letter.

"I think I know what you're about to say," Nat interrupted. "Papa Joe was the benefactor. The one who watched over Enrique Rodriguez."

"Yes, exactly."

Nat gasped for air, barely able to respond, and his face quivered. The full force of his reaction moved Renee to console him, but she held back.

"I'm speechless," Nat whispered. "I can't believe this."

"There's more," she said. "Quite a bit more. Enrique preserved a number of letters from his father, most written while Ricardo was preparing for the invasion of Germany with Papa Joe. In one letter penned to his infant son, a young boy he knew he might not ever see, Ricardo described a story carried down through the years by the Rodriguez family. The letter is imaginative and colorful: the careful effort of a father trying to talk to his son, to tell him something important, in a way a child might understand and remember. A story about their ancestor, a Mexican groom, a lost treasure, the heroes of the Alamo, and an inadvertent separation that revealed an epic clue. A story he likely shared with his friend, Joe Travis, which I'm guessing sparked Papa Joe's interest in his own genealogy. A trail that ultimately connected the Travis family to Rodriguez's through a man you've now become very familiar with—a slave named Joe."

Nat's jaw dropped even farther and he rubbed his hands across his face. "Unbelievable ... what a story. I'm so sorry, Renee. I can't believe I didn't make a better effort to listen."

"I'm not done yet," she responded, drawing a deep breath. "Enrique Rodriguez never thought anything more about that letter, which he kept and preserved over the years, until I showed up last week. I was a revelation. Suddenly, the story Ricardo

Rodriguez had written about to his son all those years ago no longer sounded whimsical but instead had a face, a history, a name. Maybe his Mexican ancestor really had obtained a treasure map from a slave named Joe. Maybe the folklore passed down through the Rodriguez family for over one hundred and fifty years *was* true. Perhaps, the vast treasure hidden by Jim Bowie was not a myth but was still out there to be discovered. All of which makes the last sentence of Ricardo Rodriguez's letter more real, if not entirely deflating—'the map was lost to a couple of sailors who stole it and left the country none the wiser.'"

"That is discouraging," Nat said.

"Yes and no. I'm not sure any map ever existed, but it sure provides a reason why someone might have been searching Papa Joe's house."

"You're right about that. It all does make sense now. So how did you leave it with Rodriguez?"

"He would like to meet you sometime … and thank you for what Papa Joe did for him."

Nat shook his head and leaned back in his chair. "Well, once I get over the fact that my grandfather never told me he paid for Rodriguez's education, I might. But I guess there's no reason to care. For all I know, Papa Joe had someone else make the payments." Nat paused and then looked Renee in the eye. "Yes, I'd like to meet him. Very much."

The heaviness of the revelation hung on Nat like news of a dying relative, and Renee could see the emotion churning through his system. Changing the subject was the only merciful thing she could do. "So look at that note you received from the security guard again."

Nat picked it up but his mind was elsewhere.

"Let's just say for grins that this note really means something," she speculated. "What if this Shakes character stole this information from Kalender? What if he really did have clues about an alternate site for the dig? Wouldn't you want to know more?"

"Of course," Nat responded. "But that means he was playing me, doesn't it?"

"Probably," she said. "Or why else pick you out of the crowd? But the fact he was murdered suggests he was onto something more, doesn't it? As were Papa Joe and his friend Ambrose, don't forget."

A chill shook them both.

"So where does that leave us?"

Renee perked up at Nat's use of the word "us," making her relax and feel more forgiving. "I suppose I should go back to Papa Joe's records tonight," she suggested, "and see if this note makes any sense based on what I've read. It takes little imagination to see that the use of the letters *BT* was intentional. Give me tonight to figure out if there's some deeper connection with this murder victim in San Antonio. I'll give you the rest of the night to soak in what you've just learned."

———◆★◆———

*B*rewton, *Alabama Cemetery—1884*
        There was no pomp, no ceremony. Under a clear sky and the canopy of a young white oak, two workers unloaded a coffin from their wagon and set it next to a rectangular hole in the ground. About thirty other men and women had been laid to rest in this small cemetery named after the country's fifteenth president, most of them without names and without any story to recognize their lives on Earth. A burial place for the most anonymous of persons, for slaves.

        "Leave it here," said the older man in charge. "And mark a spot for the headstone. We'll be hauling that thing out here later today."

        The old man's brawny sidekick kicked at the ground above the hole as instructed.

"We'll bury him tomorrow when the preacher man comes by," said the older man. "Unless the varmints get to him first." He chuckled as if amused by his dark humor.

The younger man looked down at the coffin, said a prayer, and touched the cross etched into the wood. He read the small letters carved into the casket identifying the body—Joe 1884. He then jumped back into his wagon and headed on his way.

CHAPTER 40

As her private plane descended through the darkness toward the small landing strip on the eastern side of Brewton, Angelina felt the familiar gnawing ache in her stomach, the one that plagued her whenever she realized Bowie's Treasure might be slipping away. Flying here to chase down Kalender's latest lead was rash, probably foolish, and ate at her like a ravenous cancer cell. But what options did she have? The plan they'd devised was simple—Kalender and his aides would accompany her to the cemetery, find the unmarked grave of Joe the slave, and then dig. They'd dig and dig and dig … until they found the treasure.

Angelina wrestled with another, more substantial problem—her man Kruger. Although the Serbian had served her well as her eyes, ears, and muscle—he'd actually recognized Shakes's duplicity long before she did—his methods had become far too dangerous. A murder in front of a half-dozen restaurant patrons wasn't the way she wanted Shakes silenced. Now, more than ever, she could not afford to be tied to the maniac in any way. Even then, she still needed him a while longer. If Kalender failed on this mission, there'd be one last job she'd need accomplished. Kalender and his men knew too much to be trusted.

Angelina, Kalender, and his crew loaded into a rented SUV at the local airport and then drove down a series of country roads to the obscure James Buchanan Cemetery. Kruger followed in a separate vehicle a short distance behind. The small cemetery had limited light, which suited Angelina just fine. Kalender's associate parked their Chevy Tahoe in the gravel parking lot adjacent to the cemetery while Kruger surveyed the area, pointing his flashlight into the darkness in all directions. With an arm gesture, he then directed Kalender's crew to unload the shovels and picks from the back of the SUV. Angelina looked at her digital watch; it was 1:45 a.m.

"Ms. Gentry, would you like to wait in the car?" Kalender asked.

"I'm coming with you," she responded curtly.

Angelina joined the three men as they shined their flashlights and walked toward the chain link fence enclosing the historic slave cemetery. Kruger trailed behind, keeping an eye out for signs of trouble. There was a slight chill in the air and Angelina pulled a wool cap over her head. The cemetery property was located a hundred yards off a paved farm road and was the only sign of development within miles. Angelina could see a long stretch of darkness in front of her, with a few twinkling lights in the distance from the city of Brewton. The groomed landscape near the fence belied the desolate grounds surrounding them, which were filled with knee-high native grasses. Angelina realized someone had taken care to keep the cemetery in such good condition.

"How're you going to get me inside?" Angelina asked.

Kruger stepped forward and held up a large pair of bolt cutters.

The group then walked up to the gate and waited as Kruger snapped the thick chain wrapped around the lock. Angelina charged ahead and marched to the front of the cemetery.

"Hand me that flashlight," she barked at Kalender. She strained to see the lettering on the monument at the entrance of the cemetery, a marker dedicated to President James Buchanan's service to his country. Angelina then raised her flashlight above the bronze plaque and followed it down a path that led to a huge white oak at the back of the cemetery. *JB's trail.* At least according to Kalender. In between stood approximately twenty rows of smallish headstones, situated among several tall elms. There was no sign of recent activity in the cemetery other than to the far left near the southern perimeter of the enclosure fence. There, she noticed a small American flag gently flapping in the night breeze. The grave site for Joe Travis.

"Get to work," Angelina ordered.

"You realize I've never been here before," Kalender replied. "All I have to go on are my recollections from my conversation with Joe Travis. This may take some time."

"I hope your memory's better than your research," she growled. "But I suspect you should start with that marker under the big white oak."

"Frank, we've got something here," one of the attendants said with anticipation.

"Get the damn thing out of the ground," Kalender directed.

Angelina rose from her perch to watch Kalender's men strap a couple of ropes under a deteriorated casket and raise it from the earth. The ease with which the crate moved concerned her. Surely Bowie's Treasure would be heavier.

"Open it up," she cried when the casket was laid on level ground. Kruger perked up and stood over Kalender. His looming presence had kept all of the crew on edge.

One man removed a crowbar from his bag and started working the top off the box. It took little time.

"Here we go," Kalender announced as his worker pried loose the wooden board.

Angelina hungrily stared into the casket. She hardly moved when she saw the remnants of decomposed clothing and a macabre skeleton come into view. Bugs scurried in and out of the hollowed skull when the flashlights hit them.

"Cover it up," Angelina yelled. "And go back in and dig some more. It has to be down there!"

For the next hour, Kalender's men forced their shovels even deeper into the dark hole but found nothing more than rocks and debris. The cruel realization that she'd once again failed fixed in Angelina's mind just as she noticed headlights approaching in the distance. Small dots on the horizon bobbed in and out of the darkness from the opposite direction that Angelina and her crew had come from and appeared focused on the grave robbers. "Pack up!" Kruger ordered. "Now!"

As Kalender's disappointed crew hastily grabbed their equipment and sprinted to the car, Angelina took one last look at the cemetery. She was wretched, thinking about what this failure meant—her life's work had crumbled before her eyes. Kruger abruptly signaled Angelina to head out and she reluctantly scurried back to the rental car. "Get to the airstrip," she screamed. Once safely away from the cemetery, Angelina turned to make sure Kruger was following behind as planned. She could see his car just pulling out of the parking lot but it was his next move that caught her by surprise. Instead of ducking in behind Kalender's car, Kruger appeared to pause—and then turned in the opposite direction.

CHAPTER 41

Nat headed to the practice facility Monday morning in his truck feeling worn and tired from his weekend in San Antonio. His brother had not returned his call from the previous night so he punched in the familiar cell phone number as he drove.

"What's up?" Joseph answered.

"Your text message has me a little interested," Nat said.

"Sorry I didn't get back to you last night, but I'm limited in what I can say."

"That tells me something."

"I guess it does. But I'm not sure what it means, if anything, about Papa Joe. I know this—the Alamo has a big mess on its hands. There's an investigation going on and you'll hear a lot more about it later today or tomorrow."

"Does that mean the murder you mentioned is connected in some way?"

"I'm not sure about that, but I'm told there are going to be arrests and charges brought. Seems to me there has to be some connection. I know the state's been looking into allegations of fraud and corruption by members of the DRT for some time, but the murder expedited their action. The killer's profile matches with a man who's been seen at the Alamo. He apparently knew the guard he killed. One thing I'm sure of, there's too much going on now to dismiss any single theory. But I should know more later today."

"That everything?" Nat asked.

"I'm trying to get more information but that's all I have right now. Any of it make sense to you? Have you heard anything different?"

Nat hesitated but still wasn't willing to share any more with his brother. "Not really," he said, "but call me if you find out anything else, especially if it's about Kalender. I'm wondering how deep he's in all of this."

"Not sure about that. Sorry, but I have to go. Talk to you later."

Nat clicked off the phone just as he pulled into the S.W. Niland parking lot. Practice was the furthest thing from his mind this morning but he still had a team to coach and a state championship to hunt. He just hoped Renee would find something in Papa Joe's records that would make sense of all they'd discovered over the past week.

Renee walked into the Statler Restaurant brimming with energy. She purposely subdued her excitement to avoid overwhelming Nat with her news. But it wasn't easy. He waited at a table in the corner of the steak house in his red S.W. Niland windbreaker and gray coaching pants, nursing an iced tea.

"How's practice today?" she asked.

"They're a little full of themselves after last week's big win but that's expected. We'll work it out of them. But I'm more interested in what you have to say."

The waitress took their order as Renee pulled out a spiral notebook from her large tote bag. "The possibility of a connection between the murdered security guard and some broader conspiracy at the Alamo has given me renewed hope about the note you received," she explained as the waitress brought her an iced coffee. "So I'm going to speculate a bit, although I'm confident in what I'm about to tell you." She then saw Nat refocus, training his eyes on her. "For starters," she continued, "it's clear to me that Shakes's notes do line up well with what I've learned in Papa Joe's research. I think it's safe to assume that *BT* means Bowie's Treasure, and I've made a series of educated guesses about the rest of the clue. *Not in the LBR*, however, made little sense to me so I'll leave that out for a second. But the last part of Shakes's note—*S had M*—is what really got me going. If you think about Kalender's story, and even Ricardo Rodriguez's letter, then it makes total sense to believe *S had M* means *Slave had Map*. If I'm right, then we can assume whoever Shakes got the note from thought Joe the slave died with a map to Bowie's Treasure and that Papa Joe—his descendant—had found it. And maybe that's why Papa Joe was killed. Someone was trying to find the map that Ricardo Rodriguez thought was lost all those years ago."

Nat nodded. "That makes sense," he said.

"Which points me to the one phrase I've been thinking about all day—*Find JB's trail*. I was sure that meant *Find Jim Bowie's trail*... and I'm guessing that's what the dig in the Alamo was intended to answer. Kalender thought Jim Bowie's trail led to that abandoned water well in the Alamo."

"I'm still with you," Nat said.

"But what if he was wrong? What if Kalender made a mistake. They sure didn't find any gold or silver in that well."

"Go on."

Renee drew a deep breath. "It dawned on me that the initials *JB* could mean something entirely different. Not Jim Bowie at all. And that's when it hit me."

Renee fought to keep her voice low but it was difficult to control her enthusiasm. Nat saw how her eyes sparkled, and when neither of them showed the slightest inclination to touch their food, which the waitress had quietly placed in front of them, she couldn't contain herself. "Remember when I told you that one of

Papa Joe's records suggested that Joe the slave lived in Brewton at the end of his life? The same research speculates that Joe was likely buried in Brewton when he died. Following me?"

"I think so."

"Stay with me here. Papa Joe should have died with full military honors—should have been buried in Arlington National Cemetery, or at least some comparable place, but instead chose to be interred in an old Civil War-era cemetery in Brewton, Alabama. Why?"

Nat shifted slightly in his chair and smiled widely. Renee realized she'd led him to the conclusion, which almost seemed logical now that she'd heard it out loud. "*JB* is James Buchanan," Nat said. "*JB's trail* leads to the James Buchanan Cemetery in Brewton!"

Renee's eyes met his. "The place where Papa Joe demanded to be buried. Who knows, but I think it's worth a look."

Every famous politician she'd ever read about got a break somewhere along the way that propelled their career to new heights, to new possibilities. Janet Nelson now had hers. The young woman fluffed her hair one last time, reapplied her lipstick, and headed out to her car. She had to look her best for the television crews. Although she still didn't have permission from the investigators to say anything, that wouldn't stop her once the arrest was made. Announcing that she'd rooted out the real plot within the DRT would be popular not only with her San Antonio district, but throughout the state. That's why she couldn't wait for any formal permission because she couldn't allow others to steal her glory. There was no time to waste. She'd announce her discovery of the records implicating Angelina de Zavala Gentry in the scandal—describe how her mentor had manipulated Akers and Butler to save herself—and explain that she'd left matters in the hands of the authorities. A headline-worthy story that would rocket her onto the front pages. Her political rise would be assured and, equally important, Angelina would no longer control her future.

CHAPTER 42

The Alamo—March 3, 1836
He'd lived his whole life as a warrior but neither a bullet nor a blade had ever put him down. This was different. An unseen killer inside his body, eating away at him, churning through his system like an uncontrolled parasite. Life was slowly slipping away. With Santa Anna's men looming in the distance, fate had rendered him unable to move, much less fight. Saving the hundred forty-seven brave souls sharing the Alamo with him was no longer possible; he was powerless to help his men defend against the Mexicans' attack. Cruel reality had placed his life and all of the defenders' in the hands of the incompetent Alabama transplant William Barret Travis.

Jim Bowie adjusted his position in bed and reached over for a drink from the water cup on his side table. "What day is it?" he asked his nurse.

"March third, sir," she replied.

"Where are the Mexicans?"

"Colonel Travis said they could attack any day now," the lady whispered. "They're surrounding us. What should I do?"

"Stay with me," he responded in a feeble voice. "When the Mexicans come for me, hide in the closet. Wait till I'm dead and then enter with your hands up. Even Santa Anna doesn't kill women. Now fetch me my pistols and knife. I want to be ready."

Bowie moved in and out of consciousness all afternoon, the fever knocking him out despite his effort to stay mentally ready. When lucid, he wondered if his friend James Butler Bonham had reached Colonel Fannin and whether the defenders had any hope that reinforcements would arrive from Goliad. Bonham, his great friend and confidante, who'd been the first to sign the resolution to protect the Alamo, remained the trapped soldiers' last best hope.

But even if Bonham failed, Bowie took comfort in the knowledge that his treasure was safe. The vast fortune he'd secured in the hills of Central Texas could be used to finance General Houston and the rest of his army against the Mexicans. That thought alone energized the sickly warrior and gave him hope that his death wouldn't be in vain: that his treasure would contribute to the Texans' cause for freedom far more than his body could now.

A distant cheering sound from outside his room raised Bowie from his pillow.

"Colonel Bowie, he's back," the nurse cried in excitement.

Bowie perked up. "What did you say?" he asked.

"Major Bonham just rode back into the fort!"

"Was he alone?"

"Yes sir, I believe so."

"Damn fool," Bowie grumbled under his breath. He crumpled back down into his bed. Bonham had failed; Fannin had not delivered the men Travis needed. "Ask Major Bonham to come see me right away," he told the nurse. "There's no time to waste." Bowie's eyes grew heavy as the grim reality set in on him. The Alamo would soon be in Santa Anna's hands.

CHAPTER 43

Having watched Kalender's desperate effort to locate the treasure in the old Brewton cemetery fail, Kruger decided to make his move. He'd directed Angelina into the car with Kalender's men, hurried them off, and then drove the seven hundred fifty miles back to Texas on his own. Without any new leads on the treasure, and with his identity as a murderer likely public, Kruger now had to lie low and bide his time. He'd tailed Angelina the past two days hoping she'd show him something new, and after waiting patiently for some action, she'd finally delivered. Except in this case, the revelation came in a totally unexpected way.

Kruger positioned himself outside Angelina's office building a safe distance in the shadows, but with a clear view to the dark suits in the parking lot. The surveillance team he'd spotted earlier looked ready to strike. Kruger checked his reflection in the rearview mirror and touched up the makeup covering the scar on his face. Satisfied, he then reached over to his cup of coffee, gulped down a slug, and slumped into his seat.

Twenty minutes later, the familiar black town car pulled into Angelina's parking spot near the front of the building. By this time, the suits were gone. Given the lack of activity, Angelina had no reason to suspect that she was being watched. Frankie guided the old lady out of her car and helped her toward her office. Angelina's black hair flapped in the breeze and Kruger could see she was mad about something. Fifteen feet from the front door, a man in dark sunglasses approached her and held out some sort of identification. Frankie jumped in front of the agent but was immediately pulled back by a second man who'd sprung out of a nearby van. Seconds later, two more suits arrived and surrounded the group. Kruger could see Angelina barking, but no one seemed to care. A few people from inside the building started watching the scene.

Kruger studied the agents but the distance from his car made it difficult to see their faces. One man took command and pulled Angelina's arms around her back and cuffed her. Another did the same to Frankie. A black sedan then pulled up and the leader loaded Angelina inside. Frankie was shoved into a second car.

The minute the last agent's vehicle pulled away, Kruger reached over into his console, grabbed his sunglasses, and revved up his engine. He then quietly drove his blue Taurus out the other end of the parking lot.

The crisp, wide-sky, early evening air invigorated Nat. He looked over at Renee, who had the window on the passenger's side down, enjoying the breeze on her face. With the arrest in San Antonio of the woman who'd masterminded the Alamo dig and a manhunt started for her accomplice—the criminal he now assumed killed Papa Joe—Nat felt a sense of calm for the first time in weeks. The news from Joseph hadn't confirmed Nat's speculation about Papa Joe's murder, or that Bowie's Treasure was any more real, but it did bring closure to several of the mysteries that had plagued him since his grandfather's death. And having Renee by his side also brought him peace, even as he continued to struggle with rebuilding their relationship.

"There it is," Nat said to Renee, pointing toward the small cemetery in the distance.

Nat parked his car and led Renee to the side entrance of the James Buchanan Cemetery. The only activity inside the perimeter cyclone fence was a lone worker shoveling dirt into one of the grave sites near a huge white oak in the back of the property.

"Sir," Nat said, approaching the man. He recognized the worker once he saw his face.

"Huh?" the man replied.

Nat remembered the funeral director, Jerald, from the memorial service for Papa Joe: a somber dark suit with little personality. But dressed in blue jeans and a plaid shirt with rolled-up sleeves, Jerald looked different. His taut, sinewy arms and calloused hands indicated funeral-home director wasn't his only occupation. "It's Jerald, isn't it?" Nat asked. "We met at Joe Travis's funeral."

"Yes we did. I'm the funeral director ... also the caretaker, owner, you name it." Jerald chuckled. "And you're Joe Travis's grandson? Come back to visit?"

"Yes, along with my friend Renee," Nat answered. "What happened here?"

"Grave robbers. Happens every now and then in these old cemeteries. Some of these Civil War folks liked to bury their kin with rifles, jewels, and other valuables. Times are tough."

"Did they get anything?" Nat asked.

"Not sure. The rotted casket was moved around but I have no idea what's in these old things." Jerald smiled. "Anyway, the grave robbers took off when I rousted them. Can I help you with something, Mr. Travis?"

Nat's heart stopped when he heard Jerald's explanation but Renee seemed unmoved and wandered off. "We never focused during the whirlwind of burying my grandfather," Nat started, "but we're interested in this place. Just a little curious how a cemetery in southern Alabama came to be named for James Buchanan ... and why my grandfather chose to be buried here."

"I can answer the first question easy enough," Jerald replied.

"I guess you don't know the stories about the 'Old Public Functionary.'"

"Old who?"

"Sorry, that was one of the nicknames used for President Buchanan. He had a couple of others that were much less flattering."

"Hold on," Nat said. "Mind walking with me and explaining this to Renee? She's a history professor and I'm sure she'd like to hear it."

Jerald nodded and followed Nat to the front of the cemetery where Renee was busily studying the weathered monument plaque near the entrance gate.

"Look here," Renee pointed.

Nat read the simple monument sign he'd failed to notice at the time of Papa Joe's funeral. Jerald waited while he finished.

James Buchanan

A native Pennsylvanian, James Buchanan served a long and distinguished career in politics before ascending to the Presidency in 1857. Prior to that time, Buchanan served as Secretary of State, a member of the United States Senate and as the United States Minister to Russia and England. Buchanan gained the democratic nomination in 1857 and was elected the 15th president of the United States. President Buchanan served during one of the most volatile periods in American history. During his Term, President Buchanan annexed the states of Minnesota, Oregon and Kansas into the Union. His support of the southern way of life will never be forgotten.

Cemetery dedication March, 23 1863 by Harriet Lane and the family of former Vice President William Rufus DeVane King.

Nat turned to Renee and said, "Jerald knows all of the history behind this place. Very interesting."

"I'm sure it is," she concurred.

"My family's owned this property a long time," Jerald conceded. "Actually, since the time the cemetery was dedicated in 1863. This is our little piece of history."

"You're a King?" Renee asked.

"Yep, but my interest is in the history of these grounds, not my genealogy. I also like to research obscure vice-presidents from Alabama. Especially those named King," he added with a long drawl, pointing back to the sign.

All three of them smiled. "Then maybe you can answer my other question," Nat interjected. "Do you know why Joe Travis wanted to be buried here? I didn't notice earlier but there's not a single headstone with a date after 1920."

"That question surprises me," Jerald answered. "I would have guessed it was a family decision. He always spoke so highly of you during our visits."

"I loved the man more than you know but he was secretive with much of his life. I think it was his military experience." Nat looked over at Renee for a reaction but she appeared distracted, focused elsewhere. Nat couldn't understand her attitude.

"Well, it's really quite simple," Jerald answered. "Most of the folks buried here were slaves. Few had formal names and in most cases they were buried anonymously or with limited information on their headstones. We have woefully incomplete records from the burials. Your grandfather was the first contemporary request for burial here in my lifetime."

"Why'd you allow it?"

"You really don't know much, do you?" Jerald replied. "First of all, he'd convinced me that he had family buried here."

"Family?" Nat asked.

"Like me, your grandfather knew a lot about history, about this cemetery, and about those laid to rest here. He provided me with evidence that his ancestors were buried on these grounds and it was important to him that he be put down with them. I could hardly deny that request, could I? Especially from a distinguished veteran like your grandfather."

"Let me guess which one of my ancestors." Nat speculated, "A slave named Joe."

"I guess you know more than you let on," Jerald smiled, "though I never confirmed that Joe the slave was buried here. But there was enough evidence linking him to Brewton at the end of his life that I finally gave in. Even then, it wasn't easy to convince the state to reopen the cemetery for a new burial—we'd received a protected historical designation and had been closed for years—but your grandfather was persistent. I only received approval shortly before his death."

"The old man never ceases to amaze," Renee said as if to show she was still listening.

Nat smiled ruefully and then his face tightened. "Tell me that grave site you're working on didn't belong to Joe the slave."

Renee nodded knowingly.

"I'm not sure," Jerald replied. "The headstone's unmarked." He pondered for a moment, scratching his chin. "But it's possible. The records I looked at this morning show a slave burial in 1884 so the timing's about right, but there's no way to be sure."

Renee then stood up and walked back to the dedication plaque she'd been studying earlier. Nat could tell she'd figured something out. "Let's see what she's up to," he said to Jerald. The two men walked over and stood behind Renee. Nat looked down at the plaque and then raised his head and followed Renee's eyes forward. Before him was a trail leading from the Buchanan plaque directly to the disturbed grave site. A huge white oak tree framed the solitary headstone.

"*JB's trail*," she said.

CHAPTER 44

Renee had sniffed it the minute they arrived at the James Buchanan Cemetery. She'd allowed the suspense over the mysterious note Nat received in San Antonio to override her historian's sense of good judgment. Upon seeing the isolated, century-old cemetery, she knew immediately that she'd made a mistake. And the disturbed grave site suggested to her that a desperate Kalender had probably made the same miscalculation. In that instant she'd understood that *JB's trail*, whether real or imagined, could never point to a cemetery in Brewton, Alabama. It was completely illogical. If Joe the slave had found Bowie's Treasure, why would he drag it all the way back to Alabama? Why would he have buried it in such an obscure location? No, the quixotic tale of buried treasure and the siege of the Alamo had left her reaching, not thinking. Most likely Shakes's note was part of a scheme.

Even then, Renee wasn't ready to give up. There was an uneasiness clawing in her stomach and banging on her brain that wouldn't stop. She still believed in Bowie's Treasure and she couldn't bring herself to write it off just because of an embarrassing mistake. There were too many connections and consistencies in her research to turn away. There was more to the story—she knew it.

Renee reconsidered the letter Enrique Rodriguez had given her and wondered again if she'd overlooked something. It was short, just one page, but still had more confirming information about the treasure than anything she'd read up to that point. The words were familiar to her by now:

Son,

I've met some brave, fascinating people in these past few months while stationed in England. They come from homes scattered all across our great country, and each has a unique story to tell. But one stands out. I've become close friends with a black man from Alabama who I believe has a fascinating connection to our family.

When I was a child—just a few years older than you are today—my grandfather told me a story of our ancestors and their ties to the Texas revolution and the famous battle of the Alamo. You will likely read textbooks in school about Col. William Barret Travis, Jim Bowie and Davy Crockett because all of them famously died during the siege, but my story has to do with a young slave who survived the battle. His name was Joe.

Your ancestor, a man we only know as Enrique, came to Texas some time before General Santa Anna's march on the Alamo and found work as a groom on a ranch in Bailey's Prairie. My friend claims his ancestry ties to a slave living in Texas at the same time. A young man who worked for Col. Travis—the same Joe. Why does it matter? Because Joe the slave supposedly made it out of the Alamo alive with a treasure map. And your great-grandfather told me once that Enrique saw that map while at Bailey's Prairie and searched his entire life for the trail to the lost treasure.

Tales of that map and Bowie's Treasure have now been in our family for generations and I hope that will mean something to you one day. History matters, my son. Never forget who you are ...

The letter moved on to other matters but the main premise—that a map existed pointing to a treasure that survived the Alamo—confirmed everything about Papa Joe's story. But the letter offered no details about the map's ultimate whereabouts, and she figured that's why she'd foolishly bitten on the idea that the security guard's clue led to the James Buchanan Cemetery. She looked at the note again and pondered the question:

BT - moved? Not in the LBR. Find JB's trail. S had M.

Renee had spent the last eighteen hours digging back into Papa Joe's research, trying to find a new starting place for the story. She'd pored over document after document, article after article, looking for some fresh angle before finally concluding that Kalender had been right, that the Alamo was the only truly logical hiding place. Every clue pointed there, *JB's trail* or not. After several more hours hunched over the computer screen, Renee leaned back in her chair and shook her head. Throughout her time at Emory, she often took breaks from her research, closed her eyes, and meditated for short intervals hoping to bring clarity to her mind. She leaned back now and let her mind go.

JB's trail. The words wouldn't leave her. Why did that phrase continue tormenting her brain? *JB's trail*—it had to be *JB's trail.* The key had to be in those letters.

And then Renee realized the answer had been staring at her the whole time. *JB's trail* was indeed the clue she hadn't properly deciphered. It was the single connecting point that tied all of her research together. If she was right, Papa Joe had in fact been researching the trails of many soldiers into the Alamo, but, more important, one the other direction as well. *JB's trail* wasn't a route to a location inside the Alamo; it was one leading out.

CHAPTER 45

Nat pulled into his driveway following practice. He couldn't remember a time in his career where he'd screamed so much at his players. He'd never been a screamer—always preferring to leave that to his assistants—but it had been necessary today. The Niland players had grown cocky after their big win over Riverview and the whip had needed to be applied. Nat had done his best to work the attitude right out of them.

He looked toward his garage and was surprised to see Renee leaning against her car on the street in front of his house. Realizing he was grouchy, he tried to shake himself out of his post-practice mood.

"You look tired," Renee said as he stepped out of his truck.

"Tough practice. The kids are feeling a little too good about themselves right now. That's why this will be our most difficult game of the year even though we're heavily favored. Too much confidence can make you sloppy. Amazing how much things can slide in a short time. I've got a lot of work to do in the next couple of days."

"Bad time, isn't it?" Renee asked. "I can call you later."

"Not at all," Nat replied, raising his hand in the air. "You just caught me a little raw."

"I understand," she said.

Nat realized he needed to pick up his attitude or Renee might run away. "Why don't we go grab a quick bite," he suggested. "I don't need to start studying game film yet." He forced a smile.

Renee hesitated but Nat opened his passenger door before she could respond. "Please," he tilted his head, "get in."

Nat drove them to the Oaks Café on Douglas Avenue. Little was discussed during the short trip over; conversation picked up after the hostess had seated them in a corner booth. Nat then looked at Renee and said, "Sorry about the attitude. I shouldn't take a bad practice home with me." He smiled and shrugged. "It's just a game, right? So tell me what you found out today?" He gingerly reached across the table and cupped his hand on top of Renee's. She looked at him curiously but didn't reject the advance. For several seconds, they remained quiet and stared at each other, as if the gesture needed time to breathe. Eventually, the waitress interrupted them with two glasses of iced tea.

"What's on your mind?" Nat asked, squeezing Renee's hand tighter.

She smiled and he felt a newfound confidence surge through his body.

"Okay," Renee said, "here we go. I spent the night and all of today trying to make sense of what we'd learned. Studied everything I could find about Jim Bowie and James Buchanan. At one point I wrote off Shakes's note entirely. But the more I kept putting it away, the more I couldn't let it go. I thought there had to be a clue I'd missed somewhere, especially during the period Bowie waited to die on that cot in the long-barracks room of the Alamo. But nothing explained the *JB's trail* clue, nothing but the most obvious thing in front of me."

"And what's that?" Nat asked. He leaned forward in his chair.

"What if," Renee speculated, "there was a third *JB*? What if the initials referred to another man, a man Jim Bowie and William Travis trusted as much as anyone else who fought in the Alamo?"

"I'm with you," Nat agreed.

"James Bonham. Actually, James Butler Bonham, aka the messenger of the Alamo."

"Never heard of him." Nat smiled broadly as he saw how pumped up Renee was about her discovery.

"I know it may be putting too much emphasis on Shakes's note but it makes perfect sense to me. Bonham was a confidante of Bowie and Travis, was committed to the Texans' cause, and, most importantly, had the opportunity."

"To do what?"

The natural beauty in Renee's face lit up as she dug into her story and Nat could see how hard she was trying to control her excitement. He stared at the small dimple in her cheek and watched as it seemed to pulsate with her every word. "To move the treasure," she said emphatically. "The Mexicans' siege started on the twenty-third of February in 1836. The Texans hunkered down for several days in the Alamo under cannon fire but it soon became apparent they were doomed without reinforcements. Santa Anna's attack was inevitable. At that point, Travis called on his best friend, James Butler Bonham, to take a personal message to Colonel Fannin in Goliad requesting assistance. There's not much known about Bonham's ride to Goliad but the majority of historians agree that he left the Alamo on February twenty-seventh and returned unsuccessfully on March third with news that Fannin—who was unwilling to expose his small army to what he considered certain death—wouldn't be coming to their aid. The Alamo fell and all of its men, including Bonham, Bowie, and Travis, died on March sixth. Do you follow?"

"Yes, but what's that got to do with the treasure?"

"What if Bowie's Treasure wasn't buried in the Alamo? What if Bonham had a secret mission? Jim Bowie may well have given a map to Joe the slave but it's likely he did that after he'd ordered Bonham to move the treasure to a secure location. If the map is truly lost, the only clue leading to Bonham's secret hiding place is his ride out of the Alamo. That's my answer to the inscription *Find JB's trail*."

"That's some theory," Nat gasped, "but don't you think it relies too heavily on Shakes's note?"

"A fair question, but there are more facts supporting my theory than you might think." The waitress walked up to their table and refilled their glasses. Nat finally let go of Renee's hand to add sugar and lemon to his tea. Renee then continued, "No resource I can find ever mapped Bonham's famous ride. Given that he died along with every other person he came in contact with that week, no one ever had reason to question his mission. There's plenty of evidence Travis and Bowie knew their men were doomed and that sending Bonham away for reinforcements made little sense. The Alamo needed every last man. Bonham had to have a mission of some sort beyond seeking out Fannin's help. I think he agreed to move the treasure to safety so the Mexicans wouldn't get their hands on it. That was Bonham's true mission."

"Wow!" Nat exclaimed. He drew a deep breath. "So where does that leave ... us?" he asked.

Renee smiled and Nat knew he'd finally used the right words. "If I'm right about *JB's trail*," Renee said, "we just have to find out where it leads."

CHAPTER 46

The Alamo—February 27, 1836

James Bonham knew the Texans' fading hope of surviving the Alamo rested entirely on his ability to gain reinforcements from Goliad. He also knew that Colonel Fannin was unlikely to leave the safety of Presidio La Bajia and march his limited force into the teeth of Santa Anna's army. Fannin had already turned him down once. Yet, Bonham accepted his mission without reservation, while still hoping his orders would change and he'd be allowed to stay in the Alamo to help his comrades prepare for the Mexicans' attack.

Bonham was the right man for the dangerous mission. He'd been a confidante of Travis's since their childhood days in Red Bank, South Carolina, and was loyal to his old friend. Upon hearing of Travis's plight in the Alamo, Bonham had ridden to San Antonio in December, 1835, and immediately plunged himself into the Texans' struggle. Within weeks, he received a commission as a lieutenant in the Texas Cavalry, reconnected with Travis, and gained status among the small band of defenders in the Spanish mission. His commitment was immediate and complete. And even though Bonham saw no reason to go back to the reluctant Fannin for help in late February, 1836, he would do so if asked by his friend.

But Bonham's mission changed when he was called in to see the sickly Jim Bowie on the eve of his departure.

Every soldier in the Alamo knew that Bowie was near death from an unknown ailment, but even on his last legs the forty-year-old warrior remained a revered figure among the troops. Bonham was surprised by Bowie's call. When he arrived, he bypassed Bowie's weak handshake and reached over and embraced his commander.

"*I'll bring them back, Colonel,*" Bonham proclaimed as he clenched Bowie around the shoulders, "*even if I have to tie a rope around the whole of them.*" Bonham then helped Bowie back down onto his pillow and sat on the edge of his cot.

"*You've done everything you can for the men,*" Bowie said in a feeble, barely audible voice, "*but you know good and well that Fannin isn't going to leave Goliad to help us.*"

"*Probably right,*" Bonham answered, "*but Colonel Travis has given me the order and I'll fulfill my mission. No need for you to worry.*"

"*That's not the purpose of this visit,*" Bowie responded with a furrowed brow. "*I'm not doubting your loyalty, James. But what if I told you this mission could do more for our cause than all of Fannin's troops?*"

"*I don't know what you mean, sir.*"

"*Listen, Jim, and listen closely. No one can know what I'm about to tell you. No one. Not even Travis.*"

"*I understand, sir.*"

"*Your mission is going to change.*"

CHAPTER 47

Nat flicked on his car radio. He rarely changed the dial off *The Ticket's* twenty-four-hour sports talk show but tonight he was in the mood for something different. Watching game films of his team's narrow victory the night before had temporarily dulled his appetite for Alabama football, and with the Ole Miss game near kickoff, the radio was filled with nothing else. Brewton had a few non-Crimson Tide radio stations, primarily gospel and country, but Nat had found a scratchy oldies station broadcast out of Pensacola that suited him fine. The Motown sounds were still Nat's favorites even though his players laughed at him every time he cranked up one of his favorite Spinners' tunes. He paid no mind; he'd long ago given up trying to figure out the sounds coming out of his players' headphones.

With his eyes focused down while he fiddled with the radio dial, Nat missed the small child who darted in front of him on his bicycle. By the time he looked up, Nat was nearly on top of the boy. He jammed on his brakes and screeched to a halt only a few feet away from catastrophe. Nat jumped out of his truck and ran toward the child, but the youngster sped off without stopping, never looking back. Relieved but in shock, Nat bent over, caught his breath, and clenched his stomach. He'd never come so close to a fatal accident and turned toward the skies to thank God for the miracle. Only then did he see the blue Taurus pulled over to the side of the road behind him. The car looked familiar—perhaps he'd glimpsed it earlier when he'd left the practice facility, but he wasn't sure. Was someone watching him? He could see the outline of a large figure behind the steering wheel with his head down and the sight sent chills through Nat's body. Why had the man stayed in the car when he'd likely witnessed a near-tragic accident? Nat's mind raced to Renee. Was she safe? Was someone truly after them? He picked up his cell phone and frantically dialed Renee's number.

"Nat," she answered.

"You okay?"

"Sure, what's wrong?"

The relief found in those words overwhelmed Nat and he almost dropped his phone. "Nothing, nothing at all," he said. "But I'm coming by."

Renee hesitated as if unsure of what to say. "Sure," she replied, "but what's this all about?"

"I'll explain when I get there," he said. "Give me ten minutes."

Renee opened the door to her mother's house where Nat waited on the porch sweating from the temples. He had the blank look of a frightened man. "What's going on?" she asked.

Nat said nothing but instead reached out and grabbed her around the small of the back and pulled her to him. He wrapped both arms around her waist and touched his lips to her ear. "I've been a fool," he said. "I should've done this a long time ago."

Although Renee had envisioned this moment in the stadium parking lot, Nat's aggressiveness caught her off guard. But she didn't care. She reached around and grabbed his neck and pulled him forward. Their mouths locked together, his ferocity surprising her, but she was excited to feel the strength and power of his taut frame for the first time. Their luscious, out-of-control kiss sent them staggering across the porch like drunken teenagers. Renee felt her body light up and surge in ways that eliminated all hope of self-control. She wanted to rip off Nat's clothes and explore every inch of his body that very minute but caught herself just long enough to pull away before they stumbled down the stairs. "My mother's inside," she breathlessly explained. "She might think a dog fight broke out on her porch."

"Come to my house," Nat pleaded. "Right now."

Renee inhaled. "Think that's a good idea?" she asked, although she already knew the answer.

Nat pulled her tight against his hard body and kissed her delirious a second time before separating to stare her in the eye. "You're not getting away from me this time," he whispered.

CHAPTER 48

Nat's truck weaved all over the road as Renee nibbled on his ear and stroked the back of his head while he drove. He turned one time to kiss her and after that lunge found himself halfway into the median before recovering his bearings. They finally made it to Nat's driveway where they immediately grabbed and clawed at each other as if their bodies were on fire. The soon-to-be lovers bounced from one side of his vehicle to the other, neither of them wanting to stop long enough to reach for the door handles. And then Nat pulled her from the truck and propelled her backward toward the house, unable to remove his mouth from hers even for a second. They burst through the front door, ripped off their clothes, and clenched their bodies together.

"Damn," Nat said while catching his breath, "they didn't make professors like this when I was in school."

Renee chuckled and pressed her finger against his lips. Nat then guided her to the floor and they consumed each other's bodies like wild animals. Renee's frenzy finally overwhelmed Nat and he ceded control, allowing her to steer him into position and lead him inside of her. Their bodies immediately gyrated and bucked in unison as Renee stretched her legs tightly around Nat's taut body and pulled him in deeper. Nat felt himself almost lose consciousness, panting desperately while she moaned, crying out as he climaxed with Renee's nails dug deeply into his back. He plummeted to his side and they lay together for several minutes without saying a word.

Delirious, Nat had almost missed it. Inaudible at first, but then he heard it again. A purring.

"Are you ok?" he asked, raising up to look into Renee's eyes.

She nodded and leaned into him. "I'm more than okay," she cooed.

Nat understood the message and reached out and placed her head on his chest and started gently stroking her hair. She nuzzled into his shoulder and laid her arm across his stomach. She then pulled his midsection in as if she wanted to clamp him to her side. "I love you, Nat Travis," she whispered.

"How'd I get this lucky," Nat answered in an equally soft voice. "And … I love you, too, Ms. Travis."

They'd rested quietly for almost thirty minutes before Nat said, "The kitchen's calling."

"Sounds like a good idea," Renee answered, "but I'm feeling a little exposed."

"You're beautiful." Nat hiked himself up on his arm and stared at Renee in appreciation for several seconds. She playfully pushed her hands in his face as if to shield herself from the attention. "You're more than beautiful," he gushed. Nat then stood up and sauntered to his bureau where he grabbed a couple of oversized T-shirts. After throwing the crimson jersey over her shoulders, Renee followed Nat into the kitchen. He ushered her into a chair and then walked to the counter where he started brewing coffee. He then turned and began scouring the refrigerator. "Not much here," he conceded, "but cold pizza and bologna."

"Shocking," Renee replied, before walking over and turning on the Alabama football game on the small television set between the microwave and stove.

"While I'm fixing this gourmet meal," Nat said, as he threw a bologna packet on the counter, "tell me you've figured out something new about the treasure?"

"Good thing you got off your duff this afternoon and came over," she responded, "or I was going to find a new sidekick. It might surprise you but I decided to call Kalender."

"You're kidding."

"At first, he was reluctant to talk, but when he figured out that you weren't after him, he started spilling his guts faster than I could write. I think he's so relieved that he wasn't caught up in that Alamo-DRT scandal that he wants to run as far away from Bowie's Treasure as possible. We talked a long time."

"So what did you find out?" Nat snuck a peek at the Alabama score and saw that the Tide was leading comfortably.

"We went over his research with Papa Joe, his conclusions about Bowie's Treasure, and his futile excavation project. But given my theory, it was our discussion about the Texas Revolution after the Alamo that I was most interested in."

"What do you mean?" Nat asked, while taking over the bologna sandwiches and two cups of coffee. He sat by Renee at the kitchen table. At the same time, the Alabama fullback rumbled into the end zone to make the score 52-17.

"Glad you asked," Renee said, sipping on her coffee. "Now pay attention." She smiled, directing his eyes away from the television set. "The next major battle in the Mexican war after the Alamo was the Battle of Coleto. Kalender described it to me in great detail. After his big victory at the Alamo, Santa Anna marched his troops to Goliad in pursuit of Colonel Fannin's men who were bunkered in Fort Defiance. Kalender described quite colorfully the short battle that led to the surrender of the three hundred Texans in the fort. But here's the thing that really got my attention. Fannin's troops were held captive for a week after the battle with meager rations, but with the full expectation they'd be set free to return home. Instead, as they were being released, Santa Anna led them into the streets of Goliad, lined them up in two columns, and executed them. The only man left standing was Fannin and he was taken back into the courtyard of the presidio, blindfolded, and shot in the face. The bodies of Fannin and all of his soldiers were burned that day."

"Damn," Nat exclaimed.

"But here's where it all fits into my theory about Bowie's Treasure," Renee continued. "Every article I've read suggests that Bonham's famous ride to Goliad before the Alamo fell, before the Battle of Coleto, was to seek troop support, but virtually every account also says Bonham had gone to Fannin at Fort Defiance a couple of weeks earlier without success. Why then did Bonham agree to go back? Why did Bonham make a futile effort through extremely dangerous conditions to convince a commander who'd rejected him only weeks before? That's when it hit me. No one knows what Bonham did on his ride because all of the troops in Fort Defiance, along with Fannin, were killed. No one lived to tell the story."

Renee paused to build the suspense.

"Like I told you," she explained, "I think Bonham had a different mission. He was sent to retrieve Bowie's Treasure, transport it to Fort Defiance for safekeeping, and then secondarily, to try to convince Fannin to send troops to the Alamo. That's why I'm convinced *JB's trail* leads directly to Goliad."

"Goliad?"

Renee was now rolling. "I want to go to Fort Defiance," she said. "The old fort's still standing down there and something's telling me that we need to check it out." She paused, but Nat could see that nothing he could say would dampen her enthusiasm. And he wasn't about to worry her with the story about the suspicious character he'd seen earlier that day.

"Good thing we have a bye week coming up," Nat finally said. He caressed Renee with expectant eyes and her mouth broke into a wide smile. And with that, Nat was heading off to San Antonio … again.

Nat arranged for his head of school and assistant coaches to cover for him a couple of days, explaining he'd be back by Wednesday. With an open week ahead for his team, Nat had time for a quick trip to Texas without interrupting the next game's preparations.

Nat and Renee arrived at the San Antonio airport by mid-afternoon two days later filled with ideas but short of any real plan. Even if Renee's speculation about Bowie's Treasure was correct—that buried below Presidio La Bajia/Fort Defiance was a treasure of incalculable historical significance—Nat had no idea where to start looking for it. Any plan was also frustrated by the fact that Fort Defiance was newly renovated and had very little original structure left standing. Nat figured any clues embedded in or below the stone walls of the presidio were likely cleared away during the renovation or extinguished by years of neglect and erosion. But that didn't matter. Something had crept into his brain—was it Renee?—telling him the old fort had been waiting on him for years.

Nat reserved one of the two rooms created for tourists inside Fort Defiance known as The Quarters. The rustic guest rooms had previously served as the officers' barracks in the days of the Texas Revolution and retained much of the feel of that era. By staying on site, Nat and Renee hoped to create enough time to search the old presidio at their leisure without gathering too much attention.

When they approached Fort Defiance, Nat was immediately struck by the detail of the restoration project on the old Spanish mission. Nothing short of a time warp to a distant past. Presidio La Bajia's original architecture had been brilliantly reinvented, and its centerpiece, Our Lady of Loreto Chapel, revived to its former glory. The work had maintained all aspects of the character of the mission, including the use of quarried limestone from Central Texas, so the fortress remained in perfect proportion to the original structure. The stone walls, knotty wooden doorways, and barred windows all looked authentic.

"You can sure feel the isolation of those settlers, can't you?" Nat observed as he got out of the car and stared at the building.

Renee smiled. "Kind of like living in Brewton," she replied with a wink.

Nat grabbed her hand. "Let's go see our room."

After meeting a frail elderly docent named Ethel Barnard in the visitor's center—who offered to show them around—Nat and Renee dropped their bags off and walked around the grounds. They intentionally left the excavation tools they'd picked up in San Antonio in the rental car.

Once they'd made a preliminary inspection of their surroundings, Nat asked, "So what's your plan, madam historian?"

Renee raised her eyes to the heavens and shook her head. "Not a clue, Mr. Travis, but it will come to me soon enough. I can feel it in the air."

CHAPTER 49

Nat's second full day with Renee locked in the new wonderful reality in his life. For the first time since Papa Joe had passed, he felt at peace. His ease in Renee's company gave him comfort they would be good together and that his earlier hesitation and concern about the repercussions of their relationship, especially with Joseph, had been entirely misguided. None of that mattered, not anymore, particularly not at his age. Nat reached over to the empty space next to him. He raised up and saw Renee sitting in the leather chair across the room quietly drinking coffee and reading from her laptop screen.

"Bored with me?" he asked.

"I think you've worn yourself out," she said. "I haven't heard snoring like that since that old locomotive in Brewton ran outside my window every night." She smiled. "But I love you anyway."

"Snoring? Me?" Nat shook his head as if he was trying to chase away the demons. "I guess I'll need to work on that."

"If that's your worst habit, I think we'll be just fine." Renee hiked her leg up onto the arm of the chair seductively.

"Hold that thought." Nat grinned. He then crawled out of bed and stretched out his arms.

"Get cleaned up first," Renee said to head him off. "We have a lot of work to do."

Nat lowered his head like a disappointed child before turning toward the bathroom. He showered, brushed his teeth, and threw on a pair of jeans and a T-shirt. When he walked back in the room, Renee still hadn't moved.

"What's got your attention?" he asked.

"I'm just studying all the information I can find about this place. I could be entirely wrong about *JB's trail* but I don't want to miss out just because I haven't read enough. I'm really hoping Ethel can help us and she knows things about the presidio that I can't decipher from these websites."

"I guess it's time to go find out," Nat said with mock enthusiasm.

"Don't worry," Renee said. "You'll enjoy it."

They walked to the front entrance of the presidio where Ethel Barnard waited, looking far more energetic than she had the day before. The color in her cheeks had filled up and she was dressed in a colorful Nike jogging suit and running shoes.

"You kids ready?" she asked.

Nat could tell that whatever lay ahead had already been planned by Renee and Ethel earlier that morning.

"Yes ma'am," Nat saluted, stealing a glance at Renee, who had a sheepish look on her face. Ethel then led them into the museum where she launched into a discussion about the various artifacts displayed in the room, all of which had been recovered during one of the fort's many excavation projects. Mexican army bayonets, Spanish coins, riding spurs, and numerous plates and bowls lined the walls of the small room, and it was obvious Ethel took pride in describing every one of them. To Nat's relief, after about an hour the elderly woman ran out of items to talk about. Renee, on the other hand, appeared entranced by every detail of Ethel's commentary, especially the intersection between the Battle of Coleto, the Mexican massacre of Colonel Fannin's troops, and the heroic acts of the Angel of Goliad, the woman who saved numerous Texans from slaughter at the hands of Santa Anna's men.

By the time the tour shifted to the chapel and the history of the statue of Our Lady of Loreto, Nat's interest level had dimmed to the point that he started signaling Renee to wrap it up. But she ignored him and remained focused on Ethel and her winding stories. Nat soon felt like a trapped inmate, or, worse, a man hopelessly in love.

"Care to step into the quadrangle now?" Ethel finally asked, showing no sign of fatigue. Nat wondered if Ethel had a power pack hitched to her waist.

"Absolutely," Nat answered with a touch of attitude, enough to prompt Renee to gently step on his foot.

"Ms. Barnard, you've been so nice to us," Renee interjected. "We don't want to trouble you any further."

"No problem at all," Ethel replied. "It's not often I get a young couple this interested in the presidio. Your questions are so detailed … they're quite a challenge. I'm happy to help you. Even wore my comfortable shoes in case you wanted to look further around."

Nat sensed he was now in for another couple of hours of boredom but nodded agreeably. Renee grinned at him.

The trio then stepped into the huge open-air area of the presidio. "This is the quadrangle," Ethel said. The large square-shaped yard was covered with groomed Bermuda grass and several paved walkways that led to seating areas nestled within the twenty-foot stone walls facing the outside world. On each corner of the fort, bastions had been erected to replicate the lookout towers used by the Texans to defend the presidio from invaders.

"Since you two seem so interested in the Alamo and the Texas Revolution," she continued, "you'll probably want to know that James Butler Bonham slept in the barracks room over there the night he rode in to deliver William Barret Travis's message." Ethel caught her breath. "And right over there," she pointed out, directing her finger at a location near the chapel, "is where the Mexicans shot Colonel Fannin in the face, after massacring his troops. There's a lot of history in these walls."

"Do you know much about Bonham's ride?" Nat asked, suddenly alert.

Ethel smiled. "Which ride?" she quipped. "I may be the foremost expert on the subject you'll ever run across. I guess you can understand that an old lady like me has little else to do while sitting around in this Godforsaken place."

Ethel finished showing Nat and Renee every remaining inch of Presidio La Bajia, including the monument to James Fannin and his men erected outside the walls of the fort. By the time they'd finished, Nat was exhausted.

"Not a full-blown tour," Ethel said as they got ready to part, "but I hope you got a sense of the place. I have another visitor who wants to learn more about La Bajia as well. Imagine that … two tours in one day. That's a week's worth of work for me." Ethel smiled as she waved good-bye.

"That woman must drink coffee by the potful," Nat said afterwards, while walking with Renee to their room.

"That she does," Renee answered. "What a splendid lady. I can assure you there's very little in the marketing material for this place that tells the story like she does. Amazing."

"Joseph called," Nat said, glancing down at his cell phone. "Hold on." They walked into their room and Nat retrieved the message privately.

"Nat," Joseph started, "the school told me that you were traveling. Where are you? What's going on? I wanted you to know that a woman named Angelina de Zavala Gentry will probably be indicted today in the Alamo mess. They have enough evidence to prosecute her for several crimes, and I hear rumors she may even be connected to that guard's murder. And what I didn't know until today is she appears to be a real fanatic. Her office is a virtual museum of historical artifacts from the Texas Revolution. If the security guard's murder is somehow connected to her, and by extension the treasure, then the shooter likely worked for her … and he's still not in custody. You need to be careful. I'm also beginning to think you're holding out on me. Call me as soon as you can."

Nat pondered Joseph's message for a moment before looking over at Renee. Fear ran up his spine as he thought back to the ominous figure he'd seen in the blue Taurus in Brewton. He still hadn't mentioned him to Renee, but he couldn't hold back any longer.

"Listen to this," he said.

After playing the call on the speaker, Nat asked, "What do you think?"

Renee held his hand.

"I'm worried, too," he said, placing his arm around her shoulder. "It sounds like we need to be extra careful from now on. If this Angelina character hired someone to kill our security guard, there's a real-life assassin out there."

CHAPTER 50

Renee tried to assure Nat that her plan to search the fort at night would be safer than doing so in broad daylight. Nat hated the idea of sneaking around the grounds like a prowler, but Renee assured him it was safe because the presidio's lone security guard never left his small surveillance room. Only the Goliad police force's hourly drive-by, she'd warned, presented any real cause for concern. The bigger problem for Nat, however, was that most of the areas in the fort he'd visited with Renee and Ethel Barnard earlier in the day carried coded alarm systems and securely locked doors. He had no idea how Renee planned to access the barracks room without tripping an alarm, but she convinced him there would be no trouble.

Nat followed Renee outside their room into the crisp night air just after midnight. There were no clouds in the sky and a full moon. Both wore climbing shorts, hiking boots, and multi-pocketed shirts. Their small shovels, trowels, metal detector, and flashlights were loaded securely into their backpacks.

"So what's next?" Nat asked.

"Follow me," Renee directed. "We just need to walk around the perimeter of the building until we get to the eastern wall where the barracks is. Ethel told me there is a secret room there that the Texans built to hide the women and children in case of an attack. She said it was rebuilt as a storage area during the renovation. She also told me that's where we'll find the manhole that will get us in. The storage room then opens into the barracks. Pretty good plan, huh?"

"So that's what you were doing while I was watching *SportsCenter*?"

"Ethel and I did a little conniving."

"Sure you can trust her?"

Renee rolled her eyes. "What do you think?"

"Okay, let's go," he said.

Nat followed Renee around the southeast corner of the fort, hugging the side of the building to stay out of sight, but his long metal detector kept snaking its way into the open. The lights shining down from the walls caught the end of the bulky contraption several times and cast a serpentlike shadow across the lawn. Nat thought he heard movement in the nearby trees but dismissed it as a small animal scurrying for cover. It took less than five minutes to reach the target location.

"That's about where the manhole should be," Renee noted, pointing to a row of hedges separating the lawn from the woods. "I guess I need a big strong guy to figure out where it is."

Nat chuckled, threw down his metal detector, and jogged over to the bushes. After tugging on several of them, he found one that felt like plastic. He then pushed the dirt away from the bottom of the plant, pulled out a small crowbar from his backpack, and yanked the manhole cover loose. "Are you sure about this?" he asked. "I think we're moving from innocent treasure hunters to criminals now."

Renee didn't answer but signaled for him to hurry.

"Ready," he said.

Renee smiled her appreciation and shined her flashlight down the tunnel. The wall-mounted ladder dropped down about twelve feet to a landing area where it appeared two corridors started. Renee wasted no time, descending with her backpack dangling from her waist. Nat then retrieved his metal detector, manipulated it through the hole along with his backpack, and then contorted himself down behind Renee.

The landing area opened up just enough for them to stand side-by-side with their equipment. "This way," Renee said, shining her flashlight down one of the routes marked *Storage Room*. Nat hooked the metal detector back onto the side of his backpack and followed.

Renee's flashlight guided their way down the pipe-filled tunnel through a series of twists and turns and seeming dead ends. Nat assumed the pipes were the electrical, sewer, and water lines serving the fort and the faint humming sound of machinery from the other corridor confirmed his suspicion. The pathway was concrete but water stood in several places and Nat's shoes sank into small puddles as he walked.

"Did you hear something?" Nat stopped and looked around.

"No," Renee answered. "We're almost there. What was it?"

"I must be hearing things. Sounded like something scraping against the wall."

Within minutes, Renee's flashlight illuminated a spiral staircase in the distance. The pathway into the fort.

"Ethel's directions were damn good," he said.

"Shhhh," Renee responded.

As they started up the stairs, Nat once again heard a scratching sound behind him. He whipped his flashlight back down the corridor but saw nothing. His heart ticked up a beat. As soon as they reached the top of the staircase, Renee motioned Nat forward so he could open the trapdoor above them.

"We're in," he said after pushing the door off its moorings. "Now what?"

"There's the door to the barracks room," Renee answered, as she ascended into the storage area. She shined her flashlight forward and illuminated a heavy-looking wooden door. She then moved her beam to the security pad on the wall.

"Well, the plan worked well up to now," Nat grumbled in an exasperated tone.

"Wait a minute," Renee answered with a knowing grin. She walked over and punched in a series of numbers.

Seconds later, the large door pushed back and the dimly lit barracks room came into view. Ethel Barnard stood before them.

"Thought you'd never make it," the old lady quipped.

"Now I'm really confused," Nat countered.

"Ethel couldn't take us through the front door because the security guard would have seen us," Renee explained. "But she has the run of the place. The old guard thinks she's out here channeling the spirit of James Fannin. We had to sneak inside on our own."

"Some plan." Nat rolled his eyes. "Thanks for cluing me in."

Ethel smiled. "It pays to be nice to your tour guide," she said.

Nat dropped his backpack and shrugged. "So what's next?" he asked.

Ethel's face turned serious. "I know things about this place that no one else does," she began. "I've been keeping notes for over forty years about every little nook and cranny. Never imagined James Butler Bonham hid Bowie's Treasure in this fort, but if he did, I should know where. This is pretty exciting stuff for a seventy-five-year-old woman."

Renee appeared to levitate from the ground in anticipation.

"And," Ethel continued, "I know how to use that metal detector of yours. I've found more relics on these grounds than any person alive. But I don't think we'll need it."

"Forty years?" Nat said.

"Yes, my father led the renovation of Presidio La Bajia in the 1960s. Our little museum is a tribute to him. Now, come on. We've got work to do."

Nat looked at Renee with his head cocked sideways.

Ethel Barnard led them across the barracks room to a small reception area for visitors. "Leave all of your gear right here, especially that big old metal detector," she ordered. "The rock used to build this fort is so dense it's virtually impossible to get any decent readings, especially to the depths likely needed to bury a cache the size of Bowie's Treasure. Frankly, I don't think Bonham would've had the time or energy to dig deep enough to bury that treasure here."

"That's discouraging," Nat said.

"Patience," Renee interrupted. "Ethel knows what she's doing."

"And why would I let you traipse through that tunnel with all that gear in the middle of the night if there's no treasure here?" she added with a grin. "I just wanted you to have all that stuff in case you were caught." Ethel walked over to the middle of the five small windows on the wall that looked outside the fort to the east. "This is the real reason we're here," she said, looking at the row of windows. "During the renovation project, which replicated this old fort to its exact condition in 1836, each limestone block removed from the walls was examined carefully by a member of the excavation team. They discovered something very interesting during their work. Many of the stones contained historical carvings and etchings on them. In some ways it looked like the soldiers were writing time capsules for us. I catalogued each one of them in the museum storeroom, although several are now maintained in the Texas State Archives. Today, when I was talking to Renee, I was reminded of a stone that's always puzzled me. The letters carved in the rock are unmistakable—*JB*—but the other markings are not. They appear to be a row of squares with a star of some sort above the box in the middle. Most scholars think the marks evidence Bonham's belief that the Texans' cause was divinely inspired. Others, me included, just think they're random doodlings. More than a few believe the stone is a fake. But I've never heard anyone suggest these markings were a map. I pulled out my pictures of the stone earlier and have changed my mind. The boxes weren't doodlings at all; they were windows. And the star wasn't the sign of the Divinity—it was a clue. A ridge in the distance. Take a look out this window and tell me if you agree."

Renee pushed her way to the small window in the middle of the wall behind Ethel and stared outside. She didn't say a word for several seconds but then gasped, "Oh my God."

CHAPTER 51

For the first time since he'd heard about Bowie's Treasure, Nat felt a sense of anticipation. The carved stone supposedly left behind by James Butler Bonham was either an elaborate hoax or a clue of epic proportions. One thing was clear: The hill that rose in the distance east of the fort squared up directly with the middle window in the long-barracks room. If Bonham had intended to point to a hiding place outside the fort, his clue had stood the test of time.

The next morning Nat and Renee waited while Ethel Barnard hunted down a local to help them navigate their search in the hills east of Fort Defiance. Nat worried that Ethel wouldn't be able to handle the physical work ahead but she'd insisted on being part of the team. After a long discussion with Renee, he'd given in. For the rest of the morning, Nat fretted over Niland's upcoming football game and spoke for an hour on the phone with his assistant coaches. "Work 'em hard," he told each of them, but he knew there was only so much they could do in his absence. Nat hoped the search would be done in a day because he was afraid to be away from his team much longer. To his surprise, Ethel showed up about 1:00 p.m. spry and ready to go.

Nat, Renee, and Ethel set out in his rental car, down Lopez Road, southeast on Barnhill, and then due east past Hensley Lake. Once there, they met up with their new guide, who was standing next to two ATVs.

"Nice to meet you folks," said Eric Hopping. The portly man was a self-described part-time plumber, full-time explorer, and longtime friend of Ethel Barnard. He wore a safari hat, oversized fishing shirt, cargo pants, and a tool belt with a dozen different instruments dangling from holsters, including a bulky satellite phone. "You can climb on with me, Ms. Barnard," Hopping said. Ethel had recommended the guide as a reliable accomplice for their expedition because no one in the area knew more about the trails, small caves, and potential hiding places in the hills surrounding Goliad. Ethel moved several sharp objects away from the back side of Hopping's belt, including a knife and a screwdriver, and climbed on his ATV.

"We'll follow," Nat said as he tied down his equipment on the back of the second vehicle. "Hope I can figure out how this thing works."

After a short ride down a semi-paved road, the group started its ascent up the hill they'd seen through the long-barracks room's window. The ride was so bumpy, Nat worried it might make Renee sick but she held on tight without complaint. Ethel appeared unfazed during her ride at Hopping's backside, rarely moving despite the rough terrain and continuously smiling. The man in the big hat eventually pulled his vehicle to a stop once they ran out of pathway. "Now we walk," he advised. "Too steep and too many trees up here to drive any further. You good to go, Ms. Barnard?"

"How do I look?" she asked.

Nat stared at Ethel and couldn't imagine a person half her age looking more fit. Meanwhile, he panted like an overheated dog. "Let's go," Hopping said.

The side of the rocky hill would've been difficult, if not impossible, to pass but for Hopping's knowledge of the area. He navigated the group through open passages and walking trails that made the journey manageable—but still exhausting. After an hour of hiking, Hopping declared they'd reached the target location—a flat scruffy area near the peak with a perfect sight line to the fort. They stopped amid a dense grove of native cypress, oak, and mesquite trees. The soil appeared loamy and the remnants of a dried-up creek bed cut through the middle of the flatland.

The group swigged water in unison before Nat asked, "Are we here?"

"Well," Ethel declared in an excited tone, "we hope so. Now I'm going to teach you kids how to use a metal detector." She flexed her muscles as if to show Nat she wasn't fazed by the hike.

Ethel and Hopping pulled out the metal detectors, put on their headphones, and began dragging the machines across the ground. They stopped a number of times to listen more closely and adjust the frequency of the search coils, but in each instance they shook their heads and moved on. Nat and Renee stayed out of the way, poked around rocks and trees, and searched for potential hiding places. It was a long, tedious couple of hours.

Finally, Ethel and Hopping walked over. "We're missing something," Ethel said.

"It's not up here?" Renee replied with a concerned look on her face.

"I didn't say that," Ethel shot back, "but I don't think this particular area makes any sense."

"I agree," said Hopping, "but I'm at a loss. What are we missing?"

All four explorers raised their eyes quizzically before Ethel pointed to their right. "The creek bed," she suggested.

Nat and Renee tilted their heads but Hopping looked like he'd been hit by a revelation.

"The source," Hopping enthused. "I can't believe I didn't think of it."

"Think of what?" Nat asked.

"The easiest place to bury the treasure would have been the pond that feeds this creek bed. It would be the most supple earth and the simplest location for Bonham's friends to track. There has to be a collecting area for the rainfall just above us."

"Of course!" Ethel agreed, as she followed the creek bed around the side of the hill. "Up there." Ethel pointed to a plateau thirty feet higher, just above the tree line. "Time for the football coach to do his work," Ethel proclaimed. "That's too steep an incline for an old lady."

Renee looked at Nat. "Mr. Travis." She grinned. "If they're right, it's time to meet your destiny."

CHAPTER 52

Nat studied the collecting area that funneled rain from the plateau down the side of the hill. The large depression had an irregular circumference, about sixty feet across at its widest point, but looked like it expanded and contracted during the rainy season. Coming off a hot dry summer, there was only a shallow pool of standing water in the center of the pond and patches of grass grew around its edges. A few scruffy trees and bushes framed the top of the hill but the area was expansive enough for a small group of pack mules and horsemen to gather and dig a hole. Nat felt his heart jump when he flicked on the metal detector. Renee and Hopping, who'd joined him after leaving Ethel behind on the level below, gave him the thumbs-up as he put on the headphones. Nat hoped Hopping's short tutorial was enough for him to understand the sounds resonating through the coils. He glanced to the bright clear sky above his head and quietly said, "This is for you, Papa Joe." He then moved the metal detector over the edge of the pond and started listening.

"Keep moving," Hopping advised. "And tell me what you hear."

"Not much," Nat replied. "Just some static right now."

Nat walked around the edges of the large depression, moving the metal detector over every inch of the dry ground, but heard nothing unusual. At Hopping's direction, he then walked into the pond, the metal detector hovering over the cracked earth, and waved its sensors around like a pool skimmer. Soon, he was up to his ankles in water.

"Anything?" Hopping asked.

Nat shook his head. Ten minutes later and deeper in the water, Nat grew frustrated with the static noise in the headphones. Slump shouldered, he threw his arms into the air and walked back to Renee and Hopping.

"No beeps, no sounds," he reported, pulling off the headphones.

"Let me see that thing," Hopping grumbled. He grabbed the metal detector from Nat, tinkered with the dials for a few seconds, and then asked, "Mind if I give it a try?" He held out his hand for the headphones. "I think you may have needed to adjust the frequency because of the water."

Nat handed Hopping the equipment and sighed, "Have at it."

Hopping eased into the water and stepped purposely toward the center of the pond. He continued tweaking the controls as he moved forward. "Nothing," he announced.

Nat looked at Renee. "I guess it wasn't meant to be," he said with a frown. He reached out and took her hand. For several minutes, he said nothing and stared at the sky.

"Come over here!" Hopping yelled.

Nat turned to Renee, pulled her forward, and jumped toward the water's edge. "What is it?" he asked.

"I'm still having a hard time getting readings in this pond. I'm not sure that I'm making the right adjustments. Can you go yell at Ethel and find out what frequency to put this thing on?"

Nat sprinted back to the edge of the plateau and yelled for Ethel Barnard. He peered over the side of the rocks to the point he'd left her behind but she was nowhere in sight. He then ran to the other side of the hill and called out, "Ethel, Ethel." Worried, Nat sprinted back to the rocky slope he'd used as a ladder and reached his foot out to start down. After his second blind step, he felt a giant hand grasp his ankle, twisting and pulling him down like the wrenching of a rip current. He kicked wildly, yanked his foot free, and then scrambled back up to Renee's side.

Looking back to the trail, Nat saw a mountainous figure emerge above the side of the hill with a gun in his hand. Nat knew he'd seen this man before.

CHAPTER 53

The man with the huge scar on his face marched toward Nat and Renee with the gun extended from his right hand. Hopping dropped the metal detector in the water and splashed his way out to his friends' side.

"Stay right there!" Kruger warned.

"What do you want?" Renee cried.

"What do you think?" Kruger sneered. "Now get on your knees. All three of you."

Nat could barely understand the man's heavy accent but sensed he'd shoot if provoked. He worried that poor Ethel was already dead. Nat dropped down first. Renee and Hopping followed.

"Where is it?" Kruger demanded.

"Where's what?" Nat replied.

Kruger hovered over them, his thick work boots staring at them like the foundation of a concrete statue. "You don't lie very well, Mr. Travis," he laughed, his tone ominous. "Kind of like your grandfather."

Enraged, Nat flinched but held his position. Unarmed, he was no match for the muscular giant in front of him.

"You murdered my grandfather!" Nat growled. "He was an old man."

"Murder?" Kruger snarled. "What makes you think I murdered him? The man was so brittle a stiff wind would've killed him. But no more questions. Tell me where it is. That pond?"

"We don't know," Nat yelled.

Kruger cocked his head and looked at Nat with a pained

expression. He then whipped around toward Hopping, pointed his gun at the chubby man, and fired. The sound of the shot echoed from the hill as the bullet entered Hopping's leg just above the kneecap. Blood sprayed everywhere as the paunchy treasure hunter fell backward to the ground, screaming in agony.

"Who's next?" Kruger threatened. "I'll save the pretty lady for last. Might want to have some fun with her first."

Renee grabbed on to Nat's arm and dug her fingernails deep into his flesh.

"Help me, please," Hopping shouted. "Please."

"Quiet," Kruger ordered. He fired another bullet past Hopping's head.

Nat needed to buy time or the next shot would likely kill one of them. "Let me make him a tourniquet," he pleaded. "You wounded the only man who knows where the treasure is. You need him."

"You have one minute," Kruger barked, "or the lady loses her arm. And I don't need this gun to snap it." Kruger snarled and pulled Renee up by the shoulder.

Nat ripped off his shirt, stretched it taut, and tied it around Hopping's leg just above the bleeding gunshot wound. The traumatized man cried in pain but Nat felt he'd temporarily stemmed the bleeding. At the same time, Nat motioned to Hopping with his eyes to roll over while he pulled the tourniquet tighter. Hopping followed his direction and created a scene by hollering and flapping his arms like a downed bird. The distraction gave Nat the moment he needed. Unnoticed by Kruger, he grabbed Hopping's small knife from his belt and jammed it in the front of his pants. He turned back toward Kruger and dropped to his knees.

"I told you to be quiet," Kruger grumbled. He fired another shot that grazed Hopping's right foot, sending the man recoiling into the shallow water.

Kruger then holstered his gun and grabbed Renee around the arm. He held her petite wrist in one hand and her elbow in the other like two ends of a small tree limb.

"For the last time," Kruger commanded, "where's the treasure?" He tightened his grip.

Nat saw the defiant look in Renee's eyes. Despite the killer's viselike lock on her arm, she didn't cower. Her bravery buoyed Nat's spirits and he lunged at Kruger, grabbing the knife from his pants in one motion while stabilizing himself with the other. Kruger didn't flinch. The Serbian held his ground, elbowed Renee in the chest, and crashed his tree-trunk leg into the side of Nat's head, crumpling him to the ground.

Woozy but still alert, Nat kept the knife under him as he struggled to get up from the muddy turf. Out of the corner of his eye, he saw Kruger preparing to kick him a second time. With all the strength he could muster, Nat rolled to his left, lifted the knife toward Kruger's incoming leg, and thrust it wildly. The blade crunched into flesh and bone, destabilizing the giant, but it still didn't stop his heavy boot from striking Nat in the abdomen. Nat recoiled several feet but was relieved to glimpse a freed Renee running toward Hopping. Unfazed, Kruger rushed toward the staggering Nat and pounded him in the head and face multiple times with his feet and fists, knocking him to the edge of consciousness. Nat tried to protect himself but he was no match for the mercenary's overwhelming power. Blood poured from Nat's nose, eyes, and forehead and his body dropped, limp, to the ground. He could no longer move. Kruger then balanced himself on his one good leg and pulled out his gun. He aimed it at Nat's head.

"Enough," Kruger yelled. "I've run out of patience with all of you. I know the treasure's up here somewhere."

As Nat tried to focus his puffy eyes on Kruger's weapon, he saw movement behind the man. Ethel Barnard had snuck up behind the killer with an object in her hand. Nat watched as the old lady whipped her body into an executioner's position and hammered a shovel down machete-like through the air. The slicing blow dislodged Kruger's gun and catapulted it several feet past Nat's prone body. Kruger roared in anger and lurched back at Ethel, striking her to the earth with a sweep of his now-bleeding arm. He then grabbed the shovel and raised it over the elderly woman's head.

A shot rang out from behind Nat. Then four more. Renee emptied five bullets from the handgun into Kruger's back. The hulking man staggered sideways and dropped the shovel. Nat could hear Renee crying and screaming at the same time. "You bastard," she yelled as she fired the sixth shot at the giant's head. Kruger's brain exploded. Renee dropped the gun to the ground and fell over just as the bullet-riddled corpse of the Serbian collapsed onto Nat's feet.

CHAPTER 54

Ethel's 9-1-1 call from Hopping's satellite phone saved her friend's life. The care-flight helicopter sped in from San Antonio and whisked the wounded explorer away to the hospital before he bled to death. Amputation of his gashed leg remained a possibility but Hopping showed significant improvement during his six hours in the hospital. Nat's injuries weren't as gruesome but they'd proven equally debilitating. Three cracked ribs, a punctured lung, damaged internal organs, and more than sixty stitches scattered over his cheekbone and forehead left him looking like a defeated prizefighter. But he was alive.

"How are you feeling?" Renee asked when Nat woke up from the anesthesia.

"Like a million bucks. Where am I?"

"San Antonio Veterans Hospital. Being the grandson of a war hero has its benefits."

"How's Hopping?"

"The poor man's in bad shape. His leg's a mess and he lost a lot of blood, but they tell me he's resting comfortably now."

"And Ethel?"

"A couple of bruises. The woman's tough as they come."

"You?"

"Damaged, but I'll recover. Killing a person, even a devil, is hard to deal with. It will take me a while, but …"

"I'm so sorry for all of this," Nat interrupted.

Renee's eyes moistened as she tried not to cry. "Are you kidding? I'm the one who should be sorry. I pushed you into this treasure-hunting fiasco … I couldn't let it go even though it was

261

none of my business. What a fool I've been. I could never live with myself if something'd happened to you."

Nat reached out from under the hospital bedsheets and held Renee's hand. Tears flowed down her cheeks.

"Thankfully," she continued, "they tell me you'll fully recover. I just hope it's in time to coach your team before the end of this season. More than anything, I want to take you back to Brewton, back to the life you love."

Nat smiled. "And what about the treasure?"

"That's all behind us now," she said.

CHAPTER 55

Renee stayed with Nat for the rest of the night, waiting at his bedside for the brief moments when he found the energy to open his eyes and communicate. As the evening wore on, she contacted all of the S.W. Niland administrators and coaching staff about the events in Goliad, as well as Eric Hopping's family, but waited as long as she could before making the difficult call to Joseph. She'd prepared herself for his shock, and sarcasm, but was surprised by his reaction. Joseph actually listened and was solicitous on the phone, far more than she'd expected, and then announced he'd be on the first flight from Love Field to San Antonio.

He arrived about 10:30 that evening.

"How is he?" Joseph asked, as Renee stepped outside Nat's room to greet him. She reached forward to shake Joseph's hand but he surprised her with a friendly embrace.

"Beaten to a pulp," Renee explained, pulling away, out of sorts over the hug. "Lots of stitches and he's having a hard time breathing, but he's resting comfortably. He's pretty drugged up."

"Can I see him?"

"Not right now; he's sleeping."

"Then why don't we visit for a minute."

Renee wasn't sure she wanted to "visit" with Joseph about anything but realized it was best for Nat if she had the conversation she'd been dreading for weeks. Joseph's years of neglecting her children, his philandering, and his intense narcissism hadn't left her, even after all of their years apart, but she didn't want those memories to color her discussions about Nat. She guided

263

Joseph to an empty area of the waiting room and slid into a chair next to a large Ficus plant. Joseph sat down next to her.

"First of all," Joseph started, "you need to relax. It's not like I haven't figured out about you and Nat."

Again, Joseph had jolted her in a way only he could. She'd almost forgotten how blunt and biting he could be. "What do you mean?" she asked.

"C'mon, Renee. I spent two days with him last weekend at that Alamo dig. It wasn't that hard to tell. And you are sitting here."

"So where are you going with this?"

Joseph looked at her carefully. "I don't have an agenda … if that's what you're asking. And even if I don't like the two of you together, no one's asked my opinion."

A typical Joseph comment. As if she and Nat needed his approval. Renee figured the conversation was likely headed some place unkind and critical, and she was wondering whether she should shut it off. But then the inspiration hit her. "I love him," she blurted out.

Joseph rubbed his forehead and his gaze wandered all around his ex-wife's face before seemingly resting on her fixed jaw. "Maybe you do," he finally said. "You and Nat … who would have guessed it." He paused again. "But I suppose we all deserve a little happiness in our lives."

"That's about the reaction I would have expected," Renee replied, "but then I've never understood that brain of yours, even when we were married."

"Damn, Renee, time to let that shit go. You and Nat have kept me in the dark for weeks and now you're questioning my sincerity. Listen, I'm not looking for another fight with you … or Nat. I've been off course with both of you for a long time. Frankly, I'm tired of it. I think both of you have misunderstood me, sometimes even mocked me, laughed at my ambition, my politics, my way of doing things, and I've resented you for it. But it's time to move on with our lives, all of us. It's time we buried all of that bullshit in the past."

"There's a lot to bury," Renee observed, still unwilling to let her guard down too much.

"Fair enough, and like I said, I'll accept my share of the blame, but ..."

"No buts," Renee interrupted.

Joseph nodded. "Whatever," he said.

"Nat mumbled something to me about marriage during the care flight here."

"Think he was hallucinating?" Joseph asked, his smile conveying a lightened mood.

"I'm not sure," she replied, "but I don't plan on giving him a chance to reconsider." Renee decided in that instant that she could set aside her history with Joseph if it meant bringing some peace to Nat's future. "I hope you'll be a better brother to Nat ... he wants, no, deserves that much."

"He's my brother," Joseph sighed. "And whether you know it or not, I've tried for years. The self-righteous coach in there hasn't done much on his end either. We won't get along all the time, maybe never, but we're family ... that will never change."

At that moment, a nurse ran into the waiting area with an agitated look. "Mr. Travis is awake and is asking for you, ma'am."

"Thank you," Renee replied while looking up at the stressed-out woman before returning her gaze to Joseph. "Here's your chance, you know. You can tell him all of this yourself."

CHAPTER 56

After two weeks in the hospital, Nat's battered body had healed enough that he was ready to retake the S.W. Niland sideline. His face remained puffy and scarred from his plastic surgery but his internal injuries no longer restricted his movements. He felt fortunate his football team had eked out a couple of wins in his absence, playing just well enough to defeat two mediocre opponents, but the players needed him. He needed them, too. The team captain stepped forward as Nat took his position in front of the huddle for the first time.

"Coach Travis," the young man said. "We know coaching football isn't as exciting as watching television in bed, but we're glad you're back." A loud cheer went up among the players. "We missed you on the sideline and we're ready for you to start yelling at us again." The players clapped in unison and then broke into a chant of "coach, coach, coach, coach, coach." Nat couldn't breathe. The team captain then leaned into him, gingerly patted him on the back, and handed him a hand-painted football previously hidden from view. "For you, coach," he said, before receding into his swarm of teammates.

Nat read the writing on the ball, nodded to his now-silent team, and tried to speak. But his voice betrayed him. A few tears formed in his eyes and then a torrent followed. The moment grabbed him and wouldn't let go, his outburst releasing weeks, if not months, of pent-up emotion. The team cheered, which steadied Nat. "Thank you, men," he said, gaining control. "This is where I belong." He then took a deep breath, paused, and scanned the youthful faces before him. "Now stop staring at me. Let's get to work!"

Nat strolled back to the locker room as practice ended, emotionally drained but the happiest he'd been since Goliad. He wanted nothing more than to take a shower, eat dinner with Renee, and fall into a comfortable chair at his house. But when he arrived in his office, he was disappointed to find a message from Athletic Director Watts instructing him to come to the A.D.'s office immediately.

Nat had worried about the headlines he'd received while recovering from his injuries and wondered how they'd been interpreted by his school's administration. If only Watts knew how much he hated the attention. By the end of his stay in the hospital, Nat felt satisfied the public had lost interest in his story, but he'd yet to have a serious talk with his A.D. about it. He dreaded the conversation.

Nat placed his new football on a shelf in his office and gathered his things before heading across campus. The words staring at him in white paint, **Welcome Home, Coach—Pirates 2013**, made him smile again. How he wanted things to return to normal.

Nat chose his customary route to Watts's office, marching to the back entrance of the school gym so he could cut through the basketball court and then veer directly to the administration building. About a five-minute journey. The second Nat stepped through the gym door, a horn went off, lights flashed, and a boisterous crowd erupted in cheering. Startled, Nat looked up and saw the bleachers full of people, more sitting in folding chairs on the court, and a raised dais at the far end of the building with a small group of men and women assembled in suits. Above the podium in the center of the wall was a sign that read:

Welcome Home, Coach Travis.

Nat stopped, took a deep breath, and gazed at his surroundings. So many of the faces in the gym belonged to his friends from the Brewton community but there were many others he didn't know. And they were all staring at him. A sudden tug on his arm caught Nat by surprise. Renee had snuck up behind him and was now steering him toward the dais.

"Too late to back out now," she said.

"What in the hell?" Nat mumbled.

"Read the sign, silly. These folks want to honor you. So do I. Follow me."

Nat trailed Renee to the podium as members of the crowd cheered and called out his name.

Nat had wondered if the Brewton community might think he'd lost his mind for abandoning his team in mid-season to go on a treasure hunt. Until this moment, he thought it would take months, if not years, to regain the community's trust. The outpouring of support overwhelmed and touched him. "What's going on?" he asked Renee again.

Renee didn't respond and pushed Nat through the crowd to the podium, where he spotted his brother. Joseph reached over and grabbed Nat around the neck when he got close enough. "Congratulations, little brother," he whispered in Nat's ear. Nat awkwardly placed his arm around Joseph's back and returned his greeting. "This is no bullshit," Joseph continued. "Dad and Papa Joe would be very proud... hell, I'm proud." Now even more out of sorts, Nat then looked at the other people on the dais and spotted the school headmaster, A.D. Watts, the mayor of Brewton, a bent-over Hispanic man with an oxygen tank, and a familiar older woman. Ethel Barnard. Nat bypassed the group in front of him and stretched out to hug the sprightly woman who'd saved his life.

Nat shared pleasantries with the other folks on the podium, except the Hispanic man, who was occupied in another conversation, before seating himself in the chair between Joseph and Renee just right of the podium. He felt embarrassingly underdressed in coaching shorts and an S.W. Niland short-sleeved shirt.

Headmaster Carlton greeted the assembled crowd, quickly introduced the mayor of Brewton, and then moved on to the program. He said, "Ladies and gentlemen, thank you for being here this evening. This is a special night for our school community. We're here to welcome back our football coach from the hospital and let him know that we've missed him. We're proud of you, Coach Travis." The crowd cheered. "The courage you displayed on that hill in Goliad, Texas, inspired us all," Carlton continued. He then stopped, clapped, and the crowd rose in unison to give Nat a standing ovation.

Nat waved appreciatively but remained embarrassed and uncertain. He wanted to slide off the stage and hide.

Carlton then turned toward the group on the podium. He said, "We also have a couple of special guests this evening to help make an important announcement about the school. One is an alumnus of this institution who currently serves in the Texas House of Representatives. Please give a special Niland welcome to the Honorable Joseph Travis the third."

The crowd clapped politely as Joseph walked to the microphone. Renee held Nat's hand and smiled.

"Go Pirates!" Joseph yelled when he reached the podium. "I hear we have an undefeated football team this year. If we can just get my brother off his back long enough to get to work, our Pirates might finish the job."

The crowd whooped and roared in response to the comment.

"I want to tell you a story," Joseph continued. "I think it will resonate with everyone here no matter your background." He paused for dramatic effect. "Nat and I are descendants of slaves. That's hardly news to this crowd, but many of you likely don't know that one of our ancestors has a special history. Joseph and Nat Travis are kin to the only male survivor of the famous battle of the Alamo. Our ancestor is popularly known as Joe, or in some corners, Joe the slave, and he served as an aide to the commander of the Alamo—Colonel William Barret Travis. Now you might think it odd that I'm talking about a slave and the Alamo the night of this celebration, but it has a great deal to do with why we're here."

Joseph hesitated again. He was milking the story for all it was worth. The cameraman filming from below the stage had Joseph locked in and playing politician.

"Let me take a step back," Joseph went on. "As you're all aware by now, my grandfather, Joe Travis, was murdered several months ago in his home here in Brewton … and the killer was never found. But due to the efforts of my brother and these brave ladies to my right, the assassin, and I repeat assassin, is dead … and Joe Travis can now rest in peace. The man they took down on that hill in Goliad was a trained killer."

The crowd cheered for a moment but then quieted as if confused by their own reaction.

"What most of you don't know," Joseph said forcefully, "was why this man was pursuing my family. That leads me to the reason we're here tonight. My brother wasn't goofing off in the Texas hills poking around for artifacts when he should've been back here coaching his boys." Joseph smiled. "He wasn't blindly following the dying request of a quirky old man as some have speculated. No, he took a couple of days off to follow leads left behind by our grandfather to track down the secret of our ancestor—Joe the slave. You see, our grandfather was onto a secret Joe carried out of the Alamo that has evaded scholars, historians, and, yes, even treasure hunters, for over one hundred and seventy years. Joe the slave was the only person who survived the Alamo with knowledge of the location of a legendary Texas fortune—a cache of silver popularly known as Bowie's Treasure. Nat Travis made it his purpose to finish our grandfather's work. That is why an assassin was after him. He thought Nat had finally uncovered the secret hiding place."

Joseph paused, building the drama, and the crowd appeared to collectively gasp.

Nat strained for air. *Could it be?*

"That's where our special guest comes in," Joseph continued. "While my brother researched Bowie's Treasure, his fiancée, the woman sitting right here next to him, Renee Travis, discovered a clue that linked Joe the slave to another man who's with us here this evening."

Nat felt faint. He looked at Renee but her face gave away nothing. *Could they have kept a secret this big from him while he recovered?*

"Ladies and gentlemen," Joseph said, "tonight I have the great pleasure of introducing a new friend, Enrique Rodriguez, a man, with a family connection to our ancestor Joe the slave, with news of a great treasure. A man whose ancestry also traces back to the Republic of Texas, much like the Travis family. And most importantly—some might say fatefully—a man whose father served bravely with my grandfather on Omaha Beach during the invasion of Normandy. Mr. Rodriguez now lives with his family in Lawrenceville, Georgia. Please welcome—Enrique Rodriguez."

The elderly Hispanic man worked his way slowly to the podium amid scattered applause. He breathed deeply from his oxygen mask and then looked out to the crowd.

"My name is Enrique Rodriguez," he began. "I'm honored

to be here in the presence of you wonderful people at this fine institution. I'm a man of few words so I will get straight to the point. Years ago, about 1838, a Mexican stableboy named Enrique befriended a slave on a ranch in Texas. The place was known as Bailey's Prairie and the slave's name was Joe. You just heard Representative Travis refer to him as Joe the slave. This Mexican boy, who happens to be my ancestor, helped Joe escape his master's ranch and maneuver his way out of Texas all the way to Alabama. Not much is known about Enrique beyond that point. We believe Joe the slave lived in Brewton and actually died here in the 1880s. Now fast forward to 1944. Joe the slave's great grandson, your Joe Travis, befriends a Hispanic man named Ricardo Rodriguez, my father, while preparing for Operation Overlord in England. They become close friends and likely shared many family stories. But after surviving Omaha Beach, my father was killed at the Battle of St. Lo in France. My mother, who I never knew despite my efforts to find her, placed me in an orphanage less than six months after I was born and I stayed there for several years. What I've now learned, all this time later, is that before D-Day Joe Travis made a promise to my father to support his only son, an infant at the time, in the event of his death. True to his word and unknown to me until I met this beautiful woman sitting next to me, Joe Travis returned to the United States and tracked me down. He found a way to get me released from the orphanage so I could attend boarding school and then provided me with a first-class education, which eventually led me to college. I was lucky, given a chance by a man I never met, who never had any obligation beyond his word and never sought recognition or gratitude for what he did. Not even his own family knew. That's the kind of extraordinary man Joe Travis was. His grandsons are right to honor his life, to honor his service, and to honor his memory, no matter where it led."

The crowd clapped roundly as Rodriguez breathed from his oxygen tank.

"I graduated from Vanderbilt," Rodriguez continued, "with an engineering degree, and thanks to Joe Travis, that allowed me to find financial success. When I recently learned the identity of my mysterious benefactor, I was immediately drawn to do something to repay his incredible generosity. With the help of Representative Travis and my friend Renee, I've now figured out what that is."

Rodriguez paused and breathed deeply, his emotions starting to overcome him. "While I don't know much about Joe the slave's secret or this Bowie's Treasure business," he continued, "I'm proud to discuss a different treasure. One that's perhaps more tangible and real. It gives me great pleasure to honor the memory of Joe Travis tonight by announcing a gift to S.W. Niland of one million dollars to build the Joe and Nat Travis Field House."

The crowd erupted into a standing ovation. Nat's jaw fell open.

Rodriguez placed his hands in the air to quiet the crowd. "And just to make sure Headmaster Carlton doesn't think I've forgotten this is an institution of higher learning, I'm going to contribute another two hundred fifty thousand dollars to purchase new computer equipment for your students and faculty. I have attached only one condition to these gifts: I want to be invited back to Niland when you win the state football championship this year. You hear me, Coach Travis?"

Nat nodded as the crowd rose in a standing ovation. He beat his hand against his heart to thank Rodriguez.

"Thank you for giving me the honor of being here tonight," Rodriguez said. "God bless you all."

CHAPTER 57

At the end of the program, Nat was too moved to stand and file out with the energized crowd. He sat quietly with Renee and Enrique Rodriguez taking it all in. Renee eventually leaned over to Nat and whispered, "We've planned a casual dinner for Mr. Rodriguez at your house tonight. Your brother and Ethel are joining us as well. Hopefully, Emmitt and Amelia, too. I've got the food ready and a server standing by so there's nothing for you to do but get in the car."

"You are something," Nat said. "I knew there was a reason I'd stayed single all of my life."

"Too late now," Renee responded, flashing the diamond engagement ring she now wore on her finger.

"And you even have Joseph acting half decent," Nat added.

Renee smiled. "Anything for my man." She patted him on the shoulder.

They both then helped their elderly guest out of the gym to Renee's car.

"This has been some night," Nat remarked to Rodriguez as they walked toward the front door of his house, where Joseph, Emmitt, and Amelia waited. "I still don't even know how to thank you."

"There's no need," Rodriguez replied as he adjusted his oxygen tank. "Truly, I'm not sure what gave me more satisfaction—when I saw your reaction on that stage tonight or when I told my greedy daughter-in-law that I was giving away a million dollars." He rolled his eyes.

They laughed as they greeted the other guests and walked

through the living area to the small dining-room table next to Nat's kitchen. The table was set with patterned china and stemmed glassware.

"Sorry, Mr. Rodriguez, but there's not much here to look at," Nat said. "We coaches get our thrills on the football field, although I will say it appears my fiancée has discovered some dishes I've never seen before."

Renee smiled and nodded. "And I thought he wouldn't notice," she joked as everyone laughed.

Once the group sat around the table, Joseph asked them to raise the champagne-filled glasses in front of them. "A toast," he announced. "To my courageous brother and his soon-to-be wife, Renee. Never have I known two people who deserved each other more." He smiled warmly but Nat still felt a trace of sarcasm in his voice. "May the two of you be happy forever," Joseph continued. "And to my new friend, Enrique Rodriguez, thank you for what you've done for this community and for honoring my family in such a special way. Your presence at our table is a profound blessing. To my children, I love you, and thank you for making the trip to be with us here tonight. And finally, to Ethel Barnard, I salute you most of all. For without you, none of this would be possible. Cheers."

Each person clinked glasses with wide smiles and thank-you nods to Rodriguez and Ethel while Nat continued pondering his brother's comments.

"By the way," Nat interjected, "I'd still like to hear exactly how Ethel managed to get up that hill with a shovel in her hands. No one fully explained that to me in the hospital."

Ethel flexed her muscles and smiled.

"Oh, you misunderstood my toast," Joseph admonished. "I wasn't talking about what Ethel did on that hill. I meant tonight wouldn't have been possible without her. This dinner, this moment, this celebration. It's all because of Ethel."

"That's worth toasting as well." Nat raised his glass. "Ethel, thank you for putting this dinner together."

"No, you still don't get it," Joseph interjected.

"Get what?" Nat was almost irritated.

At that point, Renee stepped over to a credenza and withdrew what looked like a photo album. She had an ear-to-ear smile on her face.

"What's this?" Nat asked.

"I guess you better open it," Renee answered as she handed it to Nat.

Nat expected to see drawings of the new field house but instead discovered a photocopy of a handwritten letter that appeared very old and worn.

"Read the date," Ethel instructed.

"I can hardly make it out," Nat replied. "Looks to be one-eight-three-six. Oh my God. Where did this come from?"

Ethel looked Nat straight in the eyes, smiling. "Mr. Rodriguez financed a dig on that hill near Goliad," she said. "I think you know the place."

"You mean?"

"Yes!" Ethel continued, almost giddy. "When Hopping recovered enough to talk, he told me about some peculiar readings he got on his metal detector while searching that pond. I got very excited. I talked to Renee and she suggested we call Mr. Rodriguez. He agreed to finance an excavation team to help me."

"And no one thought to tell me?" Nat faked exasperation.

"We've been a bit sneaky," Renee interrupted, "but doctor's orders trumped everything. We knew there was no way to keep you in that hospital bed otherwise."

"It took some work," Ethel said, picking up the story, "but we located the source of those readings. Believe it or not, Bonham preserved a note in one of the trunks he used to bury the silver. Thanks to Mr. Rodriguez, the original note and a fortune in silver are already in the hands of the Texas state archivists. A press release will hit the wires first thing in the morning announcing the single most important historical discovery in the history of the Alamo. A special exhibit bearing your family's name will eventually follow in the museum of your choice. Your brother has handled all of the details. I may have helped out on that hill that day, but you've done something far more important. You've saved a piece of history. Bowie's Treasure no longer belongs to a forgotten hill near Goliad ... it belongs to the world."

CHAPTER 58

The following weeks were a media whirlwind for Nat, Renee, and Ethel. Even Hopping got into the action once his leg healed. Everyone—from news reporters, historians, and treasure hunters to conspiracy theorists—wanted to know about the famous note left behind by James Butler Bonham and the cache of silver recovered from the hills of Goliad. At the same time, investigators unwound the financial web of Angelina de Zavala Gentry and the DRT leading to criminal indictments and embarrassed politicians scrambling for cover. Even Angelina's duplicitous understudy, Janet Nelson, was ensnared in the dragnet, her nascent political career dashed in the process. Yet, despite his newfound celebrity, Nat avoided the press, the investigation, and all of the other distractions arising from the discovery of Bowie's Treasure. He had a football team to coach. An undefeated one.

It was early November and Nat stood on the sideline as his 11-0 Pirates received the ball trailing West Brewton 24-18 with less than three minutes to go in the game. Niland's first championship in three decades was within reach. Threatening black clouds loomed over the stadium as Nat called time-out and huddled up his team. Thunder rumbled in the distance. Uncertain about the set of plays to call, Nat looked into the faces of his hungry players and drew confidence from them. He realized everything he cared about surrounded him in that huddle—his players, his Brewton family, and his new wife in the stands. Even his inscrutable brother paced the sideline in a red S.W. Niland jersey. Bowie's Treasure and the excitement of the past few months meant nothing to him without this group. Nat stepped back from the scrum, turned his head toward the fans, and stared at the familiar corner of the stadium. The same spot where Renee sat today, but at that moment, more important, where Papa Joe had sat so many times before.

This time, however, a different figure rose from Papa Joe's corner and returned Nat's gaze. An elderly man sitting with a portable oxygen tank, a man who'd grown very close to him over the past month. A man who'd dedicated himself to preserving the legacy of Joe Travis and helping his grandsons honor his memory. Enrique Rodriguez lifted a shaky thumb into the air and Nat felt a jolt of inspiration. On cue, the skies opened up and thick fat drops of rain pounded Nat's head and washed over the entire stadium.

Nat turned his face up to meet the rain, bathed in the moment, and then dove back in to face his players. He knew exactly what to do.

AUTHOR'S NOTE AND ACKNOWLEDGEMENTS

Every native Texan is raised on stories about the heroes of the Alamo. I am no different. And those stories have been told gloriously by authors many times over since that fateful day in 1836. Few, though, have examined the life of Joe, William Barret Travis's slave, the only known man to survive Santa Anna's attack. In researching Joe's story, it was only natural to study the exploits of several of the Alamo's most famous residents, including the legendary Jim Bowie. While the Bowie name is steeped in the lore of Texas—and is perhaps known more for the knife that bears the name than for the warrior's defiant death at the Alamo—Jim Bowie remains something of an enigma. Hero, scoundrel, leader, drunk: There is no one consistent character who survives in the pages of history. But there are two things most scholars agree on—Bowie held an intense hatred for the Mexicans and was relentless in his pursuit of gold and silver. The signpost **Bowie Mine 1832** still exists in San Saba, Texas, and bears witness to the adventurer's lifelong passion for treasure. It was the intersection of the lives of these two men—Bowie and Joe the slave—at the Alamo that led to this novel.

Much of the historical information contained in these pages is accurate. From the DRT's battle with the State of Texas to the life of Adina de Zavala, there is truth in all of the *historical* accounts in this work. When dealing with the events at the Alamo, I relied heavily on *The Alamo Reader*, a wonderful compilation of historical materials edited by Todd Hansen, and Walter Lord's classic account of the Alamo battle, titled *A Time to*

Stand. Researching Jim Bowie and his search for treasure in the hills of Central Texas was made easier by the excellent accounts by J. Frank Dobie and other writers who've devoted many pages to the lost San Saba mine. Old press articles about Joe the slave's movements after the Texas Revolution also provided historical context for this novel.

Writing a novel is not an exercise I recommend for a fully employed person. The patience and time required to bring these pages to life was daunting if not overwhelming. And effort alone is not even enough. Help comes in all forms, whether a supportive friend who hears whispers that you're writing a book or inspiring family members who never laugh too loudly when they see you slaving away at the most bizarre hours. My first reader, and you know who you are, will always hold a special place in my heart for encouraging me to keep going when no others would.

But what a novice author needs more than encouragement is good advice and sound criticism. For that, I thank Susan Leon. She pushed, prodded, and poked me into recognizing not only the great story in Joe the slave but, more important, that of Nat, Renee, and Joseph Travis. Her outstanding editing skills made this finished work possible.

APPENDIX[1]

"The servant of the late lamented Travis, Joe, a black boy of about twenty-one or twenty-two years of age, is now here. He was in the Alamo when the fatal attack was made. He is the only male, of all who were in the fort, who escaped death, and he, according to his own account, escaped narrowly. I heard him interrogated in presence of the cabinet and others. He related the affair with such modesty, apparent candor, and remarkably distinctly for one of his class. The following is, as near as I can recollect, the substance of it:

The garrison was much exhausted by incessant watching and hard labor. They had all worked until a late hour on Saturday night, and when the attack was made, sentinels and all were asleep, except one man, Capt. ----, who gave the alarm. There were three picket guards without the fort, but they, too, it is supposed, were asleep, and were run upon and bayoneted, for they gave no alarm. Joe was sleeping in the room with his master when the alarm was given. Travis sprang up, seized his rifle and sword, and called to Joe to follow him. Joe took his gun and followed. Travis ran across the Alamo and mounted the wall, and called out to his men, 'Come on, boys, the Mexicans are upon us, and we'll give them Hell.' He discharged his gun; so did Joe. In an instant Travis was shot down. He fell within the wall, on the sloping ground, and sat up.

The enemy twice applied their scaling ladders to the walls, and were twice beaten back. But this Joe did not well understand,

---

1. Printed from the *Diary of William Fairfax Gray, from Virginia to Texas, 1835-1837*. This excerpt is a literal text from an interview with Joe the slave.

for when his master fell he ran and ensconced himself in a house, from which he says he fired on them several times, after they got in. On the third attempt they succeeded in mounting the walls, and then poured over like sheep. The battle then became a *melee*. Every man fought for his own hand, as he best might, with *butts of guns*, pistols, knives, etc. As Travis sat wounded on the ground General Mora was passing him, made a blow at him with his sword, which Travis struck up, and ran his assailant through the body, and both died on the same spot. This was poor Travis' last effort. The handful of Americans retreated to such covers as they had, and continued the battle until only one man was left alive, a little, weakly man named Warner, who asked for quarter. He was spared by the soldiery, but on being conducted to Santa Anna, he ordered him to be shot, and it was done. Bowie is said to have fired through the door of his room, from his sick bed. He was found dead and mutilated where he lay. The Negroes, for there were several Negroes and women in the fort, were spared. Only one woman was killed, and Joe supposes she was shot accidentally, while attempting to cross the Alamo. She was found lying between two guns. The officers came round, after the massacre, and called out to know if there were any Negroes there. Joe stepped out and said, 'yes, here is one.' Immediately two soldiers attempted to kill him, one by discharging his piece at him, the other with a thrust of the bayonet. Only one buckshot took effect in his side, not dangerously, and the point of the bayonet scratched him on the other. He was saved by Capt. Baragan.

Besides the Negroes, there were in the fort several Mexican women, among them the wife of a Dr. and her sister, Ms. Navarro, who were spared and restored to their father, D. Angel Navarro of Bejar. Mrs. Dickenson, wife of Lieut. Dickenson, and child, were also spared, and have been sent back into Texas. After the fight was over, the Mexicans were formed in hollow square, and Santa Anna addressed them in a very animated manner. They filled the air with loud shouts. Joe describes him as a slender man, rather tall, dressed very plainly—somewhat *'like a Methodist preacher,'* to use the Negro's own words. Joe was taken into Bejar, and detained several days; was shown a grand review of the army after the battle, which he was told, or supposes, was 8,000 strong. Those acquainted with the ground on which he says they formed think that not more than half that number could form there. Santa Anna questioned Joe about Texas, and the state of its army. Asked if there were many soldiers from the United States in the army, and if more were expected, and said he had men enough to march to the city of Washington. The American dead were collected in a pile and burnt."